the iowa farmer's wife

by Bill Beaman

Cover design by Jill Schaben.
www.jillschaben.com

Printed in the USA by
Morris Publishing®
3212 E. Hwy 30
Kearney, NE 68847
www.morrispublishing.com

ISBN 978-0-615-35101-8

Second Printing
500 Copies
May 2010

To order more copies:
www.theiowafarmer.com

ACKNOWLEDGEMENT

Because I'm a fairly conscientious guy, I want to remind everybody who reads this book that the characters and the location are fictional. I have no desire to upset any bankers, DCI investigators, county police or any of my neighbors. If you write a fictional book, you must develop fictional characters. If you write a murder mystery, somebody has to get murdered. However, if at any point while you're reading this book you get the sense that I think southern Iowa is a beautiful place to live, that people here are, for the most part, extraordinarily kind, that a farm could be a great place to raise a family, I confess, that part of the book is not fictional.

Truth be told, I started on this book back in 1993. I've been a life-long reader of books, especially good murder mysteries these later years and thought I could put together a pretty good story. With pen in hand (I don't think we even had a computer back then, much less knew how to run one), I went to work. After a couple of months working on it during rainy spells and cold days, I thought I had it whipped. My wife typed it up for me and darn if the manuscript in hand didn't actually look like something! I sent off letters to major publishing houses and editors around the United States anxiously waiting their enthusiastic replies. Well, that was an education. No one seemed to get as excited about my book as I was, in fact, no one seemed to get excited at all. So my big dream lay around the house, a pile of typed paper and scribbled notes. In the following years, at some point each winter, usually during a horrible cold spell after chores each day, I'd spend a couple of hours in the house working on it, changing a paragraph here, correcting a misspelled word there, but essentially, the project was dead.

What I didn't know at that time was, to get the book edited and published, I'd have to wait for our youngest daughter, Jill, (who was probably about eight years old at the time the book was started), to grow up, graduate from college, get married and embark on a career of her own. Without Jill's enthusiasm, energy, patience and special talents this book would still be laying up in the cupboard, a dream that never materialized. So, if you enjoy the book, thank Jill. Without her, "The Iowa Farmer's Wife" would never have been. This one's for you, Jill.

PROLOGUE

Jamie stepped out onto the front porch carefully closing the screen door to prevent waking her sleeping daughter. The cool morning air, laden with the humidity Iowa was famous for, enveloped her farm in a light fog. She took a careful sip of coffee and let her eyes roam over what she could see in the early morning darkness of her one hundred and twenty acre kingdom. She was proud of the fruits of her labor. The garden had never looked better, having already produced this season nearly three times the yield of previous years, making her trips to farmers' markets much more prosperous. The flowers, in a wide variety of shapes and colors, decorated her farmstead, and she took a deep breath inhaling their fragrant odors.

She looked out at the dark-green grass in the pastures beyond the farmyard. Her flock of sheep would have to be moved to a new paddock of grass today, the same as they were every day. They would harvest the grass, fertilize the soil in the process and move on to the next patch of hillside, harvesting sunlight and sequestering carbon in the process, creating a healthy source of protein for her to market to a growing number of consumers and helping keep the farm sustainable, not to mention keeping the lives of Jamie and her daughter Andrea sustainable.

Today, as always, the amount of work ahead of her looked daunting. The chores alone were physically exhausting: milking Flossie, moving the sheep, tending the vegetables and feeding the pigs. She would also need to process twelve chickens for delivery later in the week, and twelve loaves of bread would have to be baked for the farmers' market on Thursday, not to mention harvesting the late sweet corn, digging up some potatoes, and getting a load of laundry on the clothesline. Well she would either get it done or she wouldn't, she could only try. She knew the day's workload would leave her feeling drained by nightfall, but the work was rewarding. She almost never had trouble sleeping and heck, she thought, she'd never been in better shape, enjoying every moment of slipping on jeans she hadn't been able to wear ten years prior. No exercise equipment or workout videos needed on this place she thought, smiling to herself.

And her most important task was taking care of her great love in life, Andrea, her four-year-old daughter. She felt a sense of peace as she thought about the sleeping child inside their house.

She could feel her muscles tensing and a tightness gathering in her stomach as her mind absorbed the sheer amount of responsibility she carried thinking how much the farm, the animals on it, her customers, and her daughter, all relied on her. It did indeed seem like a very heavy load for a widowed Iowa farmer to carry. So much could go wrong, had gone wrong.

She would endure. That's what her kind did. At sunrise, Ed, her rooster would crow once and only once. Ed's crowing would wake Andrea, who, in turn, would step out onto the porch to give her mom a hug. Jack, her border collie would come running from the important task of checking livestock. The sheep would spot her and start bleating, reminding her they needed new grass to harvest. Caring for her daughter, farm and animals would fill the entire day as it had everyday as she rebuilt her life after Bud's death. It was what she did and wanted to do. It was just that sometimes new problems would surface in her life and the load would become so heavy that she would long for the help of another adult.

The thought of the death just up the road that had occurred the past weekend, darkened her thoughts and almost unleashed the depression that threatened to overtake her and endanger her fragile existence.

Jamie's dark moment of thoughts was interrupted by the slightest glimmer of light through the fog as the sun quietly peaked over the edge of her universe. Ed strutted out of the chicken house, scratched the ground with alternating feet, craned his neck toward the sky and crowed loudly. She could hear Andrea stirring. Jack came running from the pasture north of the barn. She would face the day, be tough, keep her attitude positive and deal with any problems. Still, that little voice of insecurity deep inside kept whispering her need for an adult partner, a void that Bud had left.

What Jamie didn't know was that help was on the way from a most improbable source in a most unlikely fashion.

CHAPTER
1

It isn't the heat, it's the humidity they say that can make a person feel so damn uncomfortable on a summer day in Iowa; air so loaded with moisture that it's hard to tell if a person is sweating from the inside out or the outside in. The result is ample weather for growing tall, Iowa corn but not everyone grew corn in southwest Iowa. Doug Cordoe didn't. He did own a farm, however, enrolling most of the land in the government's set-aside program, to predominantly produce grass and cedar trees, although he did raise a few acres of soybeans and a lot of weeds. Like a growing number of Iowa residents, Doug didn't rely on his farm as a primary source of income. He was a banker by trade in the nearby town of Pigmy. Actually, his farm only lay a mile outside of Pigmy, right down a dead end road, but that mile meant a lot to Doug. The farm gave him isolation from people he didn't like and a job that, he felt, had no real future. The farm gave Doug a place to venture to and relax, listen to the birds sing, watch other wildlife and take quiet naps on a hammock under the shade trees down by the river.

Doug Cordoe would observe the sights and sounds of Southern Iowa for only a few more minutes. His life was coming to a violent end. He cried out in pain as he grasped the wooden handle of the forged-steel, five-tine pitchfork that had been rammed through his chest. As he slumped against his Cadillac, he heard the pointed ends of the fork tines, protruding out of his back, scrape against the car body. It made a sickening, offensive sound, even to the ears of a dying man.

Even in his pain and shock, he found it unbelievable that this had happened, that he had let it happen. He was amazed that one savage thrust, powered by the hands of an enraged human, could have done this to him.

Having failed to dislodge the fork from his chest, Cordoe stumbled forward, faltered, then once again collapsed against the side of his Cadillac. Strangely, the pain in his chest was not yet unbearable. It was the increasing difficulty in breathing, as his lungs filled with blood, that caused him to panic. Doug involuntarily coughed and spit blood all over the front of his shirt.

His mind felt like a stereo with speakers playing two different songs. One speaker blared out heavy metal, laced with pain and shock, as his heart began a wild series of irregular beats. The other speaker spun out a sad country ballad, recalling his past life with incredible speed and clarity. Megabytes of information, that had been stored in his brain since childhood, came hissing out like the air from a punctured tire. Clearly he could tell the theme of his thoughts centered around regret—regret for the pain he'd left as his legacy.

Staring across the beautiful Iowa horizon at the setting sun, but lacking the ability to focus on anything, Cordoe wondered what the thoughts of the living would be as they silently looked down at his dead body lying in a casket at the Pigmy Funeral Home. Would mourners even come? He had a sudden vision of his past clients, marching single file past his coffin, staring down at the chief loan officer of the Farmers and Merchants Bank in Pigmy with nervous glances, with no tears, at the man whom nearly sixty percent of the county's rural residents had depended on for financial advice and loans, the man who'd been their encouraging friend in the good times and their terminator when their financial plans failed to materialize. They would probably be glad he was dead, he guessed. No more foreclosures, no more forced sales, no more broken promises made by Banker Cordoe.

He watched in disbelief as his assailant took a red handkerchief and carefully wiped away any fingerprints that may have been present, from the handle of the pitchfork embedded in Cordoe's chest; no emotions, no comments, just the completion of a task. The assailant paused to look him in the eyes for one short moment, then turned and walked to the edge of the bridge and stared at the water below.

Suddenly, Cordoe found a brief burst of energy, as one last surge of hope shot through his damaged body. His slumping legs extended and he tried to turn toward his car. If he could get into the car, maybe he could drive somewhere for help, but as he turned, the handle of the pitchfork struck the car, sending one last fiery jet of pain through his body. Banker Doug Cordoe slowly slid down the side of his beloved Cadillac into a growing pool of blood and died.

CHAPTER

2

John Brightwall realized that his hands were trembling. He tried to still them, tried to calm himself, but he was losing the battle and angrily he looked across his desk for an object to throw. He grabbed the nameplate from the front corner of his desk and prepared to hurl it across the room in an effort to vent some anger. His throw ended in a balk, however, when a receptionist, her face contorted in disgust, entered Brightwall's office for maybe the tenth time already that Monday morning. The look of disgust on her face was the direct result of foul odors emanating from the containers that she carried: human urine samples, sealed in a variety of plastic and styrofoam containers. Twenty-seven specimens delivered to Brightwall's office so far that morning rested on top of his oak bookshelves beneath a portrait of the state's governor.

"Don't bring anymore of those damn things in here! Understand?" Brightwall's yell startled Sylvia and the sample she carried fell to the floor, spilling into the carpet.

"Shit!" Brightwall yelled at the top of his lungs, his temper out-of-control and running rampant.

The shaken Sylvia pulled a tissue from the pocket of her blazer and started to kneel toward the stained carpet. "I'm sorry but..."

"Out! Now!" He bellowed, pointing at the door. Then Brightwall, calming a bit, added, "Please, I'll have a janitor clean it up."

She turned and started to apologize again, but he interrupted her, "Please, just go. And Sylvia..."

"Yes?"

"If anymore of these...these damn specimens come in, don't take them. Okay? This is just a practical joke someone's playing on us, okay?"

She nodded her head, took one more look at the wet carpet, turned and quickly left his office.

Brightwall fell back in his chair, took a deep breath and tried to clear his head. He put his reading glasses on and reread the memo which, the previous Friday, had been delivered to a vast majority of the staff occupying the Iowa Department of Criminal Investigation Building in Des Moines, Iowa. Nearly two-hundred people, including detectives, lab technicians, secretaries and janitors had all received the memo, excluding Brightwall, who'd been out of town. Had he been there, the memo would never have gone out. Once again, he slowly read the memo.

EMERGENCY MEMO
TO: ALL DCI EMPLOYEES
FROM: DCI DIRECTOR BRIGHTWALL
DATE: AUGUST 10
SUBJECT: POSSIBLE EMPLOYEE EXPOSURE TO T213HS

It has come to our attention that a potentially-dangerous health situation has developed for all of our employees at DCI headquarters. Apparently, the office supply company that delivers our supplies may have, we emphasize "may have," delivered some improperly-prepared copy machine toner. The improperly-mixed toner may contain an unlicensed chemical known as T213HS, a chemical that has been proven by FDIC researchers to cause cancer in laboratory rats.

"FDIC?" Brightwall paused. "It should be the 'FDA'." He read on.

This chemical may have been transferred to copy paper used in the past

5

week and, consequently, many of our employees may have been exposed to T2I3HS. In order to ascertain how widely the T2I3HS may have spread, we are making the following request to all DCI employees:

Monday morning, August 13, between the hours of 8 AM and 9 AM, please deliver to Supt. Brightwall's office, a fresh sample of your urine. Approximately eight ounces should be adequate. Please refrain from drinking alcoholic beverages or participating in sexual activities during the weekend to ensure the accuracy of our testing procedures.

The DCI, while greatly interested in the health and well-being of our employees, takes no responsibility for the improper delivery of potentially-dangerous chemicals to our workplace environment.

Signed,
DCI Director Brightwall

Brightwall laid the memo down and removed his glasses in disgust. He figured, roughly, in his mind, about ten percent...hell no, more than ten percent...twenty-seven people had fallen for the bogus memo, and there sat the samples, 26 cups, well 25 now, plus the other one: a fecal sample. Incredible, he thought, what idiot did that? He tried to remove the sample marked, "My dog FiFi" from his thoughts. Why their dog? And the smell, it was terrible! He was beginning to feel nauseous.

Monday morning...ah yes, Monday morning, he thought. It always felt this way on Monday morning...son-of-a-bitching problems waiting to brighten the beginning of my work week. Brightwall stared out through the windows of his inner-office at the people sitting and walking around outside. Once again he sensed his heart beating rapidly and worried about his elevated blood pressure and his ulcers as they ignited their engines for take off.

Was it really worth it? He had asked himself this question six times in the last half hour. He turned the nameplate on his desk around, gently polished it on the sleeve of his jacket and laid it back in its precise position. Reading his name and title, "Superintendent John Brightwall," seemed to calm him a little. It served as a reminder of the years it had taken him to advance to his current position.

He started to recall memories of the good old days, back when he was a special agent, working in various departments within the DCI.

Ah, yes, what a damnable struggle it had been to rise through the ranks. "Was it really worth it?" he silently asked himself again. Regardless, he was three years from retirement and he wasn't going to quit now. Brightwall reached into the drawer of his desk and pulled out a single sheet of typing paper and his favorite pen. Whenever things seemed in chaos, he always followed the same procedure. He took his pen and began to list his problems on the left-hand side of the sheet of paper. Usually, the problems were listed in order of the frustration they were causing him and, as usual, most of the problems stemmed from the staff he managed. He listed three names on the left-hand margin and drew arrows from each to the right hand side where he would list his plan of action.

The first name on the list nearly caused him to snap his pen in half as he wrote it down with intense anger, "Benjamin Willoughby." Brightwall knew Willoughby was responsible for the bogus memo which led to the urine samples. At that very moment, Brightwall could see Benjamin, sitting on the corner of one of the secretary's desks outside of his office, teasing her, disrupting her performance and smoking one of his damn cigars. No smoking signs were posted everywhere and yet there he sat, puffing like a chimney.

Benjamin, fifty-seven years old, exactly the same age as Brightwall, had actually spent more years in the DCI than Brightwall had, yet he was still only a special agent. He had never even applied for a promotion and, even if he had, it was doubtful he would have been granted one. The employee files on Benjamin listed problems such as excessive alcohol consumption, workplace disruption and too many late and inaccurate reports. In addition, he was overweight, had two failed marriages under his belt, and was a terrible practical joker. Yet for some reason, everyone loved the guy. In fact, he was probably the most popular person in the DCI, Brightwall thought to himself. He was a fairly productive agent, actually one of the most productive. The problem was, thought Brightwall, too many of the previous supervisors had given Benjamin way too much slack. And, like Brightwall, Benjamin was nearing some possible retirement options and there lay the rub. In a heated confrontation, just one week prior, Brightwall had hinted that the best option for Benjamin was to take early retirement and get out of the DCI. This of course, was the reason for the practical joke involving the urine samples: Benjamin's revenge.

Brightwall sighed and looked down at the second name on his

list, "Adam Hawkett," aka Hawk. Hawkett was another detective who was causing problems. The fact that he was Benjamin Willoughby's partner, seemed to intensify the whole situation, but Hawkett's problems were more worrisome to Brightwall and the muscles at the base of his neck involuntarily tightened as his thoughts accumulated. Hawkett was morphing into what they referred to at the agency as a classic "burnout" and when that happened to an agent, he or she became unpredictable, sometimes unproductive and, even more worrisome, sometimes explosive. Sometimes, and this thought made Brightwall shudder, a burned-out detective became a suicide statistic. He'd heard Hawkett was drinking hard and that made the situation even worse.

Why is it, he wondered, so many law enforcement personnel end up with an alcohol problem. But, of course, he knew the answer to that question. There was hardly ever a happy day in law enforcement. Nobody had a smiley-face decal on his or her desk or vehicle. Even the secretaries seemed a little bit more dour than those in other walks of life. The business of law enforcement only dealt with the ugly side of human behavior and things rarely seemed to improve. Each convicted criminal was replaced by a new one who was often more cunning and violent, and... Brightwall stopped his thoughts. He'd been over this ground a million times and it was an unproductive exercise. He decided to get on to the business at hand.

He reached for a file and pulled out the letter of protest directed at Hawkett's involvement in a recent conflict with the media. Hawkett's former wife, Ann Mora, who had kept her maiden name, was a news anchor for one of the local TV stations. On the previous Monday, one week earlier, Ann had covered a touching, human-interest story involving a small girl, a kitten and a tricycle. Apparently, the kitten's leg had been crushed when the little girl, the kitten's owner, had accidentally run over it on the sidewalk of her family's home. Rushing the kitten, Mittens, to a local veterinarian, the distraught owner and her parents learned that its leg had been destroyed. To save the cat they would have to amputate its leg and, in fact, they did just that. The result was a three-legged kitten. Ann had picked up on the story while delivering her cat to the same vet clinic for its annual checkup. Someone, and it was now not certain who'd first mentioned the idea, wondered if a prosthetic leg might be developed for the small kitten, and a very hot news story transpired. The TV station she worked for milked the public's sympathy in a very professional manner.

By that Wednesday, Ann had set up a hot line number and encouraged every citizen of Des Moines to send a financial pledge to help pay for the artificial leg. Specialists at the University of Iowa Medical Clinic had determined that the artificial appendage would cost $22,000, which, they pointed out, was an amount that was far less than the actual costs. By the following Friday, the hot line had received pledges for over $30,000, and Ann's news station had a solid lead in the TV ratings for the week. Everyone was ecstatic, well almost everyone.

On Friday morning, around 10:15, Hawkett walked out of a house located on the south side of Des Moines in a poorer neighborhood, crossed the lawn and ducked under the yellow crime scene tape surrounding the front yard. Some murders were worse than others and this one was beyond terrible. Two adults and two children lay dead inside the house, one child, still in her bed, had been shot where she slept. At first glance, it appeared to be some sort of drug deal gone bad. Hawkett was physically sickened by what he saw. Even for seasoned detectives, this one had been a difficult one. The unspoken question was everywhere. What kind of bastard would gun down small defenseless children? His anger and frustration were so intense that his breathing was irregular and though he wasn't winded, he felt that way.

Hawkett, completely lost in his thoughts, stopped when he realized he was unconsciously heading the wrong way toward his vehicle. His car was parked up the block in the other direction. When he turned to navigate his way through the growing crowd of onlookers behind the barrier tape, he ran right into Ann's microphone and a cameraman and was trapped.

Staring directly into the eyes of her former husband, Ann could see the anger and pain. She sensed that another big story was in the making. Her stepping-stone career in the Midwest was about to escalate into something bigger. She could feel it.

Hawkett stopped and stared into her eyes. "What?"

With the smooth, confident voice that was Ann's trademark, she went to work. "Detective Hawkett, can you give the public an update on what's happening inside that house?"

Maybe it was just his depression, maybe it was lack of sleep or maybe it was Ann's impersonal manner. Maybe it was all of the above that led him to make the following reply to a live studio hookup.

"Nothing that would interest your viewers. They're too busy raising money for a freaking poody cat." Then he shouldered his way through the crowd and left.

The engineer sitting in the booth back at the station, who was supposed to bleep out such profanity via the seven-second delay, had abandoned his post to use the toilet. Therefore, the quote found itself played directly onto *Good Morning Des Moines* as Bob, the Morning Anchor, listened in disbelief and was momentarily speechless.

The TV station, subsequently, terminated the careless engineer and the executive director of Good Morning Des Moines fired off an angry fax to the DCI. Now Brightwall would have to deal with the situation.

Brightwall put down the fax copy and took off his glasses. What am I going to do about this, he wondered.

With no immediate solutions coming to mind, Brightwall replaced his glasses and let his eyes travel to the third item on his list. He'd written, "Doug Cordoe, Taylor County." A request had come in only twenty minutes earlier from the sheriff of Taylor County in Southwest Iowa asking for assistance. The message seemed to indicate that a local banker had been murdered. Murder investigation was his life's work and Brightwall enjoyed his occupation. Well, most of the time, he thought, as he once again glanced out at Benjamin Willoughby and a scowl reappeared on his face. But he could never understand why so many Americans murdered so many of their fellow citizens. He had recently read that every twenty-two minutes an American was shot, stabbed, beaten or strangled to death. This in the most prosperous country in the world, he thought...amazing.

Well, Iowa had made its most recent contribution to that statistic with a stabbing in Southwest Iowa sometime the previous weekend, a pitchfork stabbing no less, and the local sheriff needed help.

Brightwall leaned back in his chair and folded his hands behind his head. What to do, he pondered. Then it came to him. Yes. What was it the politicians called it? Yeah, it came to him, a "package deal." He'd solve his problems with a package deal and rid himself of two, no three problems.

Once again, he picked up his pen and quickly jotted "Murder, Taylor County" on the right-hand side of the paper and drew an arrow traveling from each notation on the left side of the paper toward it. The flare-up of his ulcer was aborted at the last instant. Yes, he would send his problems deep into the farm country of Southwest Iowa. His blood pressure began to subside and a warm smile slowly spread across his face. He stepped to the door of his office, opened it and politely asked Willoughby and Hawkett to step inside. It just might be a good week after all, he thought.

CHAPTER

3

The two detectives rode in silence for nearly an hour after leaving the center of Des Moines and turning south on Interstate 35. Each man seemed to be lost in his own thoughts. Neither was happy about leaving town. In fact, it was unusual for Brightwall to send them off to investigate what one of their staff members referred to as "a good old-fashioned country murder."

Brightwall's pleasant mood had seemed somewhat unusual. Benjamin had the uneasy feeling that he was just shipping them off to the corner of the state to be rid of them. Maybe the health-scare prank hadn't been such a good idea after all. The memory of Brightwall screaming obscenities and the defeated look upon Sylvia's face as she left the chief's office earlier that morning popped into Benjamin's mind and he found himself chuckling out loud.

He reached over to help himself to his fourth donut from the box lying on the seat between the two men. He allowed himself a quick glimpse at Hawkett, apparently sound asleep, slumped in the seat, his six-foot plus frame folded up into, what appeared to Benjamin to be, an uncomfortable position.

Benjamin pulled a cigar from his coat pocket, lit it with the car lighter and took a deep draw. Almost becoming oblivious to the passing traffic, he fell into deep thought as he stared down the unending strip of pavement ahead. Retire? How could Brightwall even think of him retiring from the DCI? Bastard! Stupid, bureaucratic bastard! Had Brightwall forgotten all of the years, all of the homicides he and Hawkett had solved, all of the times he had put his life on the line? Well, maybe not his life, but at least his reputation. Well, hell yes, he'd risked his life, damn right he had!

"Lack of performance," yes, that was what the bastard had said. Hell, when Hawkett and I were hot we.... Benjamin's head full of steam quickly dissipated as he once again came to grips with the problem. Team, yes the team spirit had ended.

Benjamin glanced once again at his sleeping partner, and like he'd done so many times in the past weeks, he tried to work through his mind and find the day, determine the point, when Hawkett had begun to decline. And, as in past mental exercises, the area was gray but certain key events rose to the surface, parts of a puzzle that he couldn't quite solve. Surely the divorce from Ann had not been pleasant, but that was an event that had been festering for quite some time and certainly came as no surprise to anyone. Thank God there were no children, thought Benjamin. No, it wasn't the divorce that led to Hawk's current mental state, although it probably played some role. It was Hawkett's stubborn belief that somehow, because of his devotion to duty, society should get better. He had this naive notion that crime rates should fall, that new laws would make life better, that people would learn to somehow be more accountable for their actions. And, of course, these notions were all fairy tales. Hawkett's problem was that he couldn't allow himself to quit trying, yet at the same time he couldn't come to grips with the fact that things weren't improving. It was not a good state of mind. Hence he found himself going through a cycle of depression and anger, followed by more frustration and more depression.

And, thought Benjamin grimly, the murder of children, six so far this year counting the two last week. Holy Father, he almost spoke out loud, how could we be letting this happen? What was going so wrong that people were killing defenseless children? Was this the bottom of the graph that recorded our society's continued moral decay? The murder of children sickened him and he knew it was much harder on Hawkett. The

13

guy ought to find a new career, get the hell out of the DCI and get a good job, maybe as a computer programmer or something.

Benjamin, in an effort to lift his own spirits, started recalling some of the spectacular successes he and Hawkett had enjoyed the past several years, a success rate nearly six times better than any other team on the DCI force. Damn, it had been great, felt great! And Willoughby knew, he had no doubt, that the success had been attributed, in part, to Hawkett's enthusiasm and capabilities. What to do? How could he help pull his younger partner out of his depressed state? What were the words he needed to speak?

He felt tears slipping down over his cheeks caused by the frustration he felt. He quickly wiped them away with his sleeve and turned to see if his partner had noticed. He worried about how much easier it seemed these days for those tears to start slipping out. With age he was getting soft, he guessed.

Still, he could take care of himself in a tight spot. Damn right he could. But Hawkett, nothing seemed to be left of his former self, the gutsy, cocky companion who had chased many a trail with him. He was now a ghost of the man he had once been, drinking way too much.

Despite two marriages, Willoughby had never been the father of a child, a fact that he had come to regret more and more with passing years. He had always secretly wished Hawkett was his son.

Hawkett's mental torture had been Benjamin's torture as well, but some things couldn't be repaired and it was beginning to seem that Hawkett's mental state was one of those things. Benjamin knew his partner was potentially suicidal. Benjamin had taken the departmental psychiatrist to dinner, bought her drinks until she was drunk, and pumped all the confidential information out of her that he needed in relation to her sessions with Hawkett. He had started making it a point to frequent the same bars as Hawkett, tailing him when necessary to keep an eye on him.

It was probably a waste of time, still he couldn't bear the thought of seeing his younger partner dead. How long could this go on, he wondered. Some days Benjamin wanted to grab Hawkett and slap him silly, some days he wanted to hug him. If only things could be like before, he thought.

Maybe I should retire, he thought. Maybe Brightwall is right. He had a sudden vision of himself in retirement, sitting around the house, watching TV, drinking too much, rotting away. His trance was broken as he spotted a sign announcing the exit to Highway 92 West which would take them even further into the hills of Southern Iowa.

As the car slowed and Benjamin veered onto the exit, the motion rolled Hawkett out of his cramped position. The small, economy-size cars being issued to the detectives were not suited to his larger frame, especially when that frame was suffering from a severe hangover.

As he awoke, Hawkett could immediately feel the black lights of shame running through his thoughts. He shouldn't have been so rude to Ann, shouldn't have said the things he said. Damn, he grimaced as he wondered what he looked like as he snarled into her camera, what the public saw, what a lot of children heard. Shit. He shook his head and opened his eyelids slowly, letting just a little sunshine filter into his bloodshot eyes. Even that hurt. Wouldn't my father be proud of me if he was alive and could see me now he thought. Hung over and wallowing in self-pity, two conditions his father never succumbed to. He should apologize to Ann, hell yes he should. He would send her some flowers and a note, let her know he was ashamed of his behavior and how he had treated her. Not to mention how he had let the DCI down, tarnishing their public image. He didn't blame Brightwall for his anger.

But then he had doubts. If he sent her a letter, would that letter be used against him? Would he find it used in one of her stories? She was capable of just such an action. Well hell, he'd send the letter anyway. His father had always said it took a bigger man to apologize when he was wrong than to brag when he was right. That would be his first step toward chipping away at his guilty conscience.

His second step would be to get off of this damned booze! These hangovers were becoming fairly regular events, occurring almost daily. He was constantly finding himself needing a drink to get over the hangover from drinking the night before. An ugly, guilty word was floating in the back of his thoughts and it had been coming to mind more and more frequently: "Alcoholism." Every bit as bad an addiction as that of the coke-heads and crack-heads that he dealt with so often in this line of work.

He would have to do it, angrily telling himself—yes, dammit he would just have to go to the next AA meeting like Brightwall had suggested. Fight this thing off. Be a man. Clean himself up. Get a life. No more denial. His mind shifted gears, sliding into neutral and he almost laughed out loud at himself. How many times had he been down this road he thought. It was like the age-old saying, "When is the most popular day to start a diet? Tomorrow." It was a funny line, but the premise behind it wasn't funny at all. When was he going to find tomorrow and how was he going to get there from here?

He went back to thinking about Ann, their break-up, the void this had left in his life. He thought it strange that the depression continued to linger even after the sense of losing Ann was gone. Strangely, he no longer missed her. He thought, he was never sure, but he thought the root of his emptiness stemmed from a sense of failure, failure to carry through with their life's plans, his role in that and how his occupational choice in life had affected hers.

And here I sit, he thought, going over all these feelings for maybe the fifty millionth time like it had just happened yesterday. The feelings wouldn't go away; they imprisoned him. But maybe it wasn't just him. Her favorite saying, especially when they were fighting, was "all men are scum." Hell why continue to think about it now he wondered, what a pointless exercise in anger.

And the nightmares, man, those damnable nightmares. At least they didn't seem so bad when he fell asleep drunk. The booze didn't heal anything, but it could sure dull the pain. His nightmares never quit though, even when he was passed-out drunk. He was sure the intensity of them was getting worse.

Every dream had the same basic plot: children were being beaten, being stabbed or were facing some other horrible attack, and all he could do was stand and watch as the children screamed out his name for help. And while they screamed, Hawkett was somehow frozen and unable to help, while Ann stood at the edge of his dream with a knowing look on her face. Unspoken words, but the look said it all. In her eyes he was a failure, and by not saving the lives of these poor children, he was just confirming her beliefs. The scene was so vivid, that he no longer thought of it as a dream. Maybe, he thought, if he could stop the dreams, he could fight the depression. But the dreams continued to come.

He opened his eyes wider and looked across the car at Benjamin who was lighting yet another cigar. The silhouette of the man was almost comical. Overweight, thinning hair, a slightly large, slightly crooked nose sitting above a neatly trimmed mustache. Hawkett guessed the word most people would use to describe Benjamin was "jovial" and he was certainly that. But he knew Benjamin and knew what he was capable of when the situation demanded it.

He'd seen Benjamin shoot three men during their career together. One had died as a result of the injuries. All the shootings had been determined appropriate by the DCI review board, and they had most certainly been deemed appropriate by Benjamin, just part of his job. Life was like that for Benjamin, black and white.

Most law enforcement personnel were never called upon to fire their weapons in the line of duty during their entire career. Those who did often suffered severe personal trauma from the event, especially if it resulted in a death. Some careers were ruined by a shooting, but not Benjamin's. He loved to shoot his guns, was an excellent marksman, and if he needed to put a bad guy down in the line of duty, then rest assured, the bad guy would go down.

Hawkett smiled to himself as he remembered again the first week he and Benjamin had worked together, the week the "stake-out incident" had occurred. Just mention of the phrase "the stake out" around the DCI headquarters and everyone would chuckle; they knew the reference. It had taken place almost thirteen years ago when Hawkett was still just a green rookie on the force.

The DCI had loaned two agents, Benjamin and Hawkett, to the Des Moines Metro Police Department. The loaning of agents was a rare occurrence, but Metro had a problem. Des Moines had a problem, a big problem. Some guy was hitting two convenience stores a week and he was a shooter. He had killed two employees and wounded seven others. It didn't make any difference that they had shown absolutely no resistance and cooperated fully. He'd shot them anyway. A real cold-blooded son of a bitch. Some stores had been hit twice already.

Thirteen years prior, at the time of the "stake-out incident," the string of crimes had been declared a crisis for the city. It was not commonplace then, as unfortunately, it would soon become.

By the time he and Benjamin had become involved with the case, it had been going on for almost a month, from late November through December. It was the week before Christmas. Hawkett remembered it well. Des Moines was white, covered by nearly a foot of fresh snow and Christmas lights were strung everywhere. People were shopping, traveling and planning for the holiday season. The Christmas spirit was high, yet many were haunted by the news of some criminal robbing stores and shooting people. He demonstrated the same method of operation every time—in fast, out fast, snap off two or three shots out of his .38 caliber—always blood spilled.

Gas stations and convenience stores had proven his favorite tar-

17

gets. Between the Metro guys and the DCI, they were staking out twelve stores per night. So there sat Benjamin and Hawkett, new partners trying to get to know each other, one rookie, one veteran, in the back room of a Go-Quick Convenience store on South East 14th.

It was nearly midnight and they were about to call it quits as the store would be closing soon. Benjamin said he had to use the can and left momentarily. Hawkett, alone, peeked out through a slightly-opened door to where the female clerk was totaling her cash register receipts and preparing to close the store.

Hawkett remembered yawning, then stretching his arms up and back behind his head just as it happened. Suddenly and silently, the man appeared, no ski mask, no loud intimidating threats. In the door he came, appearing out of nowhere, and immediately aiming his gun at the female clerk behind the counter.

And, just as fast, the girl, though she'd been warned not to, turned and looked right at the door Hawkett was attempting to quietly open. The criminal turned and there stood Hawkett, gun raised. That night, Hawkett learned a lesson about hesitation that he would never again forget. In that second, as he tried to decide whether to yell "Freeze, DCI!" or "Drop it!" the criminal, without hesitation, turned and fired at Hawkett. The bullet barely missed as it ricocheted off of a can of chili beans. Hawkett dived for cover, stumbled and crawled across the floor, trying to get to the other end of the short aisles to get a shot at the guy, save the girl—Do something!

And then, there he stood, the man, smiling, pointing the .38 right at Hawkett's face, not three feet away. And there was Hawkett, on his hands and knees, his gun under his hand on the floor, defenseless. The man was smiling, standing so close that Hawkett could smell the oil on the pistol. Then out of nowhere, he heard the discharge of a gun. He watched in disbelief as the criminal stumbled backwards, blood spewing from his forehead, and collapsed on top of a stack of Hamm's beer cases, dead.

Hawkett, in shock, turned and looked behind him. There stood Benjamin, his pants still down around his ankles, his gun still extended, pointed at the dying criminal, a cold hard look in his eyes. Thankfully, he'd managed to pull his underwear up. They were red and white striped boxer shorts, Hawkett recalled. Neither detective said a word. Benjamin turned and walked, rather shuffled away and Hawkett heard the toilet flush a few moments later.

Hawkett, bringing himself back to the present, turned his head to see a roadblock ahead. Benjamin reduced the car's speed and moved the car to the opposite lane to maneuver around a large group of orange DOT vehicles. As they drove around, Hawkett observed six DOT workers donning orange vests and hard hats. Three of them were carrying clipboards, one held an orange flag, and another was just standing there. The sixth had a shovel and seemed to be digging a hole in the side of the road bank. Hawkett found himself wondering if the sweating worker digging the hole hated his life as much as Hawkett hated his own. Great, he thought, keep feeling sorry for yourself.

As they cruised down Highway 92, Benjamin found himself beginning to enjoy the scenery. It was a cool day with low humidity unlike the three previous days which had been real scorchers. As Benjamin rolled down the window of the Escort, he was pleasantly surprised by the fresh air that came cascading in. He had rolled the window down because the car's ashtray was getting full and he needed somewhere to flip his ashes, but the fresh air made him forget and he snubbed out the cigar and tossed it out the window instead, an act which immediately made him feel guilty. Benjamin had breathed city air, rather city smog, for so long that he had forgotten what real air tasted like. That fact he found more than a little depressing, but the scenery—the beautiful scenery! The further they drove, the more impressive it became. Numerous trees, nurtured by ample late summer rains, were vividly displaying a multitude of green shades, Mother Nature's idea of a mixed salad. Cool rains the week before had encouraged the grass-covered hills to turn to a deep, emerald green. All of this, patchworked with fields of corn and soybeans and a farmstead here and there presented a spectacular view. It brought back images of childhood visits to his uncle's farm. Sure doesn't seem like the setting for a brutal murder, he thought.

Hawkett sat up in his seat and stretched his arms and legs as far as the small car would allow. The painkillers Benjamin had given him just before leaving Des Moines were beginning to ease his headache. The fresh air coming through Benjamin's window had given Hawkett a pleasant sensation as well. Motion to his right caught his eyes and Hawkett turned to see several young calves racing across a pasture, their tails flying out behind them.

He was puzzled to see the calves playing in this free environment. Magazine ads that his former wife, Ann, had shoved in front of his face seemed to project the notion that all baby calves were raised in some sort of confining cages. Apparently this wasn't the case.

Several were kicking their heels up as if they were full of enthusiasm and joy. He guessed they probably were.

The cool air flowing into his system must have been too much of a shock to Hawkett's stomach; he realized almost too late. When he yelled for Benjamin to pull the car over, his older partner knew what the problem was and wasted no time getting the Escort off to the side of the road, allowing Hawkett to open the door, jump out and vomit in the ditch.

With the brief, but necessary intermission over, the car proceeded down the highway, soon entering the town of Winterset, Iowa. "BIRTHPLACE OF JOHN WAYNE," a sign said greeting them at the city limits, and Benjamin steered the car into the parking lot of a restaurant. Both men climbed out of the small car, stretched and entered the establishment. Hawkett detoured toward the men's restroom.

Benjamin could just imagine him splashing cool water on his face. He would have liked to have dropped his younger partner off at the local barber shop for a shave and haircut. Then from there they could find a good men's clothing store and buy Hawkett a new pair of blue jeans and tennis shoes. A suit would have been better in Benjamin's opinion, but that would have been out of the question, of course. Even though Benjamin was a strict coat and tie man himself, he tolerated his partner's casual dress, he just wished the guy would buy some new stuff, at least attempt to look respectable.

With beads of water still lingering around his scalp and upper shirt, Hawkett walked out to the table where Benjamin was already seated. Though his stomach still felt a little queasy, he thought maybe the worst of the hangover had passed. In fact, the smell of coffee and food cooking in the kitchen actually seemed appealing. He tried to dismiss the thought that a gin and tonic might not taste too bad, but he didn't try very hard. When the waitress came, both men ordered coffee.

"Where is it we're going?" Hawkett questioned Benjamin.

"Pigmy."

"Pigmy? Have you ever been there before?"

"No, can't say as I have," said Benjamin as he gave a warm smile to the waitress bringing them their coffee.

"You know this is your fault don't you; us being sent way out here in the boonies somewhere?" Hawkett berated him.

"My fault, what makes you say that?" Even as Benjamin said it, he knew his partner was right, but damned if he was going to admit it.

"Your little gag last week. Just had to play a little funny, didn't you? Now look who gets the last laugh. Brightwall was smiling like a cat in cream when we left his office. Did you see him? I'm tellin' you Ben, he wants your ass out of the department. If he could've proved you were responsible for that little incident with the bogus memo, you'd be sitting in the park today, feeding the pigeons, and no pension. Bad enough you get us sent out here in the middle of nowhere..." Hawkett stopped.

Benjamin wasn't paying any attention to his grievances. A young mother had brought her small son into the restaurant and the two had seated themselves in a booth across the aisle from the detectives. Benjamin should have been somebody's grandpa. He would have made a great one. From a pocket in his jacket, Benjamin fished out a piece of candy. He always carried some with him. Benjamin slid to the edge of his seat and extended his hand holding the candy where the small child could see it. Then much to the glee of the small boy and his mother, Benjamin did his perfect impression of Donald Duck, talking slowly so the child could understand. Within a few minutes he knew the child's name and age, and the mother's name and had introduced both himself and Hawkett to the pair.

Twenty minutes later the two men were on the road, heading toward Pigmy. Benjamin was once again puffing on a cigar and the smoke kept Hawkett's stomach a little squeamish. He knew if the queasiness ended, the need for a drink would begin, so he decided not to complain. It would have been a waste of time anyway.

Driving a distance to begin a murder investigation was not common procedure for the two detectives. For the last several years all of their skills had been put to use in the greater metropolitan area of Des Moines. Actually, both men had spent their entire lives as city dwellers and really had little experience out in the rural areas of the state. They had little idea of some of the special problems they might encounter while conducting an investigation in a rural setting. They would soon be educated.

21

CHAPTER
4

Shortly before 11 AM, the detectives' car popped over the crest of a hill, just a few miles north of the Missouri border, and a town appeared in the valley below. A large sign stood at the edge of town introducing incoming traffic to Pigmy, "Home of the Pigmy Giants, Winners of the 1990 State Girls' Basketball Tournament."

The Taylor County Sheriff's Office was located on the second floor of the county courthouse. The courthouse was a monstrous brick building, built at the turn of the century, located near the center of Pigmy. As the detectives entered the sheriff's office, they were greeted by a shapely brunette with big, round glasses and a tight-fitting uniform. She looked at each man in turn before speaking.

"DCI?" she asked.

"That's us," replied Benjamin. "My name's Benjamin Willoughby." He opened his billfold to show her his identification and introduced Hawkett.

"My name's Jan, Jan Tenton," she replied, giving each man a warm smile.

"Have a chair," she continued. "Coffee?" Both men nodded. "Sheriff Spencer is out right now, but he should be right back. This murder has got him kind of wound up. Things have been kind of bloody around here lately and, well, he isn't really handling the stress very well." Her smile had been replaced with a look of thoughtful concern.

No sooner had she finished speaking when in walked Sheriff Spencer, short, overweight, balding and visibly shaken. The lines of tension were drawn tight on his face and he was sweating profusely even though the air-conditioned room was quite cool.

"Who are you guys?" he barked immediately upon spotting them.

"DCI," replied Benjamin. "You call—we come."

Spencer studied them silently for maybe five seconds. His hands were shaking and his breathing was coming in unnatural gasps. Hawkett wondered if the man suffered from some degree of emphysema.

"Good," he panted. He threw his arms up. "I'm done, finished, capoot. At the end of my term, I'm off to retirement in sunny Arizona. I've had enough, you understand? I'm too old for this shit, you understand? Two of them, can you believe it? Two damn bankers murdered in the last six months. Can you believe it?"

"Two?" queried Benjamin, cocking one eye and leaning forward in his chair.

"Hell, yes, two! Not six months ago, I get a call. Over on the other side of the county is the only other bank we have. Cashier, named Mitzi Miller, asks, can I come. Says they have a client who's yelling and screaming at their loan officer, a guy named Al Grist. Wants to know, can I come, restore the peace, that sort of stuff." He was breathing harder now and his face was turning visibly redder.

"Sure I says, I'll be right over. Took me maybe twenty minutes. I walk into the bank and you can hear him right away, even through a closed door. The language, man I'm tellin' you, it would have made a whore blush! I didn't need directions, walked right to the door and knocked. The yelling inside stops, so in I go. Inside I find their loan officer, Al, white as a sheet, standing behind his chair, scared shitless, I'm tellin' you. And standing there in front of him across from his desk is Emil Young, a local farmer.

"Now calm down, I says to Emil. Emil, he just stands there and looks at me like he can't figure out what I'm doing there. Sit down and

23

relax, Emil, I says. You can't be yelling and screamin' these obscenities in a public place, I says.

"Then Emil, he sits down, quiet as you please and I think, okay, no big deal. Then the banker sits down and starts to loosen his tie, glad to be able to breathe again. And you know what happened then?" Spencer's eyes were nearly popping out of his head now and his face was beet red. "I'll tell you what. Before I could move, I'm tellin' you, in the blink of a gnat's eye, Emil yanks a pistol out of his coat pocket and shoots Banker Grist right between his eyes! Can you believe it? Then Emil looks at me, turns the gun around and shoots himself, right between the eyes. And there I stand, brain tissue splattered on my glasses. Can you believe it? Two dead bodies in maybe three seconds!"

There was a pause of silence during which the two DCI detectives wondered if Sheriff Spencer was going to have a heart attack or just shake to death. The silence lingered. Spencer suddenly turned away, walked across the floor to the biggest desk in the office and collapsed into the swivel chair behind it. He covered his eyes with one hand, deep in thought.

"Jan," the sheriff spoke softly trying to calm himself down. "Have we started a file on this last murder?"

"Sure, Sheriff." She quickly crossed the room and bent over to retrieve the file from the bottom drawer of a cabinet. The strain on her tight-fitting pants was tremendous and both DCI agents' minds wandered momentarily from the case at hand. She quickly retrieved the file and handed it to Sheriff Spencer.

"Thanks, Hon," he said, taking the file folder and its contents from her. He opened it and glanced at the papers inside. "Well, let me tell you what I know about this mess and it ain't much, I'm telling you." He seemed to be directing his comments directly towards Benjamin.

"The victim is one Doug Cordoe. Cordoe was not a popular man, bankers generally aren't anyway, and the past four or five years especially. Believe me, farm country has gone through one hell of a financial shake-up. I can't tell you how many second and third generation farms have been lost, all of them different verses to the same song: borrowed against inflating property values, inflation dived, property values dived, and bingo, no collateral, poor cash flows, hellish financial losses. Banks who had encouraged expansion ten years ago, turned on their same customers and, boy, has it gotten messy." Spencer rose and walked over to the window to peer out.

"Man, all the foreclosures!" he went on. "Our department seemed to be involved in all of them, one way or another."

Sheriff Spencer continued to stare out the window, then paused for a minute, took a deep breath, and once again began to speak, "Our main bank here in Pigmy failed not three years ago. Cordoe was the chief loan officer when it failed and continued working for a new group of investors who had bought the good loans and the bank for seventeen cents on the dollar. The bad loans went to the FDIC sharks.

"Anyway, after the bank failed, the new management hired Cordoe to stay on and manage it. The previous management encouraged financing farm operations; the new management wanted out of them. So they told Cordoe what to do and how to do it and he did. Man had no conscience—maybe that's a prerequisite for being a good banker, I don't know. He seemed to have no problem foreclosing on his clients, old and young alike."

Spencer turned and came back to his seat where he once again seemed to collapse into his chair.

"This morning, about 7:30, our rural mailman, Harley Whitmeyer, was cruising down a country road known as the 'Dead End Road' about a half mile south of the edge of town and he notices a bunch of vultures come flying out from under a bridge as he crosses it.

"You guys know what vultures are?" he asked the detectives. Both of them nodded.

The sheriff continued, "Harley, I guess because he's Harley, turns his car around and goes back to the bridge to see what they're after. Says the smell hit him bad just as soon as he got out of his car. Down below the bridge, partially into the water, lie the remains of our victim, banker Doug Cordoe, and I'm tellin' you fellows, it wasn't pretty. Damn!" He paused and wiped beads of sweat off his forehead with the back of his hand.

"Two of my deputies got there before I did, maybe two minutes. I doubt either one of them has ever seen a murder victim. When I got there, they were both puking their guts out all over the scene of the crime. Great way to contaminate evidence, I tell you.

"The guy had a pitchfork stabbed clear through his chest. You could see the points of all five tines sticking out the back of his shirt. We think he was killed on the road then shoved over the bridge railing. I found his billfold on him, but identification was really no problem. We all knew who he was.

25

"Incidentally, the banker's wallet had almost $100 cash in it and all his credit cards. We found his car, a 1992 Cadillac, parked in a grove of trees not two hundred yards from the bridge. You couldn't see it from the road.

"Guy like that, with that kind of job, could have a hundred enemies. Where do you start?"

Spencer glanced once again at the documents in the file now on his desk. "Jan, will you get a plat book and make a map showing the location of the crime scene?" She went to work immediately.

"Now we do have another interesting twist to this deal. Banker Doug has a son, had a son I guess I should say, Denny Cordoe, guy about 34 or 35 years of age. Crazy bastard, I'm telling you, clear off his rocker, burnt-out on drugs a long time ago, been in and out of several institutions. We've accumulated a twenty-page file that I see Jan put in this folder; you can read through it yourselves. Doug Cordoe had a house here in town where he stayed most of the time. He also owned a farm outside of town, messy place, old trailer house. Denny's been kind of living out on his father's farm the last couple of years. I guess living is not the right word, more like just existing.

"Creepy bastard out there roaming through the woods and fields, stealing food from neighbors. Been a real problem. We never really had anything solid to charge him with though.

"I don't think his old man was supplying him with much more than basic necessities, but we never quite knew. He wouldn't discuss the kid or hardly admit that he existed. Denny was a product of Doug's first marriage. They never got along even before the drug thing. I guess letting the kid exist on his property was as close as he cared to come to parenting. Probably just didn't want to have to pick up the tab for institutional care is more like it."

Benjamin interrupted him, "Was Cordoe married at the time of his death?"

"No, three marriages, three failures. Only the one child fortunately. Anyway, Paul, my deputy, found barefooted tracks upstream from the corpse that could be Denny's. The guy runs around barefooted most of the time. Strange, right? So now maybe we've got one hundred and one suspects."

"Where's the body now?" Benjamin asked.

"It's at our local funeral home, iced up, waiting for instructions from you people. I suppose your forensic boys will want to take a look at

26

it. Our local doctor thinks maybe Cordoe died sometime Friday evening or Saturday morning, but the heat's been pretty bad, so he's not all that sure.

"We're sure not professionals out in the country here, but we've done the best we could with a deteriorating corpse. This file contains pictures, measurements and timetables. There's not much, but it's the best we've been able to piece together so far. My deputies are still out on Dead End looking for Cordoe Jr."

"Dead End?"

"Yeah, you know, the road leaves the edge of town here, goes one and a half miles east and just stops. One way in, one way out, by car that is."

"And Cordoe was killed on this road?" Benjamin asked.

"That's where he was found. He'd left town last Friday evening to spend the weekend on his farm. It's located on the far end of Dead End Road."

"And his son was out there too?"

"Presumably. We haven't found young Cordoe yet, but that's where he stays."

"Anybody else live on that road?" Benjamin continued questioning.

"Oh yeah, three different houses besides Cordoe's, and any of the people living in them might have had it in for Cordoe, one way or the other, believe me, but my money's on his son, the crazy drugged-up bastard. We find the kid, we'll probably solve this thing. Still, you never know."

Yeah, that's for sure thought Benjamin. He'd investigated murder after murder and he had to agree, as often as not, the murderer could turn out to be the most unlikely suspect. Sometimes the murderer hadn't even been considered as a suspect early on in the case.

"Tell me this, Sheriff, if Cordoe lived here in town, why stay out at his farm if it was less then two miles away?"

"Yeah, I see your point. Well, they have a pond there and the river runs through the property also. Cordoe was an avid fisherman. I think he just liked to get away from his town job. Hell, maybe he just got lonely, wanted to spend time with his crazy son, who knows?"

"Well," Benjamin stood up, sensing their briefing was over, "mind if we nose around a little, see if we can help solve this thing?"

27

"More power to you. Take it and run!" Spencer shot back with enthusiasm.

Benjamin cleared his throat, "Any special rules here, Sheriff— procedure, protocol, you know that kind of thing?"

"Hell, no! Just clean this mess up. The sooner, the better, okay?"

"Sure," Benjamin smiled, shrugged, pulled out a cigar and turned to Hawkett, still slouched in his chair, silent. "Well, Sherlock, shall we proceed?"

Hawkett didn't reply but slowly stood up.

"Oh, fellows," Spencer seemed to have an afterthought, "you got any weapons?"

"Hawkett carries a .38 Colt; I've got a sawed off .870 in the trunk and my high power."

"High power what?" Spencer raised his eyebrows.

".222 Browning. I target shoot a lot, you know? I stuck it in this morning when I found out we were leaving town. Thought I might do some target shooting out here in the hills, if we have time that is."

"Yeah, well fellows, don't be shooting any of our local residents, okay? We've had enough death already. This ain't the city, you know. We're not used to killings every night. Okay?"

Both detectives nodded quietly. Neither of them had any desire to kill any farm folks. Sometimes things don't work out as planned though.

CHAPTER 5

The two detectives spotted a cafe down the street from the courthouse and headed toward it. Hawkett read through the file as they walked.

"Pitchfork. Right through the chest. Don't believe we've ever come up against a bad guy with a pitchfork before. Can you trace a pitchfork?"

Willoughby snorted, "Hell, farmers all have pitchforks, don't they? Pitchin' hay and diggin' potatoes? I think you have to own a pitchfork to be a farmer. The handle might be a chance for prints."

They started to cross the street, but stopped to let a pickup truck pulling a trailer cross in front of them. The trailer contained a giant red and white bull. The bull turned his head to look at them with a menacing stare. He had several flies on his back and attempted to alleviate this problem by taking a couple hard swats with his thick tail. Just as he swished his tail, both gawking detectives felt small bits of matter sting them in the face. As the trailer rolled forward, Willoughby could have sworn the bull was smirking at them.

The cafe had a nice, homey feeling about it. Hawkett and Willoughby settled into a booth in one corner, distanced somewhat from the rest of the crowd. A chalkboard on the wall announced that the day's special was roast beef with potatoes and gravy. Both detectives ordered the special from a waitress. The name tag on her smock identified her as June.

The two men read through the various documents in the file as they waited for their meal. Benjamin noticed that he and Hawkett were attracting a lot of attention from the other patrons. He also noticed that of all the people in the restaurant, he was the only one wearing a suit and tie. The business attire in this neck of the woods seemed to be blue jeans and pocket tee-shirts. Well, Hawkett ought to feel right at home, he thought.

Hawkett laid a map out on the table, "Okay, this road here must be the dead end road they found him on. What'd he say, a block and a half long?"

"Mile and a half, city boy. Big difference. These must be the residents living on that road," Benjamin said, pointing at small stars drawn along the road, each with a name or names listed by it.

"Okay, as I understand this thing so far, Banker Cordoe owns a farm at the far end of this dead end road. He left the bank Friday evening with the intention of spending the weekend on his farm, so he drives his Cadillac out of town and down this road. Next time we know his location, he's found dead, stinking dead, under this bridge about halfway down the dead end road, with a pitchfork rammed through his chest and his car parked in a small grove of trees not far from the body. It says in this report that the car, a 1992 Cadillac, was hidden from view of anyone driving down the road."

Benjamin pulled a cigar from his pocket, but then replaced it when he saw June bringing their meals. The food tasted delicious and the portions were generous, even by Benjamin's standards. It crossed Hawkett's mind that they probably wouldn't be eating any fast food while they were working this case. It wasn't likely that there was a fast food joint in a town of Pigmy's size.

The two men ate silently for a few minutes, then Benjamin, while smothering his homemade roll with real butter, suddenly stopped as if preoccupied by some puzzling thought, his eyebrows lowered in concentration.

"The son probably murdered his old man," Benjamin said. "Well, let's use that as a beginning hypothesis. Why didn't he murder him at the farm and bury the body there? Why kill him at the bridge and throw the body in the creek?"

Hawkett replied, "Hey, if he's a psycho boy like the sheriff said, you shouldn't be looking for any logical behavior."

"Well, let's hope Spencer and his boys find this Cordoe Jr. and haul him in. If he's not completely crazy, maybe he'll confess and we can have this little mess wrapped up and be out of here in no time," Benjamin continued.

"Wonder why the kid was living on his old man's farm if they hated each other so much," pondered Hawkett.

"Where else does he go if he's as crazy as the sheriff says and his father refuses to pay for institutional care?"

"Yeah, I s'pose. So, Benji, what are we going to do while we wait for the sheriff and his boys to haul in young Cordoe? Play a little golf? Check out the local bar? This town surely has a bar doesn't it?"

Benjamin ignored the last question. "We'd better drive out to the murder scene and look official. Have you got a tape measure and a magnifying glass?"

Hawkett didn't have a comeback. He was still thinking about the bar.

The dead end road wasn't hard to find; it began adjacent to Pigmy. Benjamin wheeled the Escort around the corner of the intersection, turned onto Dead End, and almost collided with an old woman on a bicycle. Benjamin swerved the car to the right, and the woman went bumping into the ditch, amazingly holding the bicycle upright.

Benjamin pulled the car over to the side of the road and jumped out to see if she was alright. Hawkett reluctantly joined him. The bottom of the ditch was as muddy as a swamp and that's where the old gal sat, mad as a wet hen. Her glasses were hanging precariously on the side of her face.

She dismounted the bike and turned to Benjamin, "You son of a bitch! Where'd you learn to drive?" she yelled.

Benjamin stood there staring at the woman, not quite sure how to reply. She was a small thing, couldn't weigh more than 100 pounds, and was probably seventy to seventy-five years old. Her hair was gray, she wore baggy blue jeans, a faded-denim shirt and a set of glasses that he remembered as being popular in the fifties.

Finally, Benjamin found his tongue.

"Can I help you?" he asked as he started to ease himself down the bank's edge.

She crawled off of the bicycle, a model, noted Hawkett, which must have been at least thirty years old. The bike's wide tires were so entrenched in the mud that it stood by itself even after the woman moved away. She stood back and scowled as Benjamin tugged on the bike trying to release it without soiling his suit pants. Hawkett, standing on the road bank, smiled in spite of himself; the scene was really quite amusing. The little old lady, when not nagging at Benjamin, kept giving quick, suspicious glances at Hawkett and when she saw the smirk on his face, she turned her wrath on him.

"What's so funny, asshole? Why don't you get down here and help?"

Hawkett, somewhat taken back by her rigid statement, started down the side of the ditch bank, but stopped when he saw his help was not necessary as Benjamin gave one final heave and managed to dislodge the bike from the mud, smearing both of his pant legs with grime in the process.

"You'd better hope that front wheel isn't bent, son of a bitch, or I'm suing. That's a good bike, you know. Who are you guys anyway, Laurel and Hardy?"

Benjamin, who was attempting to scrape some of the mud from his pant legs with a small pocket knife, took a deep breath to calm his temper.

"We're from the Iowa Division of Criminal Investigation, Ma'am. My name is Benjamin Willoughby, and this is Adam Hawkett. We're here to investigate a..."

"Oh, Cordoe's murder, huh?" the woman interrupted. "Say, I heard he really looked like hell. Boy, I would a liked to seen the bastard gettin' killed. Hey, you gonna push that bike back up to the road for me? I ought to make you take it to the car wash. You know, I..."

"And who, pray tell," Benjamin interrupted her in return, "may I ask are you?"

"Pearl Oldham. Was Mrs. Oldham, but no more. Husband died." That statement seemed to take some of the steam out of her. "Me and

Thelma live right back there," she turned and pointed at a large, two-story house just down the road.

"Hey, are we gonna be suspects? Well, I tell you, Bubba, I'm ready to take the lie detector test right now, then you can get off my back, okay?"

Benjamin turned and looked up at Hawkett who seemed to be thoroughly enjoying the scene in the ditch.

"Well, Bubba, are you going to haul her in right now?" he asked with a mocking tone.

Benjamin gave Hawkett a dirty look, then turned back to the little old woman. He started to say something to her, but thought it better not to, and rolled the bike up the bank's edge onto the gravel road.

"Mrs. Oldham, I apologize for running you off the road. Detective Hawkett and I will proceed with our investigation and should we need your input, rest assured, we will contact you. Good day." With that Benjamin turned his back on Pearl and made a beeline for the car.

"Son killed him, shot him dead," she yelled, "and everybody knows the bastard deserved it!" Then she swung onto her bicycle and peddled away. Both detectives watched her pump away toward Pigmy.

While opening the car door, Benjamin once again surveyed the mud stains on his pants. He pulled out a cigar and lit it. "I don't suppose they have a good dry cleaner here in Pigmy."

"Don't know. S'pose we better get on down to the scene of the murder, huh Bubba?" Hawkett chuckled as he once again mimicked the old lady's reference to Benjamin.

"Yeah, let's go."

The detectives got back inside the Escort, Benjamin started the motor, adjusted the air conditioning and they drove slowly down Dead End Road.

33

CHAPTER

According to the map provided by the sheriff's office, the first house they came to was Thelma Oldham's, apparently some relative of the woman they'd just pulled out of the ditch. It had a large, open front porch upon which sat yet another elderly woman. She wore a full-length, blue cotton dress and sat, slowly rocking back and forth, in an old, wooden rocking chair. She appeared to be reading a magazine.

Benjamin wheeled down the gravel driveway and parked the car next to a sidewalk leading to the front of the house. The woman stopped rocking and stood up facing the car.

Oh boy, here we go again, thought Benjamin, recalling the confrontation with Pearl and her bicycle. Benjamin climbed out of the car.

"Identify yourself, please," she said in an apprehensive tone.

"Certainly, Ma'am. My name is Benjamin Willoughby. I'm a detective for the Iowa Division of Criminal Investigation. This gentlemen," he turned and pointed at Hawkett, "is also an investigator. We have identification with us." He hoped his assuring tone would ease her fear. The poor woman was trembling slightly.

"It's the murder, isn't it? So it really happened. I didn't want to believe it. Somebody said he'd been killed right down the road. I just can't..." She sat down in the rocking chair, dropped the magazine on the floor and covered her face with her hands. "I just," she stopped, folded her hands in her lap and took a deep breath. "This kind of thing just doesn't happen out here in the country. I mean I've lived in this same house all my life, sixty-seven years, and we've never had any kind of violence like this," she shuddered.

Benjamin glanced back at Hawkett who was still seated in the car.

"Oh, I'm sorry," she seemed to regain her composure, "My name's Thelma Oldham, please join me on the porch." She pointed at a pair of matching lawn chairs not far from the rocking chair. Hawkett unwound his large frame from the front seat and crawled out of the Escort. He strolled down the sidewalk, climbed the porch stairs and joined Benjamin. Each man settled into a lawn chair.

"I suppose you want to question me? Do I have to make a statement or anything? I see this kind of thing every week on TV on *Murder She Wrote*."

"Oh, no," Benjamin smiled, "we don't need a statement from you, just some answers to a few simple questions to help us get a little better picture of the situation. We'll probably end up bringing Angela Lansberry in to solve this case anyway," he gave her a smile and a wink. "I take it you knew the victim, this Doug Cordoe?"

"Yes, I have for years. He owns a quarter right down at the end of our road."

"Quarter?"

"Quarter of a section, one hundred sixty acres."

"Oh, yes, I see." He didn't, but it didn't seem important. "I understand Cordoe has to drive by here to get to his farm, right?"

"Oh, yes, this is the only road in. It ends right at the Cordoe farm," she continued. "I saw him you know, Friday night about sixish. Pearl and I had finished supper and I was sitting out here stitching. I sit out here a lot in the summer. He drove by, same as always, never waves. Even if you wave at him, he just flies right on by...always was an inconsiderate person," she added, a frown appearing on her face.

"Does he come by every day then?" Benjamin asked.

"Oh no, only on weekends. He has a house in town, too. Never could understand why, makes no sense; having a house in town and one

35

out here too, so close to town."

"Was he alone Friday night when he drove by?"

"Well, yes, I mean, I think so. I didn't see anybody with him."

Benjamin pulled out a cigar, started to light it, then stopped abruptly. "Do you mind," he asked, pointing at the cigar with his lighter.

"No," she lied, "go ahead."

Benjamin took a long draw, "Do you know of anyone who hated Cordoe enough to murder him?"

"No, I don't know murderers," she answered quickly in a defensive tone.

Benjamin decided not to give her a lecture on the realm of personalities capable of committing murder. Nothing would be gained. He was beginning to think that very little information was going to be gleaned from Thelma anyway.

"Did you ever do any business at the bank with Cordoe?" asked Benjamin. He hoped the question wouldn't set off a defensive rage, still remembering the encounter with Pearl.

"Never dealt with Doug, never had any reason to. I never borrowed any money."

"Never in your entire life?"

"Not one penny, don't believe in it."

Benjamin shook his head slightly remembering the car payments he had lived with since the day he had first obtained his license to drive.

He turned to Hawkett hoping for some help, but the younger detective seemed to be lost in thought, his hands behind his head, quite comfortable, staring out into space. He turned to Thelma again.

"We, uh, we ran into your sister, Pearl, I believe."

"Sister-in-law," she corrected him quickly.

"Oh, I'm sorry, yes, she said she'd lost her husband. Let's see, he'd be your brother then?"

"Yes, John Oldham. He passed away last spring. Heart attack."

"Oh, I'm sorry. I suppose it was a severe loss, the two of you, er, uh, the three of you, living here together, all those years?"

"I've lived by myself for most of my life, ever since our parents died. John and Pearl had a farm of their own north of Pigmy. They moved here when they lost it two years ago."

"Lost it?"

Thelma took a deep breath; she wasn't sure any of this was the detective's business. "The bank foreclosed on them. John had co-signed a note for their son. John Jr. had purchased another farm way too high. He couldn't hang onto it and, well, lost his father's as well."

"Was Banker Cordoe involved in this?"

"Well, he would be, wouldn't he!" she angrily replied.

Suddenly the interview had taken on a whole new light. Benjamin wondered where to proceed. He decided to head in another direction.

"How do you take care of the farm now? The place looks really nice," he honestly noted, looking out across the mowed farmyard surrounded by neatly-painted red and white outbuildings.

"I rent it out on shares to the young man just down the road, Mike Wilson."

"I see." Benjamin took another long draw on his cigar then blew a puff of smoke out over the porch railing and Thelma watched in disgust as the small toxic cloud seemed to settle on her peonies. Benjamin was trying to imagine how much strength it would take to run a pitchfork through someone's body. Could the feisty little Pearl or ladylike Thelma commit such a heinous crime? Would they be physically strong enough? He had known less-likely murderers he reminded himself.

Benjamin detected a noise which sounded like a weak chain saw. He turned to see Hawkett, with his head on his shoulder, his eyes closed, snoring softly.

He turned quickly to see if Thelma had noticed. She hadn't. Thelma was staring down the road, looking at some unknown object, possibly toward the site of the murder. Benjamin turned and gave Hawkett a quick slap in the leg causing his younger partner to lurch ahead almost collapsing the lawn chair. Hawkett rubbed his face and his eyes focused on his scowling partner. He returned the look, got up from the chair and headed back toward the car.

Benjamin shook his head. He could remember a time when Hawkett led every interview and he, Benjamin, would only ask an occasional question. Hawkett had always been better at interrogating. He was just much more intelligent than Benjamin, a fact that Benjamin would readily admit, but to himself only. The car door slammed shut and Benjamin turned once more to Thelma.

"One last question, Thelma. Did you see any other strange vehicles entering this dead end road during the weekend?"

"No, detective, and we, that is, Pearl and I, keep an eye on the traffic. Living close to the road like this, you know, don't care much for strangers."

Benjamin nodded his head, "Well, thank you Thelma, you've been most helpful, perhaps we'll have a chance to visit again." Thelma shook her head in reluctant agreement.

"Uh, Thelma?" Benjamin turned back to her as he was walking down the sidewalk, when he realized his previous question shouldn't be his last. "Did you happen to see Cordoe drive by, going either direction, other than the time you already mentioned?"

"No, Detective," she shuddered, her voice breaking.

She watched the overweight detective get into the car. Then watched as the car backed out the driveway. Her body shuddered again and she suddenly felt faint. She closed her eyes and whispered, "Please, God, don't let it be possible."

CHAPTER
7

"Are we awake now?" Benjamin was getting damn tired of Hawkett's attitude, his moodiness.

Hawkett glanced at him, but gave no reply. He had been pre-occupied with the idea of checking out the Pigmy Tap they'd spotted across from the restaurant after lunch, assuming it was a nice, quiet, air-conditioned bar. He could visualize buying a chilled pitcher of Bud and relaxing.

Benjamin wasn't quite sure what to do next. Somehow he felt out of sync working in the country like this. Well, he guessed, they'd drive on down the road to the scene of the murder. It couldn't be far.

Off to his right, Benjamin could see another farmstead sitting up on a hill with a long driveway winding down to join the road. The name on the mailbox read "Mike Wilson." There were large, black and white cattle grazing in a pasture along the road. Benjamin had the feeling that they were the kind of cattle used primarily for milk production, but he wasn't sure. They drove on by.

Down the road, they could see a bridge with a pickup truck

parked on it. A man in baggy clothing was leaning on the bridge railing, staring over the side. Benjamin pulled the car over to the side of the road near the bridge and shut off the engine. He turned to Hawkett, "This must be the murder scene. I wonder who this guy is."

There was no response from his companion. "Well, we'd better take a look and see," Benjamin suggested anyway.

The man gazing over the side of the bridge turned abruptly to stare at Benjamin, looking almost surprised. Round-lensed glasses were positioned low on his nose. He wore a safari-type, tan, straw pith helmet on his head. Benjamin had never seen a hat like it anywhere except in old Tarzan movies. The man appeared, to Benjamin, to be in his sixties. A cloth emblem above the pocket on his shirt read "U.S. Mail" and in his pocket was a pen holder with different marking tools protruding. Stitched on the pocket of his gray shirt was the name, "Harley."

"Harley, would you be the fellow who discovered the victim's body?" Benjamin broke the silence.

"Yes," Harley answered with a smile. He always smiled, as Benjamin would come to learn. That voice, those half-closed eyes, that smile reminded Benjamin of Mr. MaGoo, the cartoon character. Yes, he thought, the one who was half-blind, constantly oblivious to his surroundings and drove an old jalopy.

He held out his hand toward Benjamin, "Harley Whitmeyer, United States Postal Service, Rural Delivery Specialist. And who, might I inquire, do I have the honor of meeting?"

"I'm, er uh, we are detectives from the Iowa Division of Criminal Investigation. I'm Benjamin Willoughby and this," he turned and pointed at Hawkett, who had emerged from the car and was standing nearby, "is Adam Hawkett, my partner." Hawkett said nothing, but at least nodded his head toward Harley.

Benjamin turned back to Harley. He noticed Harley's fly was wide open exposing his underwear and he couldn't help but smile. This Harley appeared to be a character, the type who would indeed stop a car to see what vultures were feasting upon. Benjamin decided to try and catch him off guard.

"Harley, who do you think murdered this banker, Cordoe?"

Harley smiled and shook his head, "Don't have any idea who done it, but they done it all right, for sure."

"I believe you're the one who found the body?" Benjamin felt a little foolish realizing this had already been established.

40

"You believe right, Mr. ahhh,"

"Benjamin, just call me Benjamin."

"Yeah, well, I found him, Benjamin," he chuckled nervously. "Drove right down to Jamie's and called the sheriff."

"Jamie's? Where's that?"

Harley pointed on down the road beyond the bridge. Benjamin could see yet another two-story farm house flanked by several outbuildings.

"Isn't that Cordoe's farm?"

"No, his is beyond it another quarter of a mile, around the bend. You can't see it from here."

Benjamin turned and looked up and down the road. The road wound through trees, tall corn and other obstacles, but still, it was difficult to believe that none of the neighbors had witnessed the murder. Well, it was probably done at night, he told himself.

"Harley, it would appear that the farm back there, the one with the big black and white cows is closer than this...Jamie's. Why didn't you go there to call for help?" Benjamin thought it probably a worthless question but still, he was curious.

Harley smiled as if somewhat embarrassed, "Oh, I know Jamie better. I help her out around the farm. She lost her husband a while back, and I kind of feel sorry for the kid. Wouldn't made no difference, Cordoe wasn't gonna get any better, I mean bein' dead like that."

Benjamin nodded. He took out a cigar and lit it while walking over to the bridge railing where Hawkett was already peering. Hawkett pointed down at a flagged area not twelve feet below them and showed Benjamin a picture he had pulled out of the file. "Looks like that's where they found him."

"Yep," replied Harley, who had joined the two detectives staring over the bridge railing. "Both eyes clean gone. Buzzards got 'em." He stared into each of the detective's faces to get their reactions and was disappointed. Both detectives had seen worse, much worse.

"Harley," Benjamin paused to take a draw on his cigar, "do you deliver mail every day?"

"Every day except Tuesday and Sunday."

"Have you noticed any strangers driving up and down this road?"

"Can't say as I have, no, can't say as I have."

41

Benjamin wondered if he should tell the mailman that his fly was unzipped. He found a smile creeping back on his face.

"Harley, do you know this Cordoe's son? I believe his name is Denny."

"Well, yes and no. Guy gives me the creeps. I seen him a few times, just kinda standin' off the road starin' at me. I never talked to him. Don't know if anyone has. Sheriff's deputies, they're trying to find him right now."

"Where?"

"At Cordoe's farm, on around the bend from Jamie's," he said pointing in that direction. "They got their work cut out for them. I tell ya, he's a slippery bastard, that Denny is."

Hawkett had backed away from the bridge's railing and leaned against Harley's pickup. His watch read nearly 1:30 PM and he was wondering how long his partner was going to keep them out there. He was toying with the idea of suggesting they go on down to the Cordoe farm and help the detectives hunt for this Denny, catch the bastard and get this case wrapped up. His train of thought was interrupted by a low, whining noise coming from Harley's pickup. It almost sounded like a small child whimpering.

"What's that?" he interrupted Benjamin and Harley's conversation.

"What's what?"

"Oh," said Harley, "that'd be Daniel." He started towards the pickup. When he opened the passenger-side door, out jumped a plump, black and white rat terrier with a smiling mouth and sad eyes. The small dog looked at each man in turn, then walked to the right front tire of the pickup and lifted his leg. Hawkett was amazed at the accuracy with which the dog was able to spray the tire.

"Uh, what did you say the dog's name was?" queried Benjamin.

"Daniel," Harley answered in a matter-of-fact tone which implied no explanation was necessary for the small dog's name.

Benjamin engaged Harley with more questions concerning the murder, but Hawkett was preoccupied with watching the small terrier. After the dog finished the front tire, he moved to each of the other three, lubricating the lug nuts with zest. Hawkett was amazed.

The sad-eyed dog, apparently having completed his mission, walked around to the half-opened door and hopped back onto the seat.

The dog slowly spun around twice and snuggled down onto the seat, closing his eyes almost immediately. Why would a guy name a dog Daniel he wondered. Not Spot or Fido or Pooch, but, Daniel. He yawned and turned to find out what Benjamin and Harley were discussing, though he really didn't care.

Benjamin and Harley had once again been looking over the edge of the bridge discussing some point concerning the body. The two men were now walking back toward the mailman's pickup and Benjamin was thanking him for his cooperation. Hawkett found himself smiling. This Harley character was quite amusing. Walking along with his fly wide open, his shirt buttoned crooked and that jungle helmet, bouncing around on his head like a China bowl on a trampoline. The man was almost clown-like. Hawkett wondered how capable he was at delivering mail.

Benjamin handed Harley his card. "This is the DCI phone number in Des Moines. If you think of anything else, call this number and they'll know where we are. We'll probably stay in Pigmy tonight, or do they have a motel?"

"Good motel," Harley replied, "Small, only three apartments, but nice place."

Harley started to place the card in his shirt pocket but dropped it. He quickly bent over to pick it up and the exertion not only caused his jungle hat to fall off, but at least half of the pens in his pocket fell out and judging from the sound coming from his posterior, the crotch seam of his pants ripped completely out.

To make matters worse, his butt had bumped the half-opened door of the pickup, slamming it shut hard enough to frighten the sleeping terrier, who yipped twice and leaped out the window on the opposite side of the pickup.

Both detectives laughed heartily. Benjamin laughed until he felt tears in his eyes. The sight of Hawkett laughing sobered him somewhat. He couldn't remember the last time he'd seen his younger partner laugh like that. Benjamin went to the Escort and turned to see if Hawkett was coming. He was surprised to see Hawkett following the little terrier around the back of Harley's pickup. Daniel was once again working on his third tire.

CHAPTER

"That Harley, he's a character, huh?" chuckled Benjamin, as he slipped the Escort into drive and headed it further down Dead End. He slowed down as they neared the driveway of the next farm. This had to be the residence of the lady named Jamie, a widow Benjamin believed, who was some sort of friend of Harley's.

Benjamin could just about imagine the old widow lady, probably cast from the same mold as Thelma Oldham. There was possibly some romance between her and Harley although he didn't know what Harley's marital status was.

Benjamin started to turn the car into the farm lane, but as they rounded the bend in the road, he could see what had to be Cordoe's farm further ahead. There was a patrol car parked out front. He stopped the car, backed up and proceeded down Dead End Road.

"Let's go see how the sheriff's boys are getting along hunting for young Cordoe. Maybe we can wrap this baby up and be back in the city tonight instead of in that three-room motel Harley was talking about."

"Sounds good to me," Hawkett responded.

Benjamin turned and looked at Hawkett. "Sounds good, aah, a positive statement. That's what I like to hear. Hard to believe you're still in such a good mood, seein' as you haven't had a drink for over twelve hours." Benjamin wished he hadn't said those words the instant they'd left his mouth, but it was too late. The arrow had been shot.

Hawkett felt a rush of anger pump up from his soul and, for a brief second, he balanced on the edge of telling Benjamin off. Who the hell did he think he was? Damn it anyway!

"I'm sorry, I shouldn't have said that," Benjamin added in his most sincere, apologetic tone. "It's just that I know you've been through a lot, but you've been drinking too much lately." He pulled the car into Cordoe's driveway behind the county patrol car. The two men sat in silence for a few moments until at last Benjamin broke the uneasy tension, "Let's see what's going on."

The two detectives climbed out of the car. Unlike the other farmsteads they had viewed before, this one was not well-kept. The lawn apparently had not been mowed the entire summer and tall weeds stood everywhere, almost entirely covering the windows of the dilapidated trailer house. An old pickup with a broken windshield and four flat tires was parked by the trailer house. Beer cans and trash were strewn everywhere. The rest of the farmstead looked like hell as well with gaping holes in the barn roof and a corn crib collapsed into a pile of splintered timber.

Hawkett noted, as promised, the dead end road ended right at Cordoe's driveway. Three large posts with reflectors mounted on them blocked the end of the road and beyond them was a field of some type. Hawkett believed the field was for growing soybeans, but tall, yellow sunflowers stood so thick in it, he wasn't really sure.

Benjamin walked to the trailer house and knocked on the door. He was not surprised when no one answered.

"Where's everybody at?"

"Up there." Hawkett had just spotted two uniformed men high on a hill beyond the soybean field. They appeared to be working their way through dense brush in a wooded area. Just as he saw them, they disappeared again into a group of trees.

"Where?" Benjamin turned his eyes in the direction of Hawkett's.

"Can't see them now. You want to walk up there?"

45

Benjamin took a look at his mud-stained suit pants.

"No," he replied emphatically. "Let's let those local boys play cops and robbers and we'll go find somewhere to detect things." He turned around and looked back down the road.

"I suppose we could go back up the road and visit the good widow, Harley's lady friend. Jamie, wasn't it? That's an unusual name for a woman don't you think?" Hawkett didn't reply. "Well, she's probably on her back porch, sitting in a rocker, knitting herself a new shawl."

Once again, Benjamin squeezed behind the steering wheel and Hawkett folded his large frame into the compact car.

It is very convenient, Benjamin thought to himself, to have all of the people who need to be interviewed, living on one road like this. In less then two minutes they were back up the road at Jamie's house. The mailbox at the end of the driveway had the name "Chambers" on it.

"Must be Jamie Chambers then," Hawkett mused.

The car proceeded down the driveway. They stopped in front of the Chambers' house and, once again, both detectives climbed out of the car.

No sooner had they stepped out of the car, when out from the large red barn sprinted a small girl in bib overalls, bare-footed, with her pigtails flying straight out behind her.

"Harley," she yelled, "Mom needs your help with..." She slid to a stop, both pigtails flying ahead, as she spotted the two strangers. A look of apprehension developed on her face, and Benjamin quickly attempted to make the small child feel safe.

"Hello, young lady. My name's Benjamin. Is your mother's name Jamie?"

She said nothing but nodded her head up and down once. She didn't like having strangers around. Her mom had made clear the rules about strangers. The apprehensive little girl turned and sprinted back into the barn just as fast as she had sprinted out.

"Damn, I hate to scare a kid like that." Benjamin closed the car door. "I suppose this Jamie's in the barn."

"Knitting her shawl?" Hawkett questioned with a smirk on his face as he lumbered around the front of the Escort.

Benjamin gave him a frown, tossed his latest cigar on the ground, and smothered it out with his shoe.

The barn was a massive, red-boarded structure with a green-shingled hip roof. It had a rock foundation mortared at the base. Most

46

of the windows were trimmed in white. Some sort of escalator was positioned on its wheels so that it climbed from ground level through an open door into the second story of the barn. Near the peak of the roof, in white numbers one could read "1896," presumably the year the structure had been built. Benjamin was impressed. The building was over a hundred years old. He didn't know of anything that had stayed around for a hundred years, except for, he thought, possibly Brightwall.

The men could see a white-board fence stretching away from the side of the barn. Within the pen, a large group of sheep were eating some sort of forage from a wooden rack. Baby lambs were racing back and forth across the pen, bouncing and jumping like rabbits.

"Look at that dog," Hawkett said as he pointed at what he was fairly certain was a border collie sitting on top of a small stack of rectangular bales of hay. The dog's keen eyes followed every move they made.

"Suppose it's mean?" Benjamin had witnessed police attack dogs at work, but this one didn't look as vicious.

"Well, I suppose we'd better find Jamie anyway, just in case." Hawkett turned toward the house. He looked back at the dog. Its stare was almost chilling.

"She's probably in the barn, but I'll knock on the door first, just in case." The house had a white picket fence surrounding the front lawn. The lawn, like the rest of the farmstead, looked immaculate. Hawkett couldn't believe the number of different flowers growing around the yard, not a weed to be seen anywhere, quite a contrast to the mess they'd just left. Hawkett opened the gate and proceeded down the sidewalk to the front porch. He walked up three steps and across the wooden porch floor and knocked three times on the screen door. He could see inside, but nobody appeared.

"Must be in the barn." He trotted down the steps, through the gate opening and both men walked across the barnyard toward the large red barn. The border collie never made a sound, but they could both sense its icy stare. Fifty feet from the barn, Benjamin stopped, cleared his voice, and yelled, "Anybody home?"

The little girl appeared at the barn doorway once again and in a voice almost too soft to be heard said, "Mom's in here." Then she disappeared.

Benjamin looked at Hawkett who shrugged his shoulders and both men proceeded through the barn door. It was darker inside and their eyes had to adjust to the change. What they saw next caused both men to look at each other once again and Hawkett could hear Benjamin mutter under his breath, "What the hell?"

Deep inside the barn, on her knees, was presumably the young girl's mother, Jamie. She was certainly not the older lady that they had initially anticipated would be living on this farm. Instead they saw a slender woman, with an athletic build, wearing faded-blue bib overalls, a light-blue tee-shirt and a pair of dark tennis shoes. Benjamin guessed she was in her mid thirties.

This part of the initiation was a mild shock compared to their bewilderment concerning what she was doing. She turned and looked at the two detectives, a difficult task since she had her arm inserted in the rear end of a straining ewe sheep.

Benjamin, somewhat shocked, cleared his voice, then said, "Yes, ah hello, we're from the Iowa Department of Criminal Investigation. I'm Benjamin Willoughby; this is Adam Hawkett. Uh, have we come at a bad time?"

She started to reply, but just then the sheep sat down pulling Jamie with her. Jamie's reply turned into a curse, "Damn." She needed help and she knew it. Jamie glanced back at the two detectives quickly assessing them. The fat one with the tie on would be no good, but the younger one in blue jeans looked stout enough.

She looked straight at Hawkett. "Could you help me please?"

Hawkett, caught completely off guard, started to turn and look behind him as he replied, "Me?"

"Yes. This ewe has been trying to lamb for over an hour and I just know something's wrong, so I'm trying to help her." She still had her arm inside the ewe, and she could feel the small leg of the lamb, bent back under its belly instead of extended outward as in a normal delivery. It was with some difficulty that she had even managed to locate the leg, let alone get a grip on it. She didn't want to let go of it now.

Hawkett started across the straw-covered floor, full of apprehension. Hell, he wasn't a veterinarian, what was he going to do?

"What do I do?"

"Untie her halter and let her lie over on her side. Then hold her there."

Hawkett turned to look back at Benjamin who shrugged and pointed an unlit cigar at the front of the ewe. With reservation, Hawkett walked to the front of the ewe and started to untie the rope halter from the metal ring on the barn wall. The ewe was breathing hard and he could see a look of fear in her eyes.

"Get a good hold on her head, okay? I don't want her taking off."

Hawkett gripped the woolly animal's head.

"That's good, now let's roll her over on her left side." The ewe rolled over easily, but started struggling to get up.

"Hold her," Jamie ordered.

Hawkett put one hand on the ewe's shoulder while pinning the ewe's head between his other hand and his knee. He could tell Jamie was trying to manipulate something inside the ewe.

"Okay," she said as she seemed to be achieving some success. "Here we go." She started pulling outward and Hawkett could see first one, then two legs protruding from the ewe's backside. Then, a head popped out and Jamie pulled the rest of the lamb out and placed it gently on the straw behind the ewe. Immediately she inserted her arm back inside the ewe, a movement not to the ewe's liking, and it almost got away from Hawkett who tightened his grip.

"Yep, I thought so," Jamie said. She gently pulled out another lamb, identical to the first one and laid it beside its twin, who was already attempting to stand. Once again, she reached into the ewe's backside, gently probing, then withdrew her arm.

"Guess that's all of them," Jamie said to Hawkett. "You can let go of her now. Thanks. Oh, slip that halter off of her head, okay?"

Hawkett released the ewe as Jamie rose to her feet and walked toward a bucket of soapy water sitting on top of a bale of straw. She began vigorously scrubbing her arm and turned to observe the ewe. It rolled to its belly then quickly jumped up and turned around to face the lambs. The ewe started softly bleating to the little slime-covered newborns, licking them and smelling them as well. Hawkett noticed a smile on Jamie's face as she observed the new family.

Hawkett watched the animals with a look of perplexity. In his entire life he had never witnessed the birth of any creature. His gut reaction was that he should be feeling nauseous, but in actuality, he found himself thinking how spectacular the whole event had been. He turned to see Benjamin, one foot resting on a sawhorse, with a smile on his face, watching the little lambs struggling to stay on their feet.

"You can wash up here or in the house if you got dirty or anything," Jamie said to Hawkett.

He turned and looked at Jamie, drying her arms off with a towel, straw tangled in her brunette hair. For a moment he was unable to reply, almost in a trance as he stared into the dark brown eyes of this farm woman. One thought kept running through his head—this woman is really quite beautiful. He suddenly realized that he was dumbly staring at her and that she had said something, but he had no idea what it was.

"Uh, beg your pardon?"

"I said, thank you for the help. I'm not sure I could have gotten the job done by myself," she replied with a warm smile on her face.

"Oh, sure, no problem." He wanted to say more, but found himself tongue-tied. Benjamin saved him.

"You know, Jamie, you are Jamie Chambers, aren't you?"

"Yes, and this is my daughter, Andrea," she said pointing at the barefooted, pig-tailed child, sitting on a bale of hay, with her arm curled around an older pet lamb.

"Jamie, I have been with the DCI for nearly twenty-five years and I believe this may be one of the first cases in which one of our men was called upon to help deliver an animal. I think you may have missed your calling, Hawk." He turned to look at Hawkett who was still staring at Jamie.

The Dorset ewe, meanwhile, was desperately trying to persuade her new babies to move away from the human beings. Although she felt greatly relieved, the pain with the delivery had been intense. Her perspective of what had transpired was completely different from that of her human caretakers. She attempted to corral the little lambs, but they were still too weak and wobbly. She glanced up just in time to see the scoundrel, the border collie, trot in through the barn door, another enemy capable of hurting her babies. Enraged by the instinct to protect her babies and disoriented by a difficult birthing, the ewe decided to take action. She turned toward the humans, tilted her head down slightly and charged hard at the nearest danger, Hawkett.

Hawkett neither saw nor heard the ewe's imminent attack, but when her front hooves left the ground and her rock-solid head drove straight into his groin, he most certainly felt it. He gasped in surprise and started to move away, but the pain of a direct hit dropped him like a rock.

Jamie grabbed the ewe by its chin, quickly backed it into a pen and latched the gate. She picked up the twin lambs and gently laid them in the pen with their mother. With horror, she turned to observe Hawkett, on his hands and knees on the barn floor.

She had absolutely no idea what to do. The other detective, the older, heavy one, still had his foot propped up on her sawhorse, as he watched his partner. Did he have an amused expression on his face, she wondered.

Jamie picked up the towel with which she had dried her hands, took it to the barn hydrant and soaked it with cold water. She took it to Hawkett who, by then, was up on his knees, his hands resting on his thighs, beads of sweat running down his face. "I'm so sorry," she said as she handed him the towel. "Are you going to be okay?"

Benjamin had to fight to prevent himself from bursting out in laughter. He couldn't recall ever having a murder investigation begin with a day quite like this. Could it be a sign of things to come, he wondered.

CHAPTER

Jamie set a pitcher of iced tea and four plastic glasses on a tray. Through the kitchen window she could see the two detectives slowly making their way toward the house. It looked like the younger one, Adam, was walking fairly normally again. She suspected the ordeal had been quite painful. That darned Dorset ewe...of all the times to lose her temper.

"Andrea," Jamie called to her daughter. "Get about ten cookies out of the cookie jar, please, and put them in a bowl. Be sure to wash your hands first, then bring them out to the porch."

"Yes, Mother," answered the small girl in a tone that implied she had better things to do.

Jamie walked over to the mirror on the kitchen wall and looked at her reflection. She ran her hands through her hair and tried to make it look right. She noticed a large stain on the right knee of her bibs. That wouldn't do. She didn't know these two men, but still, she took pride in her appearance. She trotted into her bedroom and changed into a comfortable pair of khaki-colored, cotton shorts and slipped on her good tennies. The light blue tee-shirt seemed to look okay, so she left it on.

Having reached the picket fence, Benjamin turned to Hawkett, "Feeling okay now?"

"Yeah, I'm okay." He looked at Benjamin to see if there was even the slightest hint of amusement in his partner's face.

"Well, she said to meet her on the porch," Benjamin said, "Ah, there she is now."

Jamie had appeared on her front porch with the tray of tea and glasses. "Come on up and take a load off your feet." She pointed to a white wooden porch swing, suspended by two chains, hanging from the ceiling of the porch.

The two detectives walked up the sidewalk and climbed the steps to the front porch. Benjamin looked at the swing suspended by two chains. He had serious doubts concerning the ability of the swing to hold their weight. A large wooden chair, built to match the swing, stood nearby and Benjamin eased into it instead.

Hawkett, having no other option, gingerly placed himself into the swing. He ached, he needed a drink and he was tired. His facial expressions portrayed anger, and Jamie could sense his hostility.

She felt guilty and once again tried to apologize. "I'm sorry. Those sheep generally aren't that aggressive. Are you okay?" She started to look down at the area injured by the blow and then quickly looked away again, meeting Hawkett's eyes as she did. A red tint rose on her cheeks, visible even through her tan. Benjamin had to turn away to hide his smile.

"Would you fellows like some iced tea?"

"Sounds great, Jamie," Benjamin replied, "Uh, is it okay if we call you Jamie or would you prefer Mrs. Chambers?"

"No, Jamie is fine."

She poured two glasses of iced tea and handed one to each detective. Hawkett could smell a light fragrance of soap as she handed him a glass and it lightened his mood somewhat. He tried to give her a warm smile.

"Thank you, I'm fine. Really," he said as reassuringly as possible.

She returned his smile.

A lot of smiling going on around here thought Benjamin, who couldn't help but smile himself.

Jamie sat down in the only place left available—next to Hawkett on the swing. She felt uncomfortable placed between the two men like that, but they both seemed to be gentlemen.

"Well, what brings two detectives from the FBI out to my sleepy little farm? Is it the murder, I suppose?"

"Yes, uh we're from the DCI, not the FBI," Benjamin corrected her.

"Oh, I'm sorry."

"Don't be. It happens all the time," Benjamin assured her.

"Did you know this Doug Cordoe?"

"Sure, well, you probably know, he owned the farm right down the road. Of course he was only out there on weekends mostly. And we, that is my husband and I, did borrow some money from the bank when we first moved here."

She could have said a lot more about Cordoe, but instinct told her to answer their questions briefly. What was it they always said? Anything you say can and will be used against you? If it weren't for that, she'd tell them what a jerk Cordoe really was, and she wouldn't be brief about doing it.

"Did you see him at his farm this last weekend?" Benjamin inquired.

She paused as if in thought, then said, "We didn't get together socially." She looked him straight in the eye to make sure he got her drift.

"Yes, uh, I understand. We're just trying to develop a pattern of Cordoe's movements over the weekend. What I meant was, did you physically see him driving by, working on his farm, you know?" Benjamin never put more into a question than he had to, always leaving as many blanks as possible for the other party to fill in.

"Oh, I see. Well, he drove by here late Friday afternoon, I remember. I was hooking up the mower to Harley's John Deere."

"What time would that have been?"

She frowned. Better get it right or not say it at all, she thought. "Well, Andrea was in the house watching *Sesame Street*, so it had to be between four and five. I'm sure of that."

"Did you see him drive by any other times?"

"Oh, yes, he drove back toward town within five minutes. I recall thinking he must have forgotten something in town." She glanced to her left at the younger detective and discovered he appeared to be staring at her legs. He was doing just that, admiring her tan, well-muscled legs and suddenly his eyes met hers. He immediately felt guilty and quickly looked away.

Benjamin, taking in the scene, found himself frowning as well. There's an awful lot of frowning going on around here he thought. He liked the smiling much better.

He tried to give Jamie a warm smile to lighten things up a bit. "Uh, Jamie, do you know the younger Cordoe, this uh, Denny?"

She looked at Benjamin for a few moments without saying anything as if trying to collect her thoughts. Both men could sense her uneasiness. Was it fear, Benjamin wondered.

"Denny is spooky. We've always tried to avoid the guy. As far as I know he's never hurt anyone, but still he's scary. I'll be working around the farm and all of a sudden I'll see him, standing off in the distance staring at me." She shuddered. "It gives me the creeps. My husband and I used to wave at him, you know, at least try to be friendly, but, he never waves back, just stands there and stares, then turns and disappears into the woods."

"Does he come onto your property?"

"Never has as far as I know. His father's farm borders ours, so he can get fairly close just walking around on it. When my husband was alive, he talked to the sheriff about Denny. The sheriff said there wasn't anything he could do as long as Denny didn't break any laws. Still, we're talking about a guy who's burned-out on drugs and probably should be institutionalized somewhere, instead of roaming around out here."

"Do you know anything about the relationship between Denny and his father?"

"Probably less than you. We never got together socially. Doug stayed at his house in town during the week and out here on most weekends. He did a little farming on the weekends. I suppose he brought supplies out to the trailer house for Denny to live on." She didn't tell the detectives that Zelda, the grocery store clerk in town, had said that he purchased a case of beer every Friday night.

"Have you ever seen Denny off the farm?"

"I haven't. Have you met Harley, our mailman, yet?" They nodded. "Harley says he's seen Denny all up and down Dead End Road, but, I don't think the guy's ever gone all the way into town. Doug had probably threatened him with being sent back to the institution if he did."

"I see." Benjamin wondered if threats of that type hadn't actually been the basis of the relationship between the father and son. "Jamie, have you noticed any strangers around the neighborhood in the last weekend?"

After pausing to think, she shook her head and answered, "No."

"Did you see Cordoe return to his farm once again Friday evening?"

"I don't recall seeing him at all after that, now that you mention it."

"Are you sure he was alone when he drove back by here, going back toward town, that is?"

"I'm not sure. I was having a heck of a time hooking up the mower to the tractor." She shrugged her shoulders.

Benjamin glanced at Hawkett, who appeared to be staring off across the pasture somewhere. Daydreaming again, thought Benjamin. It'll take a six-pack to get him back among the living.

Actually Hawkett was enjoying himself. He didn't know why, but it was pleasant to sit there on the porch swing by this lady and watch the farm activity. Andrea played with a small bob-tailed lamb on the lawn. He gathered that it was an orphan and a pet of the child's. He heard her refer to the lamb as "Junior." So far he had seen three cats, several chickens, the sheep, a cow and even a wild rabbit dashing across the far side of the barnyard. He wondered where the caged animals were that Ann had bemoaned every time she'd returned home from some sort of an animal rights meeting. These animals seemed quite content.

There seemed to be vegetables growing everywhere, tomatoes, peppers, melons and a variety of other plants growing in different raised beds around the farmstead. He wondered what she did with all this food she was growing.

The lawn had been mowed recently and had that pleasant smell to it. The smells were as varied as the sights, especially Jamie's perfume, if, in fact, it was perfume he smelled. It could be, he realized, that he was smelling the multitude of flowers growing everywhere around the farmstead.

He supposed he should ask a question or two, but what the hell. He didn't care who killed this banker; he'd probably deserved it. Come to think of it, he didn't care if he ever asked another question in any more of these dirty little murder games. Let Brightwall fire his ass, what the hell. He took a deep breath.

Yeah, he thought to himself, maybe he'd just buy himself a little place out here in the country. He wondered what a farm would cost. He didn't know, but it certainly would be nice to have a place as pretty as this one, a place with a swing on the front porch, no blood, no murder, no lawyers, no noise, no smog, and no crowded streets.

He had a sudden vision of himself standing in the middle of a large garden, all kinds of vegetables planted by his own hand, a straw hat on his head and a garden hoe in his hands. He wondered, could he sell products from a garden? What would a person do for his income? His daydream was broken by Jamie's voice.

"Andrea, can you hear me?"

"Yes," came the answer from the small girl who had been busy whispering a secret to her pet lamb.

"Would you go in the kitchen and bring the cookies out please?"

In a moment the little girl appeared on the porch, the screen door slamming behind her. Without being told, she offered a cookie first to Benjamin, then her mother and finally to Hawkett. The child stood directly in front of Hawkett as if wanting to say something.

"One time my dog Jack ate some rat poison. Did you know that?"

Hawkett, caught off guard by her question, simply shook his head back and forth.

"Yes, well, Jack, he got really sick and kept throwing up all over the barn floor. Did you eat some rat poison?"

"Andrea, he doesn't want to hear about Jack," Jamie admonished. "I'm sorry, Jack's our border collie. Kind of a member of the family."

Hawkett smiled at her. She smiled at Hawkett. Benjamin smiled again. Good work, Andrea, he thought, we need all the smiles we can get. He wondered whether or not to probe into Jamie's financial dealings with the bank. He also was curious about what had led to her husband's death. These were ugly, unpleasant questions, and this was too beautiful of a day for such nonsense.

Hell, the son killed his old man anyway. Cordoe probably threatened the boy with institutionalization one too many times. He took a large bite out of his oatmeal cookie. Wow, it tasted good.

From the porch, Jamie and the two DCI agents could see a pickup approaching. It seemed noisier than normal and appeared to be bouncing as if on railroad tracks. Quickly they could tell it was Harley's pickup, and it bounced into Jamie's farmyard, with the rear right tire completely shredded.

"I wonder how far he drove with the tire flat," Jamie said, shaking her head.

"Gone quite a ways. It'll be a wonder if he didn't ruin the wheel as well," replied Benjamin as he lit his sixth cigar of the day, causing Jamie to wrinkle her nose.

Harley climbed out of the car, followed by the small rat terrier and started toward the house.

"Flat tire, Harley?" Jamie yelled at the mailman. At that, Harley turned and looked back at the pickup, bobbing his head in surprise as he saw the shredded tire on the lopsided truck.

"Damn, I thought she was riding a little rough." He turned and smiled to the trio on the porch. "Reckon I'll have to change it." The little rat terrier was already lubricating the hub bolts Hawkett noticed.

"What did he say that dog's name was?" Hawkett inquired.

"Daniel. Real sophisticated name for a dog," answered Jamie, still shaking her head and staring at the mangled tire. "He used to have a pair of those dogs. He hauled them with him everywhere.

CHAPTER
10

Twenty minutes later, the two detectives were back in Pigmy. Benjamin parked the Escort in front of the courthouse, left Hawkett with the car, and entered the sheriff's office.

Deputy Jan greeted him with a smile. She presented him with the search warrant for Doug Cordoe's town residence that Benjamin had requested at their earlier meeting. He spent a little time flirting good-naturedly with her and tried to get her to come with the two DCI agents to search Cordoe's house. She declined, but gave him a wink and went back to her computer. Benjamin left the building whistling.

Squeezing behind the steering wheel, Benjamin tossed the search warrant to Hawkett who checked for an address and they quickly located the residence. It was not a difficult task in a town as small as Pigmy. The two detectives sat quietly in the car for a moment and studied the Cordoe residence. It was a pale-green-colored, ranch style house surrounded by a thick hedge.

"Well, a hell of a lot better looking place than the farmstead, huh?"

Hawkett didn't reply but nodded his head slightly, and both detectives climbed from the car. A county patrol car was parked in the driveway adjacent to the house and a fairly large man in uniform sat in a lawn chair near the front step. As they walked up the sidewalk, the man dropped the magazine he had been reading, locked his hands together and rested them on his large belly. He wore no cap and his head was completely shaved. A name tag pinned on his pocket read "Deputy Carlton Cog."

"Sheriff Spencer around?" Benjamin asked.

"Nope." No smile. No other reply. Benjamin had an apprehensive feeling that they might be dealing with a fun one.

"Who might you be?"

"Depends. Who might you be?" replied the lawn chair guardian in a mocking tone.

Benjamin sighed and shot a glance at Hawkett, then turned again, pulling out some identification.

"We're both DCI agents. We've come to take a peek at the banker's house and..."

"Well, you've had your peek, now why don't you boys just turn around and get the hell out of here?" the man replied with menace in his voice.

Benjamin turned again, glancing at Hawkett. Well, so much for cooperation, he thought.

"We uh, have a search warrant in the car and..."

"Sheriff didn't say nothin' to me 'bout no search warrant. I'm s'posed to watch the house, keep everybody out he said. Reckon you guys would be part of everybody, right?"

Benjamin was starting to get really irritated. This was totally unnecessary. The guy in the lawn chair had one of those smart ass smiles beaming from his face, enjoying his fleeting moment of power.

"I take it you're a deputy. Am I correct?" Benjamin asked.

"Shit, you DCI boys are smarter than I thought. Haven't been here five minutes and already you detected something. Zowwee, I'm impressed! Yes, sir, I am!" Still the same smart ass smile on his face.

"Well, deputy, we have a search warrant in that car. We've visited with Sheriff Spencer and now we intend to search the deceased's residence."

"Don't believe so," the smile disappeared from his face as the deputy stood up and extended his bulky body. He made it a point to turn his body slightly to the right, letting both detectives see him lift a large hand and rest it on the service revolver hanging from his left hip. The deputy was bigger than Benjamin had earlier estimated, standing a good 6'4" and weighing in the range of 280 to 290 pounds. Mostly fat, but still big.

Benjamin shook his head in disgust, turned and looked once again at the quiet Hawkett, then turned back and began to step around the obstinate deputy. The bluff failed and, quickly, quicker than Benjamin would have thought, the deputy grabbed the lapel of his jacket and yanked Benjamin backwards causing him to lose his balance and nearly fall down on the lawn.

Hawkett didn't say a word but quickly moved toward the large deputy. Caught off guard by Hawkett's nonthreatening, calm approach, the bulk was completely unable to block a punch to his giant mid-section, a punch, developed from experience, that used the muscles from every part of Hawkett's body. He drove his fist into the soft flesh in a manner designed to go clear through. The deputy let out a loud gasp, grabbed for his mid-section and doubled over as a massive quantity of air was knocked from his body. Hawkett then delivered an upper cut with his right fist to the detective's jaw. The hit made a bone crunching sound and the deputy dropped straight backwards, unconscious, destroying the lawn chair as he fell.

Benjamin quickly moved to the deputy's side, checked his pulse and peeked under one eyelid. Seeing that the man was knocked out cold, but still breathing, he felt somewhat relieved. They probably wouldn't need to call an ambulance, but maybe they should. This was a mess. He turned to Hawkett. "What the hell got into you?"

Hawkett shrugged. "The guy was a piss ant, needed an education, so I gave him one. He'll thank me later, I..."

"Oh shut up!" Benjamin checked the bulk's pulse again and turned to survey the neighborhood. Surprisingly no angry crowd was converging upon them. "Here, help me," he said as he bent down and grabbed one of the deputy's legs. "Let's drag him behind those bushes by the door." Together, they drug the unconscious deputy behind a large bush adjacent to the house and left him there in the shade, where he would be less visible from the street. This, of course, was completely the wrong way to handle this situation Benjamin told himself. He should call an ambulance, call the sheriff, begin a process that would include several review boards, countless lawyers and a real heyday for the press.

"What now?" Hawkett asked, starting to feel a bit of remorse for his physical outburst.

"Shit, I don't know," was Benjamin's answer. "Let's do what we came here to do. Search the damn place while I try to come up with a way out of this mess."

Surprisingly, the door was unlocked and both men walked right into the house. With all of the shades drawn the house seemed quite dark, but they didn't need much light to know that the place was a mess. It smelled of stale, greasy food. Empty pizza boxes and beer cans were strewn everywhere. For fifteen minutes the two detectives efficiently searched the small one-story domicile.

The search revealed only two distinct pieces of information. The first being the fact that the murdered banker had been a slob and the second, that he had loved pornography. The sex-filled material was everywhere. Piles of dirty magazines and books, stacks of porno tapes and calendars picturing nude women were everywhere. Disgusted, Benjamin opened the front door and took another peek at the unconscious detective. He was still lying peacefully under the shade bush snoring.

He stepped back into the house and turned to Hawkett. "There's no garage and no basement, but I think he's got a backyard of some sort. Let's take a look at that, then decide what to do with your punching bag out front."

A sliding glass door led to a cement patio and beyond that lay a small backyard, heavily littered, and surrounded by a tall, solid, board fence. On the patio was a lawn chair with a BB gun propped up against it. One lone, proud oak tree stood in the middle of the yard, seeming quite out of place among the discarded beer cans and dead birds. As Hawkett walked around the base of the tree, he counted nearly twenty dead birds in varying stages of decay. Mostly sparrows, but he spotted one cardinal and two goldfinch as well.

Sickened, he turned to Benjamin who was examining the BB gun, an old Daisy model, and said, "Can you believe what a jerk that son-of-a-bitch was? Gets home from work, brings out a six pack, sits in a lawn chair and shoots birds. Look at this. Hell there's nearly twenty of them lying around here!"

Benjamin shook his head in disgust as well. "I suppose, what with the tall board fence and this relatively noiseless weapon, the neighborhood had no idea what he was up to." He took the toe of his shoe and turned the cardinal over, somehow wishing it would come back to life.

Nothing else in the backyard attracted much interest, except for a lone metal bucket turned upside down near a corner post of the back fence.

He walked to the bucket which was embedded in the ground, thinking that he could overturn it for a look underneath. Benjamin started to do so when he noticed a pair of binoculars hanging by a black leather strap from the top of the corner post. Having developed a fairly good idea of the kind of pervert the deceased must have been, Benjamin quickly deduced what the bucket had been used for.

He lifted the binoculars from their resting place and carefully stepped up onto the bucket. Not surprisingly, the additional altitude allowed him to peek over the top of the board fence and into the neighbor's backyard. What Benjamin saw as he glanced over the fence shocked him at first, but then also amused him.

There was an abandoned lot between the Cordoe residence and his nearest neighbor, and the neighbor's backyard was completely surrounded by a tall, thick hedge. Yet, standing in this particular spot, from this distinct angle, one could see through a rather significant gap in the foliage.

Through that gap, using the binoculars, Benjamin could spot a man and woman lounging in their lawn chairs, enjoying cold beverages and taking in the late afternoon sun. Both the man and woman were completely nude. Probably some kind of body worshippers thought Benjamin. This was probably an after-work type of ritual the couple did each late afternoon. It had been just by luck, the two detectives showed up at the right time of day to discover what Cordoe had discovered.

Benjamin watched them for a moment as he contemplated handing the binoculars to Hawkett and making some wise crack about studying nature. However, when he turned toward Hawkett, he remembered the unconscious deputy laying on the ground in front of the house and his mood quickly soured again, but only momentarily.

Somehow, from somewhere, a scheme flooded through the gray cells of his brain, a scheme that might alleviate their problem of the deputy out front, or a scheme that might at least muddy the water enough to cloud Hawkett's misconduct. Hell, it was worth a try he thought.

He stepped down off the bucket, walked back to the patio and picked up the BB gun, which judging from the sound of it, was still loaded with miniature pellets. Hawkett had gone back into the house and was looking around aimlessly. Benjamin opened the door and yelled, "Hawkett!"

"Yeah?"

"Get some water, wake up that deputy and see if you can get him to stand up."

"What?"

"Do it now and hurry up!"

Hawkett shrugged his shoulders, got a glass of water from the sink and headed out the front door.

Benjamin turned and trotted back across the lawn, carrying the BB gun with him, and climbed back up onto the bucket. He laid the barrel of the BB gun atop the fence, cocked it, and aimed it through the neighbor's hedge. He was fairly certain that the small weapon, at this distance, would hurt, but not harm. Hoping the sights were accurate, he aimed the gun at the woman's right buttock. He squeezed the trigger, the little gun gave a muted popping sound and almost instantly the woman screamed. She jumped up from her lawn chair and extended her hand to examine her injury.

As quickly as he could, Benjamin cocked, aimed and fired again, this time hitting her left buttock. Again she screamed and by this time her nude partner had abandoned his lawn chair and was standing beside her. Benjamin cocked the gun yet a third time and aimed at the man's groin, but some inner instinct caused him to veer to the left slightly. His last shot hit the nude sun bather in his right thigh. The man yelped in pain as well. Holding the BB gun up to block his face from view, Benjamin cupped one hand to his mouth and yelled, "Don't you assholes know public nudity is against the law?"

Benjamin turned quickly, still carrying the BB gun, and ran into the house and out the front door. By this time, Hawkett had revived the deputy and the big man was leaning against the house, still in a daze, rubbing his chin.

"Here deputy, hold this weapon for the sheriff." With that Benjamin, still running, shoved the BB gun into the deputy's arms and made a beeline for the car. "Come on Hawkett, move!" he ordered.

Hawkett, completely confused, trotted to the car and jumped in.

Benjamin started the Escort, slammed it into gear and sped down the street bringing the car to an abrupt stop about a block away. Benjamin glanced back toward the Cordoe residence and decided to turn the car around in order to get a better view of what was about to transpire. Hawkett was still completely baffled.

They didn't have to wait long for the drama to unfold, as suddenly the front door of the neighbor's house flew open and out marched the sunbathers, no longer nude, but clad in jogging suits. The man was carrying a baseball bat and the woman, a heavy frying pan. Both had expressions of intense anger and retaliation on their faces as they marched down the sidewalk in front of their own house, across the empty lot and up to the dazed deputy holding the BB gun in front of Cordoe's house. The confrontation wasn't a pretty one.

Benjamin dropped Hawkett off at the small motel on Main Street. Hawkett was supposed to line up a room for the night, while Benjamin checked in with the sheriff's office.

Hawkett quickly accomplished this task, securing one of the three rooms available from Ed, the manager. With the room keys in his pants pocket, Hawkett walked to the only tavern in town to purchase two six packs of cold beer and then returned to the motel. He unlocked the door, surveyed the room and set the air conditioning.

Having kicked off his shoes, Hawkett made himself comfortable on the bed and drank two beers, barely taking time to breathe. The bed was pleasantly soft and the sheets had a sweet, alluring fragrance. It reminded him of the smell radiating from Jamie. He closed his eyes and thought of her.

Benjamin stepped through the half-opened door and observed his partner, lying on the bed with his arms folded behind the back of his head, eyes closed with a stupid-looking smile on his face. "Smiling. Must be into the booze already," murmured Benjamin to himself. He shook his head in disgust at the large hole in Hawkett's left sock, his little toe breaking through for freedom.

"Sheriff's boys haven't found young Cordoe yet," Benjamin informed him. "They think he's moved out into the woods somewhere, hiding."

Hawkett opened his eyes, the smile had left his face. "Can't they get some more help? I mean, they need to get about a hundred volunteers and start combing those woods in some sort of organized manner."

"I agree. Sheriff says it's hard to get volunteers out here. Most of the young people have jobs in neighboring towns or work all day on their farms. Most of the older people are retired folks who can't do a lot of walking, especially in the heat of the day."

65

Hawkett opened his third beer and handed one to Benjamin who was loosening his tie. "You gonna call Brightwall or should I?"

"The way you're putting down those beers, I think I'd better do it." He tried to hold the criticism out of his voice, but still, it was evident. Hawkett seemed unaffected. Benjamin reached for the phone on the nightstand and dialed Brightwall's number. His secretary had gone home, so Brightwall answered the phone.

"Brightwall here."

"Yeah, this is Willoughby. Thought I'd check in."

"What have you got?"

"Not a lot yet. Best suspect seems to be the deceased's son, a kind of mental case running wild out here somewhere. The sheriff's boys have been looking for him but no luck so far. They're going to need more help."

"Is this son dangerous to the rest of the community?"

"There's no indication of that."

"Why would he kill his own father?"

"It seems the father pulled him out of institutional care because of expense. Then he kept the kid out in a dilapidated trailer on his farm. His welfare wasn't a big item with his father. The kid wasn't allowed to go into town."

"Was the murder on the farm?"

"No, but close."

"How did he die?"

"A pitchfork through the chest."

"Pitchfork? Oh yeah, I guess I already knew that."

"Yeah."

"No witness?"

"None that we know of. We've been working the neighborhood. No one seems to have seen anything unusual."

"How's the local sheriff to work with?"

"Seems fine. A little wound up, but fairly competent."

"What do you need from here?"

"Better get somebody down here to do an autopsy."

"Already scheduled. Benson will be there tomorrow morning."

"Good."

Benjamin wondered what else to say. He hated to say he honestly had no other leads. The silence lingered. Finally Brightwall broke it.

"How soon will you have it wrapped up?"

"Probably a couple of days."

"Good. Well, keep in touch and stay out of trouble, okay?"

"Yeah."

"Is he sober?"

Benjamin turned and glanced at his partner, draining the last drop out of his fourth beer. "Yeah, he's okay."

"Keep him that way." The line went dead on Brightwall's end. Benjamin scowled at the phone and replaced the receiver.

"How's the almighty chieftain?" Hawkett asked.

"Same stupid bastard he was when we left," Benjamin replied. "You hungry?"

"Yeah. Where are we eating? Back at the restaurant we had lunch in?"

"It's probably the only place in town to eat. Lord, this is a quiet little town, isn't it?" He heard no reply. He continued anyway, "I'm going to take a quick shower, then we can go eat."

Fifteen minutes later, when Benjamin stepped out of the bathroom, his partner was sound asleep, snoring. Benjamin shook his head as he counted the empty beer cans on the floor. He dressed, walked to the restaurant and ordered sandwiches to go. Half an hour later he returned to the room to find Hawkett still sawing logs.

"Hey!" He slapped Hawkett on the foot. Hawkett awoke with a start, rubbed his face with the back of his left hand and sat up on the bed. He could smell food and it smelled good. Benjamin handed him a paper bag and Hawkett looked inside to see a roast beef sandwich and an order of fries. Benjamin also handed him a cup of hot coffee with a plastic lid on it. Once again the food from the small town restaurant didn't disappoint.

"You know, I've been thinking," said Benjamin, as he made himself comfortable in the only chair in the room. "Maybe we shouldn't be so quick to accept this young Cordoe as the bad guy."

Hawkett gingerly sipped at the hot coffee. It was review time. Benjamin always liked to talk over their day's work. They had done this for years. It was probably one of Benjamin's strongest points in detection, Hawkett had always thought.

"What'd you think of the Oldham sisters?" Benjamin asked him.

"Pearl's a nut case or close to it. Motive? Possibly she and her husband had a bad time with Cordoe's bank. Thelma seemed like she had other things on her mind that may come out with a little more pressure. Same motive as Pearl's, I guess, only her brother, not husband. Neither one of them said anything bad about the other."

Benjamin nodded his head and pulled his second roast beef sandwich out of the paper bag. "That Harley's a character, huh?" He chuckled silently.

"Doesn't seem to be able to give us much information. He may have missed something though."

"Jamie Chambers. Very pretty lady. Suppose Cordoe was hitting on her? Her being a widow and all?"

Hawkett frowned, he knew he should answer that question objectively, but somehow it upset him. He shook his head trying to clear his thoughts.

"Well?" Benjamin wondered what the head-shaking was about.

"She doesn't look like a murderer to me." Hawkett finally responded.

"We've seen a lot of people before who didn't look like murderers, some of them women."

"I know. I know."

"Besides young Cordoe, we still have one farmstead to visit on Dead End, that place in between Jamie's and the Oldham sisters' that had the big black and white cows."

"Yeah, probably better hit there first thing in the morning," Hawkett suggested as he wadded up his sack, napkin and cup and shoved them into the small trash can under the desk.

"Yeah, I'd like to take a look at the car too. Sheriff says they've got it locked up in a shed behind the courthouse. And the body. Brightwall says Benson's supposed to be here in the morning to do an autopsy. Should be fun on a decaying body."

"Won't bother Benson any."

"No," Benjamin agreed.

Hawkett yawned and looked at his watch. Nearly eight o'clock. He was surprised it was that late. Benjamin stood up.

"I'm going for a walk, want to come?" He already knew the answer.

"Think I'll pass, thanks," replied Hawkett as he rolled his back flat onto the bed and locked his hands behind his head.

68

CHAPTER 11

Hawkett woke with a start, momentarily forgetting where he was. He tried to sit up, but a sharp pain in the back of his head halted his movement. Hangover time again. His stomach had that familiar, queasy feeling that greeted him almost every day as of late.

He was tired. The nightmares had attacked again last night in a big way, making for a restless night.

As he lay on the bed looking at the ceiling, the room slowly filled with the light of the morning sun. Hawkett wondered to himself how much human trauma from insomnia occurred in the world. How much human error was caused by overtired workers, doctors, machinery operators, automobile operators? How many deaths resulted from the mistakes of people whose senses were dulled by inadequate rest? The list would be endless he decided.

He knew his inability to rest was probably at the heart of his problems. At any rate, he knew he felt tired and his head hurt like hell. And he also knew there had been a time in his life when each day hadn't started like this.

Hawkett, ever so gently, rolled over on the side of the bed and eased his body upright into a sitting position, knocking several empty beer cans off of the bedside table in the process. Benjamin was nowhere to be seen, but there was a bottle of aspirin sitting on top of the TV. Hawkett opened it and slid four of the pain relievers into the palm of his hand. He placed them on his swollen tongue and chewed the dry tablets. Breakfast. His watch said 9:05. He willed himself into a shower and shaved.

Benjamin had been busy. Though he had spent the preceding day believing that Cordoe's son had murdered his father, doubts were now beginning to creep into his head. Things just didn't feel right.

Ironic, he thought. Three years ago, his younger partner Hawkett would have been taking the lead in this case, looking under every un-turned stone for clues. Now he shook his head in disgust thinking of his hungover partner back in the motel room.

At 8:00 in the morning, he had met with Sheriff Spencer. He had learned two things: one—young Cordoe had still not been apprehended and two—Spencer's nephew, or "Deputy Sheriff Dumbass" as Spencer had described him, had taken a pretty good beating. Surprisingly, Spencer was neither upset nor irritated. In his words, "The dumb son-of-a-bitch probably deserved the beating." He didn't even bother to question Willoughby about the details, but did add a warning, "Deputy Cog is bad blood and you probably haven't heard the last of him, so be careful, okay?"

By 8:30, Benjamin had polished off three eggs (sunny side up), four strips of bacon, three slices of homemade bread (toasted and smoth-ered in strawberry jam), and two cups of freshly-brewed coffee at June's Restaurant. He felt pleased with himself for passing on the freshly-baked homemade cinnamon rolls covered in melted butter. After all, a person had to watch what they ate.

Between 8:30 and 9:00, he had carefully examined the murder victim's Cadillac parked in a locked storage shed two blocks from the sheriff's office. He'd found only two things of interest there: one was a loaded .44 Smith and Wesson he found stuffed up under the driver's side seat, and the other was the apparent blood stains on the steering wheel.

A little after 9:00 he called DCI headquarters in Des Moines and requested that they send the mobile lab investigative team to examine the car. By 9:30, he had Hawkett eating some toast and drinking coffee back at June's Restaurant, at which time, Benjamin polished off two large cinnamon rolls and yet another cup of black coffee.

"How's your toast?"

"Tastes good, homemade bread, huh?" Hawkett replied.

"Yeah, you can't get that just anywhere."

Benjamin lit his second cigar of the morning. "I took a look at Cordoe's car this morning. Had a .44 hidden up in the seat. Sheriff's gang must of missed it...loaded."

Hawkett, finishing his toast, looked at Benjamin and cocked one eyebrow. "So that tells us our victim got out of his car, for unknown reasons and was stabbed through the chest by someone he didn't fear. His son, no doubt."

Benjamin only nodded in reply, a look of puzzled-contemplation on his face. June came over and refilled both men's cups.

"There appeared to be dried blood on the steering wheel."

"Dried blood, are you sure?"

"Not 100%, but pretty sure." He'd seen enough of it over the years.

Now Hawkett was puzzled. "If Cordoe got out of the car, approached his son, his pitchfork-bearing son, and was stabbed through the chest, then dumped over the edge of the bridge, how did blood end up on his steering wheel?"

"Maybe they'd had a prior scuffle and the father chased the boy down the road in the car. Say he had struck the boy maybe and had blood on his hands."

"Yeah, but if they'd become violent with each other, say the old man's after the boy, and the boy has a pitchfork in his hand, why doesn't Dad grab the .44 out from under the seat when he leaves the car? I think it's more likely that young Cordoe got blood on his hands when he threw his father over the edge of the bridge, then got blood on the steering wheel when he was hiding the Cadillac."

"At any rate, I've got the mobile crime lab on the way and there should be DNA samples and fingerprints taken off the steering wheel."

Both men remained speechless while they tried to picture in their minds the last events leading to the pitchfork being plunged through Cordoe's chest.

Benjamin broke the silence. "Maybe somebody besides the son killed Cordoe." He stubbed out his cigar, finished his coffee and slid his

71

chair away from the table. "We'd better go take another look.

Back in the car, the two detectives once again headed down Dead End Road and once again met Pearl Oldham peddling her antique bicycle towards town. Upon sighting their vehicle, she quickly braked to a stop, pulled her bike well off the road, and glared at Benjamin as they drove by, ignoring his friendly wave.

"She's not happy to see you, Bubba." Despite a bad mood caused by his hangover, Hawkett couldn't resist kidding Benjamin about the previous day's encounter.

As they approached the Oldham house, both men could see the other sister, Thelma, busily hoeing weeds in her garden. She glanced their direction when she heard the car approaching, but then quickly looked away again and intensified her efforts in the garden.

"Wonder what that woman's keeping to herself. She's trying to pretend she doesn't see us. We're going to have to visit her again. I know she's holding back some little tidbit of information," mused Benjamin.

Benjamin turned up the long farm lane at the second residence on Dead End. A sign along the lane read "Mike Wilson- Grade A Dairy." Large black and white cows of various sizes grazed the green grass in the pastures on either side of the lane. Several of them, chewing their cud and swishing their tails at pesky flies, paused to watch as the car crept passed them. Each appeared to have a bored expression on its narrow face. Benjamin was impressed by their shiny, healthy appearance.

At the end of the lane set yet another two-story farmhouse made entirely of brick and topped with a red-tile roof. Across the lawn from the farmhouse stood an equally-impressive two-story brick barn. In fact, noted Benjamin, every building he could see was made of brick. The lawn was well-kept and a productive garden stretched out from one side of the house. A plump, young woman was digging in the garden. She wore faded jeans, a tee-shirt and work boots. A wide-billed, straw hat protected her head from the hot, late-morning sun. Alongside her were two small children, one boy and one girl, both barefoot and wearing bib overalls.

The woman looked at the detectives with a suspicious stare. Benjamin crawled out of the car and attempted to disarm her apprehension with a smile and a warm greeting. Upon hearing their intentions, she informed Benjamin that he needed to talk to Mike. "He's walking up from the south pasture," she explained and pointed to a man coming their direction. She turned back to her task and the two detectives watched silently for a few moments as she stabbed a pitchfork into the rich soil. With considerable ease, she lowered the handle and forced a fresh chunk of ground out of the soil. The two children then sorted through the overturned soil searching for fresh potatoes.

Even from a considerable distance, the two detectives could tell Mike was big, wide at the shoulders and narrow at the waist. If there had been any doubts about his physical assets, the bone-crunching grip he used when giving each detective an introductory handshake would have quickly dispelled them.

Benjamin had always considered Hawkett a pretty fair specimen, physically, and he had proven this to be true in a couple of different physical confrontations with criminals, but this Mike Wilson stood taller and wider than Hawkett, and there wasn't an ounce of fat on him. He was just the kind of guy who could put a pitchfork through someone's chest with one hand.

"Mike, we're here looking into the murder of Doug Cordoe. I assume you knew him?" asked Benjamin.

"Yeah, I knew him." The big warm smile left his face and was replaced by a somewhat-menacing frown.

"Did you do any business with him at the bank?"

"Did, but no more." The angry look remained.

Benjamin continued to probe. "Any special reason why you don't anymore—don't do business with the deceased?"

Before Benjamin could correct the obviously-stupid question, Mike interrupted, "Yeah, he's dead." The scowl started to lift, but the smile that began to replace it was just as disturbing.

His reply had irritated Benjamin, but the detective in him told him to press on. He took a deep breath, "Yes, I realize that. What I meant was, were you doing business with him just prior to his death?"

"No, the bastard sold me out." The smile was gone again.

"Sold you out?"

"Yeah, you know, forced auction of all my machinery and all three of my Harvester Silos." He pointed to three circular, concrete pads setting firmly in a row next to the barn. Benjamin could only surmise that those pads had been the foundations for the silos that Mike spoke of.

Benjamin continued, "But you're still farming?"

73

"Oh yeah, still got my cows, never did mortgage them like I did the machinery. Still got my milking set up too. I still sell milk."

"Am I fair in assuming you didn't think much of the deceased?"

"Hated his freakin' guts. The world is a better place to live now that the rotten, lying son of a bitch is dead. But I didn't shoot the son of a bitch; somebody else had that privilege."

Shoot him, thought Benjamin. Hadn't somebody else mentioned the banker being shot? Had they just assumed that was how he'd died? Well, regardless, this young Wilson is giving us pretty straight forward answers, thought Benjamin. "Any idea who killed him?"

"Nope."

"See any strangers on this road over the weekend?"

"Nope." All the while he talked, his eyes radiated a defiant look as if he were begging someone to doubt his word.

"Have you been home all weekend?"

"Yep, been building fence on the back slope." As he stated this, he nodded his head in the direction, back over his shoulder towards some location beyond the barn.

Benjamin turned and looked at the woman who continued to work in the garden with her children.

"She never seen him either," stated Mike following Benjamin's line of vision.

"Cute kids. How old?" asked Benjamin.

A somewhat warmer expression spread across Mike's face. "Matt's eight, Megan's six."

Benjamin pulled two pieces of candy from somewhere in his jacket. "Can they have these?"

"Sure."

While Benjamin visited with the children, Hawkett was left standing by Mike and an uncomfortable silence lingered.

Hawkett cleared his throat. "You know this Chambers gal, uh, I believe her first name's Jamie; she lives just down the road?"

"Sure, I know Jamie."

"Mailman said she was a widow, what happened to her husband?"

"Hung himself."

Mike watched as the two detectives drove away. There were things he hadn't told them, but then, they hadn't asked about those things. He wondered if he should talk to Jamie, try to sort some things out, help her in some way.

He glanced at his wife who had begun hanging clothes out to dry. She wouldn't like him going to Jamie's...no, not one bit. She was jealous of Jamie. Well, he thought, hell, Jamie was a good-looking woman.

He remembered the day Jamie's husband Bud had died. The image of his body swinging from a rope attached to a haymow beam was forever implanted in his brain. The call had come midmorning. He knew something terrible had happened when his wife came running out of the house waving her arms frantically at him. His first thought had been that something had happened to one of the kids. He'd dropped his feed buckets and had run to meet her.

She was crying, having difficulty breathing, hysterical, as she tried to tell him that Jamie had called and Bud was hanging in the barn. He knew right away what she meant by hanging...suicide. He yelled to her to call for an ambulance as he ran to the four-wheel-drive pickup that they had owned at that time.

Mike had driven the pickup out onto the gravel road with so much speed that he'd nearly rolled the truck. He was at the neighbor's barn in less than three minutes, but it was too late. Bud had already turned a bluish gray, the rope remained tight around his neck.

He remembered Jamie, screaming, completely out of control, trying to lift Bud's body up and loosen the rope. She couldn't. Hell, he'd had to use a ladder and an axe to cut the rope, to lower the body, while Jamie frantically tried to break Bud's fall.

He figured that Bud had been hanging there for nearly an hour before Jamie found him. Thank God the child, little Andrea, wasn't home. Jamie had taken her to stay with the Oldham sisters while Jamie had planned to help Bud pick corn.

Shit, he still couldn't believe Bud had done it. Hell, he had a beautiful wife, fine child...but then again, Mike thought, he had known what depression could do to a man. Suicide had crossed his mind more than once over the past few years. He knew the worthless feeling that could cloud a man's soul when he found himself financially-unable to pay debts to trusted friends. He knew the gnawing, everyday pain of his wife as she constantly reminded him of all the things her relatives in the city had that she didn't: the minivans, the camcorders, vacations. It was always something. His wife had let him know all right, never let up.

They had begun this farming operation together, just as his parents and grandparents had, with the philosophy that hard work and honesty would guarantee them a good, middle-class livelihood. In the beginning Mike had loved his wife and loved his farm.

He had to be a farmer; it was all he'd ever done. As a tot, he played with farm toys in the sand pile as he watched his dad and grandpa using the real machines in the outlying farm fields. As he grew, he was allowed to take on more and more responsibility. He developed into a strong young man and gradually took over the jobs that his aging father could no longer handle.

This farm had been in his family for over one hundred years now. His great grandparents had started out with next to nothing and had farmed the land with horses. His grandparents had switched from horses to steel-wheel tractors. His father had witnessed the evolution from old gas tractors to more efficient diesels. Before Mike had lost his machinery, he'd owned a $70,000, four-wheel drive, diesel tractor with an air conditioned cab, AM-FM radio, and digital monitors.

Now he had virtually no machinery and was starting all over again, just like his great-grandparents. Somehow, this knowledge tied him closer to his farm, his family roots. Now he had no machinery, but he had no debts as well, and he felt like a free man again. He once again found farming enjoyable; his life had more purpose.

Of course, he'd had to change the way he farmed. He no longer roared back and forth across the hillsides in his powerful tractor, trying to grow crops of corn and soybeans. The grain-farming part of his operation had been a big loser financially anyway, and had caused severe soil erosion as well. Now the hillsides were covered with grass, and he spent most of his time managing his cow herd's grazing pattern—harvesting the sunlight via his grass.

In the winter he dried up the milk cow herd and spent his time doing other jobs like cutting firewood and working for other farmers. Financially, their livelihood had improved and most certainly their quality of life had improved as well. Even his wife had changed, the nagging and feelings of discontent had disappeared. They'd grown closer than ever.

Ironic, he thought, that most of the decisions he'd made to liquidate assets, learn more sustainable farming systems, pay more attention to net profit instead of mass production had been initiated the week after Bud's suicide. Yes, he thought, the impact of one man's failure had caused another man's survival. Ironic, yes, and very sad.

Yeah, thought Mike, he'd made it through the tough financial time. He'd survived. Some farmers did, some didn't. Bud hadn't.

CHAPTER
12

Denny Cordoe sat perfectly still and, except for his slightly irregular breathing, made not one sound. Sitting up high in an old cottonwood tree observing the world was one of Denny's favorite pastimes. It was his special, secret place. Not even his father had known about it.

The tree was located less than fifty yards from Dead End Road, and he had spent much of his time the last two days watching various law enforcement people drive by. He knew they were searching for him, and he liked that. It was the most excitement he had experienced in years.

And he knew why they were searching for him; they wanted the murderer of his father. The thought of his father's corpse lying in the creek, the grotesque expression on his face, brought a thin smile to Denny's face, exposing his yellow, decaying teeth.

Though Denny was only 26 years old, he could have easily been mistaken as someone much older. At the age of twelve, Denny had already taken to drinking and smoking. His mother had left by then, and his father hadn't given a damn about him. From that age on, he had experimented heavily with every drug he could get his hands on.

He had first been institutionalized at the age of twenty two after he had cut off two of his fingers with a pocket knife while hallucinating on LSD. He later told doctors he had thought they were snakes biting his hands. By that point, his brain had been permanently damaged and Denny spent the next two years in different institutions.

To his father's regret, Denny's parentage was well known, and Doug had to pick up the bulk of the boy's expenses. When he quit paying the bills early on, the government stepped in and garnished his wages to cover the expenses. Doug had considered fleeing the area to escape the financial burden, but he liked his job and didn't really want to leave. Finally, he'd decided to bring the boy out to his farm and take care of him there.

At first Doug had done a good enough job of feeding and clothing the boy. Denny had a few small animals to take care of and a garden to tend. The situation appeared almost ideal to the overworked welfare workers who checked in on Denny periodically, and they finally placed him on their twice-yearly checklist, but it had been two years since the last visit. For the previous two years, Denny had lived on beer, potato chips, candy bars and cigarettes. He needed a cigarette badly right now, but his last one was gone.

Denny squirmed uncomfortably and carefully touched the inside of his left leg. In his haste to flee from the scene of his father's murder, when the deputies had arrived, Denny had carelessly run through a patch of poison ivy and now had a nasty, burning, itching rash spreading down the front of his body.

Denny was becoming more and more of a thing and less and less of a human...a "thing" waiting to die. Somehow, he knew he would die soon too, now that his father was dead. He really didn't care; he had nothing to live for, never had really. All he had at the moment was the excitement of his father's murder, the thought of the fresh, red blood quickened his pulse.

He also had hunger. With his father dead, no one was bringing him anything to eat. Tonight he would have to steal food from somewhere, probably from the Chambers woman he guessed; she would be the most unlikely to hurt him if she saw him. Not only that, but Denny knew a tree he could climb just up the hill from Jamie's house. From there he could see directly into her bedroom, and some nights the view made his heart pound.

Denny's breathing stopped short; a car was coming. It was the fat man and the tall guy who'd been driving up and down the road visiting with his neighbors. He knew they must be some sort of investigators looking for his father's murderer. Well, Denny could help them, he sure could, for Denny had watched his father die.

CHAPTER
13

Jamie was upset. One hundred and twenty-four square bales of alfalfa hay lay out in her hay field north of the barn. She had baled them the previous afternoon with Harley's tractor and baler. Harley had promised to show up first thing that morning, it being his day off, with two high school boys, to help her stack the bales on hay racks and haul them in from the field. Then they would elevate the hay into the barn mow, stack it and store it there until it was needed for winter feed.

But it was nearly 10:30 and there was still no sign of Harley. Though she was upset, she wasn't mad at Harley. Harley was her salvation, he seemed to love coming out to her farm and would help her any way he could. Harley spent most of his free time since Bud's death working around her farm and much of the machinery she used was borrowed from his small farming operation. She was pretty sure that between his postal job and helping her, his small farm went pretty much neglected. Still, he shared many meals with her and never left without a thank you, and some fresh produce or baked products and it seemed to be an ideal relationship for both of them.

This was Harley's day off from delivering mail and he could have spent it puttering around on his own farm north of Pigmy, but instead he had eagerly volunteered to help Jamie put up her hay, hay she badly needed to feed her flock of Dorset sheep during the cold, snowy days of winter.

She heard a car and glanced up the road. The car stopped at the bridge and she saw the two detectives she'd visited with the day before emerge. A grim feeling went through her mind as she remembered the incident in the barn. She wondered if any kind of permanent injury could result from her ewe's assault on the younger detective. Could she be sued? Was he the suing type, she wondered. Wouldn't that be the berries, she thought.

All she had left in the world now that Bud was dead was Andrea, her farm and her animals. Her best hope in life was to make enough money with the animals to hold onto her farm and raise Andrea. It would be just her luck to be sued and lose it all and...she stopped herself. She was feeling sorry for herself again, and she had made a resolution to stop doing that. Positive steps, that's what she needed to take.

Well, she would just have to start picking up the hay herself and hope that help was on the way. As she started toward the tractor, she heard the phone ring. She trotted toward the house but when the ringing stopped, she assumed Andrea had answered the phone. Before she reached the house, Andrea came sprinting out the screen door and across the lawn to deliver a breathless message.

"Mom, Harley can't come today."

"He can't? What about the boys he was going to bring, did he say anything about them?"

"Nope, just said he had to go to the doctor cuz his hem, hem-er-hoids, I think he said, was flaring up. What are hem-er-hoids?"

"Oh, part of your body." Jamie didn't feel like explaining any further. She knew that one question would only lead to another. She glanced at the sky and noticed darkening clouds far in the distance. That, combined with the uncomfortably-high humidity, made the likelihood of rain probable.

If it rained and the hay got wet, it would seriously decrease its feed value and the rain-soaked bales would be very hard to handle. Yes, no doubt about it, she'd better get on with the job. There was really no one else she wanted to ask for help.

Jamie instructed Andrea to play in the yard where she could see her from the adjoining field. She pulled on her leather gloves, climbed onto the tractor and pushed the starter pedal. The John Deere 530 came to life, its motor making the popping noise unique to two-cylinder tractors. Jamie eased the hand clutch forward and headed toward the hay field. She glanced at the cloud bank forming many miles to the southwest and wondered if this was going to be a hopeless task.

The bales lay in straight rows, though spread unevenly, where the old baler dropped them. Jamie pulled the hay rack between the first two rows, geared the tractor into neutral, locked the brake and stepped down off the tractor. She began to pick up the bales, one at a time, lugging each to the hay rack and heaving them onto it.

The old baler had done a nice job and the two lengths of twine wrapped around each fifty pound bale were tight. Jamie decided she could carry eight bales in succession to the rack before she moved the tractor to the next location. After throwing eight bales on the rack she climbed onto it and stacked them as orderly as possible beginning at the rear of the rack. She knew it was possible to stack at least seventy-five bales on the rack if she could hoist them high enough.

With the sun beating down on her, and the humidity very high, Jamie was soon sweating profusely. She tied a red handkerchief around her head to keep sweat out of her eyes. Jamie had worn blue denim bib overalls and a long sleeve denim shirt to prevent chaffing from the hay and they had proved to be the right clothes for the task. However, they weren't good clothes to wear if she was trying to keep cool. Nevertheless, her resolve remained firm as she loaded another eight bales and glanced back at the house to check on Andrea.

At that moment, Benjamin and Hawkett, having failed to uncover any new clues from their tour of the murder scene, were driving down the road toward Cordoe's farmstead. From the road, both men could see Jamie loading the hay bales and Benjamin decided to stop.

"Lord that brings back memories," Benjamin said as he stared across the field where Jamie was driving the tractor.

"What?"

"That old Johnny-Popper she's driving. I used to visit my uncle's farm years ago and he taught me how to drive a tractor a lot like that one."

"You can drive a tractor?" Hawkett asked, amazed at what he was hearing.

"Hell yes! Well, I mean, it's been a while. It's kinda like learning to swim, once you learn how, you pretty much remember, I guess."

Benjamin slipped the car into gear and drove into the hay field, taxiing directly to the area where Jamie was picking up bales.

Jamie was standing on the hay rack stacking hay when the two men got out of their car. She turned to face them, resting her hands on her hips. The sky had formed a darkening blue background. Hawkett would never forget the picture of her standing there, the smile on her sweat-streaked face and the bits of hay caught in her hair.

"Looks like a pretty big job you're tackling here, Jamie," said Benjamin, surveying the situation.

"Hadn't figured on doing it by myself," she half yelled trying to make herself heard over the rhythmic popping of the John Deere. "Harley was supposed to come with a couple of high school boys, but he can't make it. What can I do for you?"

Benjamin had suddenly became uncomfortable. Here, he and Hawkett had just climbed out of an air-conditioned car and were slowing Jamie's progress. It didn't help that he realized he was sweating nearly as badly as she and he wasn't doing anything physically-demanding. The temperature had risen to nearly seventy-five degrees already and the humidity made it feel almost unbearable.

"Why don't you wait for some cooler weather and line up more help?" Benjamin asked her.

She didn't answer right away. Her eyes had turned toward Hawkett, standing on the other side of the car staring at her, a slight smile on his face. It seemed to take him a few seconds to realize she was looking at him, almost as if he was caught in a daydream. Then suddenly, reality hit, and he turned and pretended to be observing the bales of hay laying across the small field.

"Can't wait," she finally replied pointing to a cloud bank far off on the distant horizon. "If this hay gets rained on, it'll be nearly ruined, and I'll be severely short of winter feed."

Benjamin nodded. This made sense, but still, it looked like one hell of a job, especially for a woman by herself. He wondered how heavy the bales were. He wondered just how physically strong some of these farm women were. For a brief moment, Benjamin tried to imagine a team of women from the DCI, or from any organization for that matter, spread across this green hay field, heaving bales onto wooden wagons.

"What can I do for you?" she repeated, bringing Benjamin back to reality.

"Oh, you haven't seen young Cordoe, have you?"

"No." She shivered involuntarily as she always did at the thought of the drug-scarred neighbor.

"Oh, well, let us know if you do, okay? Or, if you think of anything else pertinent to the case, let us know. Okay?"

"Sure, no problem."

With that said, the two detectives climbed back into the air-conditioned car and Jamie moved the John Deere forward toward the next eight bales. As the car bumped toward the road, Hawkett looked back at Jamie climbing off of the tractor. He couldn't believe the next statement that came out of his mouth. It was almost as if some spirit had entered his body and was talking for him.

"Ben, let's go back and help her."

"What?" Benjamin almost yelled, looking at his partner, "You're kidding, right?"

"No, hell, it wouldn't take long. You can drive the tractor and I'll help her load."

"Why in the hell would we do that?"

"She needs the help," Hawkett responded pleadingly.

Benjamin stopped the car, "Hawkett, we work for the DCI, remember? We investigate, we report, we arrest bad guys. We don't load hay."

The two men sat in silence for nearly five seconds, eyes locked on each other's.

"Well, I'm on vacation!" declared Hawkett almost matter-of-factly. He opened the car door, stepped out and slammed it behind him. Without looking back, he started marching across the hay field toward Jamie and her John Deere.

Benjamin was caught between disbelief and anger.

"What the hell," he turned in his seat and looked at his partner. "What the hell," he repeated silently to himself four times. "Damned idiot. Damned idiot. Now what? The damned idiot," he kept repeating to himself. Had he gone crazy, completely crazy? Booze didn't eat your mind up that fast, did it? Now what?

Jamie had just thrown a second bale on the rack when she noticed Hawkett marching across the hay field toward her.

"Now what?" she whispered to herself. The expression of intensity on Hawkett's face looked a little unnerving. Was he mad about the ewe butting him in the groin yesterday, was that it? Probably yes, and now she was going to get chewed good, threatened with a lawsuit, maybe even issued a citation. Could she be charged with assaulting a police officer? That damned ewe!

She waited for the barrage of threats, but none came. The detective stopped at the first bale he came to. He picked it up, clumsily, almost tripping, and laid it on the rack without saying a word. He turned and retrieved a second bale while Jamie watched, dumbstruck.

"What are you doing?"

"Helping."

"You can't be doing this."

"Stop me," he replied, still carrying bales and never once looking her in the eye.

"But you have a job, your responsibilities."

"I'm on vacation."

She couldn't believe the scenario that had transpired. She didn't know how to handle it. Hawkett threw his fourth bale onto the rack and turned and looked at her.

"Look, I don't know how to stack them up on the rack, so you'll have to do that, okay?" With that he seemed to dismiss any further debate and went back to work. By that time Benjamin had returned to the car and parked it by the tractor. He got out of the car, but was not quite sure what to say. He didn't get a chance.

"You drive," Hawkett pointed toward the tractor.

"What?" Benjamin shouted in absolute disbelief.

"Help or get the hell out of here!"

Benjamin stood dumbstruck, much the same as Jamie, for nearly thirty seconds while they watched Hawkett load another bale onto the rack. Then, without another word, he took his jacket off, threw it into the backseat of the car, loosened his tie, hiked up his pants and climbed up onto the seat of the tractor, cautiously, as if he was mounting a wild horse. He turned and once again looked at his partner.

"We get caught doing this and our careers are over, you know that?"

"Drive," Hawkett pointed toward the waiting bales of hay that laid ahead.

CHAPTER

14

With the two men helping, loading the first rack wasn't too much of a job. The biggest problem was Benjamin's difficulty in handling the tractor's hand clutch. Twice, his ineptness with the machine made the rack lurch, nearly causing Jamie to fall off.

Hawkett's adrenaline was running low, and without it, his physical drive sunk quickly. He hadn't worked out with his weights nor done any running for months, and his stamina was low as well. The booze hadn't helped either. Still, he never broke stride throwing bale after bale onto the rack for Jamie. Three times he had even climbed onto the rack to lift bales up to the higher tiers that she couldn't reach.

The gray polo shirt he was wearing was soaked with sweat and he was tempted to take it off, but the hay had already scratched his arms and he didn't want to expose any more of his body. His hands were developing blisters from grasping the bale twine, and he realized why Jamie had worn a pair of leather gloves. Glancing across the hay field, he estimated they had gathered nearly half of the bales. A feeling of accomplishment ran through his body.

Jamie was having trouble placing the last bale onto the rack. She had little room left to stand and the hay was stacked five bales high. Hawkett jumped onto the front of the rack to help her.

The tractor was still proceeding along slowly until Benjamin decided to stop the wagon, thinking it would help them to position the final bale. Instead, it threw both Hawkett and Jamie off balance.

Jamie would have fallen off of the wagon and landed on her back, had Hawkett not instinctively thrown an arm around her. He pulled her back toward him and, in an effort to regain her balance, she lunged in his direction. She grabbed hold of the haystack and steadied herself. She felt safe and secure. For some reason, Hawkett's arm lingered around her waist a few more seconds than necessary, and he had to physically will it away. For the second time in an hour, he again felt as if he was not quite in control of himself. She looked straight into his eyes and smiled.

"Thanks, Adam."

He found himself delighted that she had remembered his first name. Then, just as quickly, he wondered why such a trivial thing had excited him.

Hawkett was totally disoriented as he climbed down from the hay rack. He knew what he was thinking, and it felt strange. He kept thinking how good Jamie had looked and felt, even when she was soaked in sweat and covered with bits of dried alfalfa leaves. He felt a smile begin to form on his face and quickly looked to see if anyone else had noticed.

Ben had; he didn't miss much. He could see something happening that had the potential to be really good or really bad for Hawkett, not to mention his own personal career. Still, he decided not to speculate. He turned to Jamie who was brushing hay from her denim bibs.

"Now what?" Benjamin asked her.

"Oh, well..." she surveyed the remaining bales not quite sure what to say. And no wonder, thought Benjamin, with two strange detectives popping into her field like this, almost physically forcing themselves into her presence.

"You fellows probably need to get going. I appreciate the..."

"Have you got another hay wagon?" interrupted Hawkett in a pleasant, but firm voice.

"Yes, but..."

"Let's go get it. You drive. I'm afraid Ben might unload all these bales the way he's handling that clutch."

Benjamin, pretending to be hurt by that comment, climbed down off the tractor. "It's been over thirty years since I've driven anything like that. I thought I did a fairly respectable job!"

"You did fine, Benjamin," assured Jamie. "It sure made the job easier." She took another look at Hawkett and saw the resolve in his eyes. She shook her head, somewhat still in bewilderment, climbed onto the tractor and pulled the load toward her farmstead.

Andrea was sitting in the swing, barefooted, dragging the tips of her toes on the ground as she watched her mother pull the load of hay near the elevator by the barn and unhook it. The border collie, Jack, lay motionless to one side of her and her pet lamb, Junior, contentedly grazed grass in the lawn on her other side. The two detectives followed her mother into the driveway in their car. Benjamin got out and visited with Andrea about Jack and Junior, while Hawkett helped Jamie hook the tractor to an empty hay rack.

Jamie approached her daughter, restated a list of safety warnings, which Andrea had already memorized, then left again with the two detectives, in their car, following behind her.

The second load went onto the hay rack quicker than the first, primarily because Benjamin was getting the hang of driving the tractor and Hawkett was learning to place each bale in a better position for Jamie to load. Hawkett felt fortunate that there were no more bales to load. The physical effort had taken a heavy toll on his out-of-shape body, and he was starting to feel weary. He knew there would be sore muscles to deal with the next day. Still, it gave both Hawkett and Benjamin a feeling of accomplishment to see all of the bales neatly stacked on the two hay racks.

Jamie looked up at the sun. "Looks like it must be nearly noon. You fellows want a bite to eat? I've got plenty of good food in the house."

"Oh, no," both detectives answered almost in unison, then Benjamin continued, "We can eat at June's, no need to trouble you."

"No trouble, I was figuring on having Harley and some boys for lunch today anyway. If you don't help me eat some of the food, it'll go to waste. Heck, it's the least I can do, the way you've helped me."

Benjamin turned and looked at Hawkett who merely shrugged his shoulders seeming to feign indifference. In reality, he very much wanted to join her for lunch. Benjamin looked at Jamie and winked.

"I have to warn you; Hawkett's a pretty big eater."

Hawkett laughed out loud at that statement and Jamie replied, "Great, follow me into the house then."

As they followed her up the front steps and onto the porch, Benjamin, although enjoying himself immensely, couldn't believe the actions they were taking. For all practical purposes, this woman should be considered a possible suspect in their murder investigation, yet here they were, loading hay with her, eating dinner with her. He shook his head silently. He reckoned he'd done less intelligent things.

Andrea had moved with her pets to her makeshift sandbox, an old tractor tire laying on its side filled with sand. When she saw the detectives approaching, she sprinted across the lawn and up the steps to the porch, with the border collie and lamb at her heels. Both detectives stopped to visit with her while Jamie continued into the house.

Jamie stepped into the utility room, just off the porch, to wash her hands and face. Looking in the mirror, she was appalled at the amount of alfalfa bits caught in her hair and brushed them out. She remembered the detective's arm around her. She smiled. It had been a long time since she'd had a man's arm around her waist.

"Andrea, show these fellows where to wash up. I'm going to check dinner," she instructed her daughter as she walked by the screen door.

Both men in turn washed their hands. Hawkett winced a little as he bent over the sink, already feeling some soreness in his lower back. The cold tap water felt good, but the blisters on his hands burned when he rubbed the soap across them. He tried to remember how long it had been since he had done any physical work of this magnitude.

When the two men entered the farmhouse kitchen, they were pleasantly surprised at the look and smell of dinner. Jamie had been up early that morning baking and there was nothing as fragrant as the smell of homemade bread, thought Benjamin. She had prepared a lamb roast in the crock pot and was slicing it when they entered.

"Have a seat, wherever you're comfortable." Each of the men took a seat at the large, round oak table. Andrea began setting plates around the table as if it were her job.

"Can we help?" asked Benjamin, although in truth he didn't have the slightest idea how to prepare a meal.

Hawkett found himself reminiscing, remembering meals prepared by Ann—a lot of microwave, a lot of tofu. Man, he hated tofu.

"No, just relax," Jamie replied. She turned and checked the roasting ears of sweet corn that were just starting to boil in a pan on the stove.

Gradually, an approaching vehicle could be heard turning into the driveway. Jamie peered through the kitchen window to see who it was. She saw Harley, slowly getting out of his pickup, his little dog right behind him. Jamie wished he would leave the small dog in the pickup. It always started a fight with her border collie, Jack.

"Oh, Harley's here. Andrea, tell him to come in for dinner, and then set another place at the table please."

"Sure, Mom."

Benjamin smiled. He liked to see a child pleasantly respond to her parent in that manner. Some of his nieces and nephews, well, they were a different story.

By the time Harley found his way into the kitchen and had exchanged pleasantries with Jamie and the two detectives, Jamie had covered the table with food. Hawkett's mouth watered as he observed the homemade bread, the sweet corn, the roast, the sliced tomatoes and the baked potatoes. She passed a pitcher of iced tea around the table and told them to help themselves.

"Mom?"

"Yes, Andrea?"

"Shouldn't we pray?"

"Well, uh sure, will you say a prayer for us?"

"Okay," she sighed.

She looked up at Benjamin, "Bow your head and hold your hands like this, okay?"

Benjamin, with a look of earnest on his face, nodded his head and did as the child had requested. She turned to see if the other adults were following suit and began her prayer.

"Dear God, thank you for this food. Take care of me and Mom and Junior and Jack. And say hi to Dad for me and tell him I miss him too, okay? Amen."

Hawkett looked up in time to see Jamie quickly brush a tear from her eye before passing him the roast.

CHAPTER
15

Hawkett couldn't believe how delicious the food tasted and told Jamie so.

"It's almost all home grown," she said, "farm-fresh so to speak."

Hawkett watched in silent amazement as the ever-smiling Harley loaded his plate almost beyond capacity, stacking tomato slices three high on top of two golden ears of sweetcorn.

"Whoops!" Harley exclaimed, suddenly squinting through his thick glasses at the clock on Jamie's kitchen wall. "Time to take my pills; left them in the pickup."

He excused himself from the table and started to leave to fetch his medication. As he pushed his chair back, he bumped into Daniel who had followed him into the house and had fallen asleep under Harley's chair. He reached down and affectionately petted the small dog.

"You stay here like a good boy and guard my food while I'm gone." He winked at Hawkett. "It's such good food; these other fellows might snitch it if you don't, okay?" He proceeded to laugh at his own statement.

He looked across the table at Andrea and winked, then proceeded out of the kitchen to retrieve his pills. Just after Harley had left the house, the screen door slamming behind him, the little rat terrier leaped onto his chair. Hawkett thought, momentarily, that the dog had taken his master seriously, and was, in fact, guarding the food.

Little Daniel, however, had other plans. He lifted his two front paws onto the table, dropped his head and began lapping hungrily at the food on Harley's plate. Hawkett, not quite sure what to do, his mouth full of sweet corn, turned to Jamie, assuming she would handle the situation. However, Jamie had gone to the freezer for more ice cubes and could not see what was transpiring.

Both Benjamin and Andrea were also witnessing the small dog's feast; Andrea, with grave interest, and Benjamin, silently laughing so hard that Hawkett thought he might roll out of his chair. Seeing that no one else was going to take steps to rectify the situation, Hawkett decided he would have to reprimand the dog. However, to his amazement, the dog had already eaten everything except the tomatoes and the sweet-corn. In fact, he was already leaving his master's plate, taking one of the ears of sweet corn with him. The little dog trotted off into an adjoining room, the golden ear of sweet corn bobbing in its mouth.

Hawkett once again turned to Jamie, who was just returning to the table apparently completely unaware of the small dog's coup. The screen door banged once again and Harley shuffled in, jabbering about his pills as he returned to his chair. He didn't notice the missing food until he had a fork in his hand and was reaching for his first bite. The fork, however, came to a halt in midair when he realized that all that remained on his plate were three battered slices of tomatoes.

For nearly five seconds, he stared at the plate, the fork still lingering above it. Then slowly, ever so slowly, his gaze rose from the plate to Hawkett, sitting just across the table. Nothing was spoken aloud, but the accusing stare said it all. Hawkett was speechless. He hated to admit that he'd let the dog clean Harley's plate, yet it was ludicrous to let Harley suggest that Hawkett had stolen the food.

Benjamin, watching the drama develop, nearly choked on his roast lamb as he tried to refrain from outright laughter. He excused himself and stepped out on to the porch to regain his composure. Jamie, with a quizzical look on her face, noticed Harley's empty plate and started passing things to him. She could see Harley staring at Hawkett but couldn't quite figure out what had transpired between the two men.

Finally, Harley shook his head as if disgusted, reached for the baked potatoes and once again started to heap food onto his plate, a half smile slowly returning to his face.

Hawkett glanced at Jamie and caught her looking at him. She smiled; he smiled. Benjamin returned to the table. His eyes were brimming with tears from laughing so earnestly. He looked at Hawkett and almost started laughing again, but then regained control of himself. What a day this was turning out to be, he thought to himself.

The rest of the meal was consumed with almost no more embarrassing interruptions. Benjamin was finishing his second piece of fresh, homemade apple pie, smothered in vanilla ice cream, when Jamie asked if any of the men would like a cup of coffee. All three replied that they would and she rose to get it.

Before she could slide away from the table, however, Hawkett, uncharacteristic of him, jumped up and said, "I'll get it! I feel guilty, you know, us sitting here like it's a restaurant, you jumping up and down."

"Well, thank you, Adam, but you don't have to."

"No, point me towards the cups," he replied, cutting her off. He felt a warm feeling etching through his soul and once again it puzzled him. What was it about her calling him by his first name that gave him such a buzz? It seemed like the last woman who had called him "Adam" was his mother. Then suddenly he remembered, surprised that he'd forgotten, there had also been Ann.

He poured four cups of coffee for the group while Benjamin watched in amazement. Had Hawkett had too much sun, he wondered.

Harley leaned back from the table, tipping himself up on the two back legs of his chair. He rocked, dangerously, on the legs and Jamie worried that if he lost his balance, it would likely result in an injury. Furthermore, it annoyed her to no end, listening to the joints on the old oak chair creak in misery. It was a bad habit of Harley's. He had done it after every meal that they had shared. She knew that she should say something to him about it but she wouldn't today in front of the other two men.

Harley reached down and scratched little Daniel behind his ears and the dog licked his hand in return. Then, surprisingly, the little dog lifted his head and let out a low-pitched howl.

"Now, now," Harley snatched the small dog up with one hand

94

and laid it across his lap, as he continued to teeter on the back legs of the chair.

"What's he howling about, Harley?" asked Jamie, with genuine concern in her voice.

Indigestion, thought Hawkett, with more than a little satisfaction.

"Oh," sighed Harley, stroking the small dogs back, "he still misses his buddy, Edwin."

"What happened to Edwin?" inquired Benjamin before Jamie could cut him off.

Harley didn't answer for a moment. He just sat there, stroking the rat terrier. Finally, he lifted his head and Hawkett was alarmed to see tears forming behind his thick glasses.

"Well..." Harley started to reply, his voice thick with emotion. He took a deep breath. "Well..." he tried again, but he didn't have a chance to finish the statement.

If they hadn't witnessed it themselves, they may not have believed the events that transpired next. Before Harley could complete the sentence, Daniel suddenly jumped up to lick his master in the face. This caused a notable change in weight distribution on the tipped chair. Before anyone could move to help, in the flash of an instant, Harley's chair tipped over backwards and he landed on the kitchen floor.

Hawkett would always remember that scene, staring at the bottom of the mailman's tennis shoes and right up his pant legs as he toppled over. Even more bizarre, however, was what happened to Daniel. With a thrust of his arms, initially trying to grab for support, Harley inadvertently tossed the small dog straight backwards over his head. The little dog was catapulted through one of Jamie's kitchen windows. Thankfully, the window was open, and the dog crashed through only the metal screen covering it.

The remaining three adults rushed to assist Harley, while Andrea sprinted out of the house to check on Daniel. Harley, his glasses thrown off, seemed to be disoriented as he tried to get up. "I'm okay, no problem. Anybody see my glasses? Ouch, dammit." Embarrassed, he tried to regain his position and rebalance the chair.

By then, Hawkett was on one side of Harley and Jamie on the other, attempting to help him up.

Calming a little, Harley looked around and with help from Hawkett and Jamie, regained his footing. With his glasses still missing, he was a little disoriented. He squinted his eyes at Hawkett, attempting to focus. Outside the window, the adults could hear Andrea's voice.

"He's all right, no cuts or anything; he's just kind of going to the bathroom on our cherry tree."

Harley seemed to regain his senses, "Sorry," he chuckled awkwardly. "See my glasses anywhere? Can't see a thing without them. Where's Daniel, is he okay?"

Hawkett bent down and picked up Harley's glasses. They were lying near the wall and were, surprisingly, undamaged. Harley was apparently still disoriented because when Hawkett handed him his glasses, he placed them on his face upside down. It was incredible, thought Hawkett, how well the glasses resided there, completely upside down on Harley's nose. Jamie reached towards his face to correct the problem, but Harley, obviously unaware of his error, stopped her.

"No, I'm okay."

"But," responded Jamie.

"No, I'll be going now. Thanks for lunch."

With that, he ambled out of the room, the glasses bouncing precariously on the bridge of his nose. Hawkett silently shook his head while Benjamin turned away and tried to control his laughter.

They listened to hear the screen door slam and the pickup start before anyone uttered a word.

Benjamin, having regained his composure, asked, "Did I upset him? Was it something about the dog? I'm, sorry if I..."

"Oh, no," Jamie replied, "I should have probably said something, interrupted him, I don't know. Harley's other dog, Edwin that is, died last weekend. I think, I'm not sure, but I'm probably right that Harley ran over it with his pickup. If not that, something else, the tractor maybe, I don't know for sure. He tried to tell me about it Monday and the tears got in the way just like today. You can tell how crazy he is about his dogs. They're just like children to the old fellow."

"Anyway," she shrugged, "I don't think he got hurt, do you? I mean I couldn't see anything wrong with him."

Both men agreed that yes, amazingly, he had seemed unscathed following the acrobatic accident. Benjamin knew that, until his dying day, he would never forget the sight of that small dog flying through the open window. He chuckled quietly to himself.

CHAPTER 16

Jamie refused any offers to help wash the dishes. She decided that they had done too much already, although she secretly wished that the two men could stay and help unload the hay as well. Both of the loads still needed to be elevated into the barn's haymow and stacked. She had no idea how she would accomplish that task alone but, nevertheless, the hay had to be sheltered before the rain came.

"Thanks again!" she yelled, standing on her front porch as the detectives got into their car.

"Anytime," replied Benjamin, who in fact was actually thinking to himself, never again. But, he had to admit, he'd enjoyed driving the old John Deere, the feeling of its power under him, the rhythmic "pop-pop-pop" of its engine and the smell of the fresh hay.

Benjamin shook his head; he was getting as crazy as Hawkett. It had to be the heat; the humidity had cranked up another few percentage points. He rolled up his window and flicked on the air conditioning. He shifted the car into reverse and started to back down the driveway, waving at Andrea and her pets as he went. The trio, lamb, dog and little girl, were running toward the barn. Remembering Harley's bad luck with his other dog, Benjamin made it a point to back well away from the child and animals, swinging a wide arc into the farmyard as he kept a watchful eye on them. Just as he was about to apply his brakes, with a rather sudden jolt, the car came to a crunching halt against Jamie's hay elevator. Benjamin and Hawkett looked back and then at each other. Not a word was spoken out loud, but the look on Hawkett's face was not a pleasant one. Benjamin, somewhat shocked, shrugged his shoulders, then the two men climbed from the car to survey the damage.

Jamie walked slowly across the yard, dread written all over her face. She knew that if anything on the hay elevator was broken her day had just gotten a whole lot longer.

All three adults silently congregated at the junction of the elevator and the rear of the car. The car, amazingly, somehow remained unscathed, blemish-free, but that wasn't the case for the elevator. The dump on the elevator was badly bent with some of the sheet metal torn completely loose. That in itself wouldn't have been a major problem, thought Jamie; she could have somehow pounded out the dents. No, it was the bent power takeoff shaft, shoved clear back past its cast iron coupling that was the killer. It indicated that repairs, major repairs would be in order. She felt tears welling up in her eyes, but forced them back as she walked away from the scene and took a deep breath. It seemed she was always taking deep breaths, starting over, trying again. She was mad, irritated as hell, but still, it had been an accident. It could've happened to anyone. She took another deep breath and turned back toward the two detectives. Both of them had expressions of guilt.

"Hurt your car any?"

Benjamin cleared his throat and refrained from lighting the cigar he'd pulled from his pocket.

"Uh, no, Jamie. Gosh I'm sorry. I was trying to stay well clear of the little ones and I just didn't think to look back. We have insurance, er uh, the DCI does anyway." Lord, he thought, how he hated the thought of reporting this to Brightwall.

"Oh, don't worry, I think Harley and I can fix it up somehow." It was the tone of her voice, when she said "somehow" that gave the detectives an assessment of how bad the damage really was.

"What does this contraption do?" asked Benjamin, further attempting to assess the damage.

She couldn't believe anyone would ask a question that silly but reminded herself they were city slickers.

"It's an elevator. I was going to use it to hoist those bales on the hay racks up and into the barn." The two detectives turned to glance at the loaded hay bales then back to the elevator climbing up into the top of the barn. They were beginning to understand the seriousness of the situation, and Benjamin asked the dreaded question.

"What will you do now, try to fix the elevator?"

"I can't do that by myself. I'll have to wait for Harley and he probably can't fix it either, but he'll know who can. No," she paused looking back at the barn, "I guess I'll throw them through that side door over there, drag them across the barn floor and stack them on the north side of the bottom story." Even as she said it, she knew she couldn't do it by herself before the rain came, even with a positive attitude. The clouds were already getting darker and thicker on the horizon.

"I'll help you."

Benjamin spun around and looked Hawkett square in the face.

"Hawkett," Benjamin replied, barely keeping the anger out of his voice, "We have a murder investigation to conduct. We can't spend anymore time here, okay? I screwed up, yes, I know. I'll report the damage and make sure the insurance claim is promptly filed. Okay?"

"I'm helping her," Hawkett replied, in a voice quiet enough that only Benjamin could hear.

Benjamin was in a real quandary. What he wanted to do was give Hawkett a really good chewing. The man was losing touch with reality and he hadn't even been near any booze for the past twenty hours. On the other hand, Jamie and her daughter, standing behind him, were undoubtedly going to suffer through extra hours of labor because of his carelessness.

"What am I supposed to do?" Benjamin asked.

"Investigate."

"By myself?"

"Sure."

"What if Brightwall finds out about this?"

"He'll probably fire me. I don't care."

"He'll fire me too, especially if I don't report you."

"Then report me."

Benjamin didn't have a response to that. He pulled his handkerchief out of his pocket and wiped the sweat from his brow. The heat was becoming unbearable. He had no response. He knew what he wanted to say, but he could tell it would be a waste of time. What the hell, he thought, this was going to happen sooner or later anyway, yet he had always assumed that Hawkett would get fired for a different reason, specifically something related to booze, not for unloading hay while he was supposed to be conducting a murder investigation. His temper had peaked now, but he managed to hold his tongue. He took one more look at Hawkett, climbed into the car, turned the air conditioning on full blast and quickly drove down the driveway towards the road.

Hawkett watched the car speed up the road towards Pigmy, then he turned to see Jamie, hands on her hips, staring at him. Suddenly he felt like a real fool.

"Adam," she started to speak then shook her head as if confused.

"Yes?"

"I need this hay. It's important that the rain doesn't destroy it. But you don't need to risk your job, your career. It's not your fault the elevator got broken. I mean, well, why?"

Yeah why? Hawkett wondered to himself. Twenty-four hours before, he hadn't even known that this woman existed. Her sheep had damn near ruptured him, his back hurt like hell, he was starting to get a bad sunburn and he had a slight headache. Yet, he couldn't force himself to leave. What was it about her that attracted him so much? Was it physical desire? Well, hell, he thought, probably. No, it was something else.

Had he become this screwed up? No, that wasn't it. It was this woman, standing there staring at him, seeing him for the damn idiot he was. Yeah, it was this woman; he felt a strong attraction to her. Somehow she seemed so different, so independent, so purposeful, so...well, Lord, maybe he really was screwed up. Yeah, he needed help; he probably should contact...

Her voice interrupted his train wreck of thoughts. "Hey, is there anybody in there? Are you okay, Adam?"

He took a few steps away from her, turned, then spoke. "Look, I've been having a few problems with my life. I'm not a psycho or anything but, well, things haven't gone very good for me. I'm sick of my job, hell, I'm sick of my life. For some stupid reason, I can't explain it, but for some reason I just feel good helping you. And feeling good hasn't been something I've done very much lately." He paused. She said nothing. Yes, he thought, I sound like a damn babbling fool. "Look, I'll help you unload the hay, then I'll get out of your life, okay?"

She turned around and looked at the barn and took a deep breath, then turned around and looked at him again, shaking her head in bewilderment.

"Okay, partner. We'll pull the hay rack as close to the barn as possible and get on with it. You change your mind, though, it's okay with me."

"Sure." He tried to smile a little. She tried to return a little smile.

CHAPTER
17

Benjamin had thoroughly lost his temper. He was tired of Hawkett's erratic behavior. He cursed his younger partner vehemently all the way out the driveway. He slammed the brakes and stopped the car on the bridge under which Cordoe's body had been found. The car's air conditioner was cooling the interior and was helping Benjamin cool off as well. He pulled out a cigar, lit it and took several deep draws. That helped more. "Now what?" he asked himself. Dammit to hell, he knew what, he'd continue on by himself. Yes he would, hell yes. Dumb son of a bitch wants to get fired, let him do it. Hell, Benjamin knew he was a good detective. He'd straighten this mess out by himself. Screw Hawkett, he thought. He was a big boy, he could take care of himself.

He got out of the car and stared across the horizon. He watched a large hawk glide across the skyline and then something else caught his eye. Instinct told him not to stare, but he was positive somebody was sitting in the tall tree back from the road. Who the hell, he wondered, taking occasional glances. It didn't look like a child, too big. Now what he wondered. He took one more casual glance in the direction of the tree and yes, the somebody was still there, almost completely camouflaged by leaves.

Benjamin returned to the car and spent some time studying his rear left tire, then shook his head as if disgusted. He removed his car keys from the ignition and used them to open the trunk of the car. Out of sight of the tree dweller, he reached for the case containing Hawkett's pistol. He opened it and jammed a loaded cartridge into place. He wasn't sure who he was dealing with, probably some harmless fool, but still, he couldn't be too careful. He shoved the gun into his belt on the left side of his pants and pulled the spare tire out of the trunk. Keeping the gun out of view, he started rolling the tire around the side of the car, then tripped and pretended to lose his balance. The tire went bouncing down the ditch crashing into and through the barbed wire fence adjoining the pasture. Benjamin once again shook his head and started carefully working his way down toward the tire. Reaching the fence, he crawled over it, still giving the pretense of retrieving the tire. He now was within fifty yards of the tree and decided to make his move. He turned and started to sprint toward the tree, but actually almost tripped in doing so and slowed to a clumsy trot, drawing the gun out of his belt as he went.

Up until that point, Denny had been enjoying the show immensely. He actually had to cover his mouth when he saw the clumsy, fat man let the tire go rolling into the ditch. "Shit," he whispered when he realized what was happening and started untangling himself from his hiding place. Real fear consumed him as he saw the gun emerge, but it was too late. The fat man could barely run, but the element of surprise had placed Benjamin in the position of power. By the time Denny reached the bottom limb of the tree and began swinging to the ground, Benjamin was already waiting, gun pointed directly at his target.

Benjamin was gasping for air and sweat poured from his brow. He took one look at the mangy specimen before him and knew it had to be the missing Denny Cordoe. Denny quivered like a scared animal, yet a small evil grin, exposing yellow, broken teeth, remained on his face. He was wearing dirty black sweatpants, a ripped tee-shirt and no socks or shoes. He stood slightly stooped and his hands hung loose at his sides in a most unnatural manner. But even more grotesque was the smell. Benjamin was slightly downwind from Denny and his odor was nauseating.

After catching his breath, Benjamin finally said, "You're Denny Cordoe, right?" There was no answer. "Answer me," he said in a firmer, louder, demanding tone.

Denny nodded, meekly, still displaying the evil little smile. Benjamin knew he was the type of guy he could never turn his back on.

"What were you doing up in that tree?" There was no answer. "Can't you talk? Answer!" he again demanded.

In a whiney, high-pitched voice, Denny finally replied while looking directly at Benjamin's revolver, "I watch things."

"You watch things?" This guy was crazier than Benjamin had anticipated. "You got any weapons?"

Denny shook his head back and forth.

"Turn around," ordered Benjamin. He supposed he ought to search the guy for weapons but that smell, wow. He couldn't wait to have the fugitive locked in his car, he thought with dread. "All right, start walking toward my car, and don't try anything funny, okay? If I have to shoot a hole through you, you won't be able to walk, what with your guts laying all over the pasture. Then I'd have to drag you to the car and it's too damn hot for that, so just don't do anything stupid, okay?"

Denny, still trembling, nodded in understanding, then started towards the car; then stopped. Wherever that car hauled him to, he would again end up locked in a cage or tied up. No, no never again. His trembling became worse. No, he thought, they're not going to cage me again. He remembered the injections, the shock treatment, the perverted orderlies. No. He stopped, turned, and faced Benjamin, "No."

"No? No what? I've got the gun here, boy; get moving."

Denny shook his head side to side. "Leave me alone, okay? I didn't kill him. Please, I didn't kill him. Leave me, okay? Denny didn't hurt nobody."

"How'd you know he was dead?"

"Denny seen him die. Seen him roll around and scream little screams." The ever-present evil smile grew as he spoke. Maybe he believes me, thought Denny. His spirits began to pick up. Yes, he was going to be able to convince this gun-toting fat man that he didn't kill his father.

"Seen him die, huh?"

Denny bobbed his head up and down.

"What killed him?"

"The fork, you know." Denny turned sideways to Benjamin and started thrusting his hands out as if shoving something. Benjamin realized that Denny was play-acting, showing him how the pitchfork had been shoved through his father's chest. Then Denny turned, and began playing the part of his father, pretending to grab at the fork buried in his chest, a shocked expression on his face. Denny moaned a little bit, then uttered a series of short, quiet screams. His play-acting was so good, it scared Benjamin. There was no doubt in his mind that Denny Cordoe had witnessed his father's death. Finally, Denny dropped to the ground on his knees, rolled over on one side and lay there, still grasping the imaginary fork in his chest, paddling his feet as if riding an extremely slow bicycle.

Then the acting stopped and Denny lay motionless, staring up at Benjamin with a questioning expression on his face. Benjamin pitied the guy lying there like that. If his father, Doug, had been a contributor to Denny's poor physical health, he couldn't help thinking somebody had done the world a great justice by killing his father.

"Well, get up."

Denny scrambled to his feet but remained in a somewhat crouched position, not fully standing up.

"To the car," Benjamin waved his gun in the direction of the car.

Denny took off running, but not toward the car. Let the fat man shoot me, he thought. I'm not goin' back. He headed for the dense timber on the hillside.

Benjamin had the time and he had the ability. He extended his arm and aimed the .38 at the fleeing figure, running, bent over with his arms flailing back and forth. As Denny ran, he emitted a low-pitched, steady whine that sounded somewhat like a rabbit crying in distress. Benjamin lowered the sights from the middle of the fleeing man's back, down to his lower left calf, knowing he could cripple the escapee even at the ever-increasing distance. Then he dropped the gun to his side and watched Denny Cordoe disappear into the trees.

There was no use chasing him. He knew that he just wasn't physically able. Too bad Hawkett wasn't there; he would have been able to. He turned and walked slowly back to the car. Well, he knew more now than he had, there was that anyway. He knew that Denny had at least witnessed his father's murder. Had he committed it? Denny said no. Had he been lying? Benjamin didn't think so. Had Denny killed his father and yet was so mentally unstable that he couldn't accept that he had performed the deed? Benjamin thought that could be possible. He had one glaring regret. If Denny hadn't committed the murder, he damn sure knew who had, and Benjamin had failed to gain that information in the confrontation. Damn, maybe he should have shot the guy. Maybe he was getting too old for this kind of work.

CHAPTER
18

A man in her life? Was this what was happening she wondered. Jamie was tossing bales of hay off of the rack and through the side door of the barn, while Hawkett was lugging them to the far wall and stacking them up as high as the ceiling. His job was undoubtedly harder than hers, but he hadn't complained. She noticed that Hawkett's pace was slowing as the job progressed and they had only unloaded half of the first rack of hay. She wondered where Andrea and her gang had gone. They'd been near the rack only a few moments prior. Then she recalled Andrea asking if she could walk up to the hill pasture. Hawkett appeared at the door, his shirt already completely soaked through with sweat.

"Pretty warm in there, huh?"

"Yeah, I'm okay. Mind if I take my shirt off?"

"No, but those bales will chew a hole in any bare skin they touch. Might be painful."

He didn't reply, simply yanked his polo shirt off, hung it on the barn door, grabbed a waiting bale and disappeared.

Jamie realized she was staring at Hawkett's bare chest and was surprised by the sexual awareness that she felt. His skin could sure use some sunlight, she thought, but he has a fairly nice build. She shook her head. She felt guilty for thinking such thoughts. What the hell is wrong with me she wondered. There had been no other men since Bud had died, and she had assumed that there never would be. The emotions she felt troubled her. Her world had remained barely stable since Bud's death. Was it now collapsing? A murder right down the road, a stranger working side by side with her. What else? Should she throw this guy out, chase him away?

It took just over an hour to unload the first rack. Hawkett was dog-tired, soaked with sweat and aching in a lot of places. Still, despite the fatigue, he felt a good sense of accomplishment while surveying the tall stack of green hay bales he had helped Jamie stack in the barn.

She started the old John Deere, pulled the empty rack out of the way, and hooked onto the second load. This load she pulled up along side of the barn, as she'd done with the first, and shut the popping tractor off.

She was about to ask Hawkett if he wanted a drink before they started on the second load but was interrupted by her daughter's voice coming from far away. She turned, shaded her eyes and stared up the hill toward the noise.

"Mom, Mom!" Andrea screamed as she sprinted down the lane from the sheep pasture up on top of the hill. Her lamb and border collie were running alongside her. "Mom!" she screamed again. Jamie knew something was wrong. Her first thought was that her daughter had been stung by a bumblebee. Jamie jumped off the rack and ran to her daughter.

"Coyotes, Mom! They got our sheep." Jamie knelt down, took her daughter in her arms and tried to calm her. Tears were streaming down her face. "There's blood and stuff," she sobbed.

"Where honey? Where?" she repeated holding the trembling child as she spoke.

"Up there," pointed Andrea, "at the end of the lane, under the big tree."

The border collie turned, stared back up toward the hill and growled, the hairs bristling on the back of his neck.

Jamie wiped the tears from Andrea's face.

"Did you see the coyotes, Honey?"

"Yeah, we seen two big brown ones running away into the trees.

I was scared they might try to get Junior, so we ran, fast as we could. Jack barked at them real mean and started chasin' them but I told him to come back. I was scared, Mom." The child was still trembling and Jamie held her tightly and patted her back.

"Okay, Andrea, you guys go back to the yard and play by your sand pile. I'll go see how bad things are." She tried to sound calm for the child's sake, when in reality, she felt full of dread. Coyotes, the bastards. She had heard stories of coyotes, destroying entire herds, but until now they'd never bothered her sheep. Startled, she realized Hawkett was standing just behind her, a concerned look on his face.

"Something scare the child?" he asked.

The child? She didn't like that description for some reason. It seemed so cool and impersonal, like the kind of classification you'd expect from a man who had made a career out of dead bodies.

"Andrea says coyotes have attacked some of my sheep. I don't know how bad it is. I have forty ewes and my buck, Otis, up in the top pasture." As she spoke, she pointed up the hill where the lane led. "I guess I'd better get up there." Unsure of what else to say to Hawkett, she set off, walking up the pasture lane. Glancing behind her, she could see him following, becoming even more deeply involved in her life.

At the end of the lane, Jamie's dreaded apprehension turned into genuine sickness. There seemed to be blood-stained wool everywhere. It was thickest in the spot where the herd had been chased through the fence surrounding the pasture. Ewe number sixty, a seven-year-old Suffolk, lay dead, right at the base of the old cottonwood tree. Jamie felt tears trickling down her cheeks as she knelt by the dead animal, her belly ripped open where the coyotes had been eating, one ear ripped completely off. Old number sixty had always been a cantankerous ewe, butting at Jack whenever he tried to herd the flock. Had she turned and tried to fight, wondered Jamie.

Hawkett surveyed the scene from behind Jamie. For some reason, it reminded him of the Bennett Park murders he and Benjamin had investigated two winters back; then he remembered why. The murder victims both had goose down coats on and they had been ripped by the killer's knife, the lining, blood-stained, lay all over the murder site. But those had been human lives lost; these were only sheep.

He glanced around into the timber bordering the edge of the pasture. Somehow, he could feel their eyes, could sense the coyotes, lying somewhere out there right at that very moment, watching them. He'd

109

felt this way before, an instinct that he was close, very close to the killer. He turned back to Jamie and cleared his voice, unsure of what to say.

"Where are the rest of sheep?"

She pointed to the fence. She had thought the answer was obvious, broken wire and tracks leading into the adjoining field. "They've been chased through the fence into that field, the neighbor's CRP ground."

Hawkett wondered what CRP meant, but didn't ask.

I'm going to go find them. She turned and looked at the other end of the pasture. Far across the hillside, Chief, her horse, was grazing. At least he hadn't been hurt in this business. She blew three short, loud whistles and the paint gelding turned and came loping towards them.

Hawkett watched the large black and white horse running directly at them and felt concerned for their safety. Jamie, however, seemed unconcerned as she unclipped a lead rope from a nearby gate. When the horse reached her, he stopped and stood as Jamie patted him on the neck and hooked the lead rope to his halter. She turned to Hawkett.

"Gimme a lift will you?"

Hawkett was caught off guard. Nevertheless, he walked toward her, assuming the lift had to do with getting her onto the horse. Awkwardly, he started to reach for her waist, not knowing where else to grab her in order to assist. She stepped back, slightly irritated.

"No, hold your hands like a stirrup, like this." She locked her hands together and Hawkett got the picture. He did as instructed and she boosted herself up onto the horse with ease, putting very little weight on Hawkett's hands. She looked out across the CRP ground, tall grass waving at her. It would be easy to track the flock. They would stay close to each other and mash the grass down wherever they went. She collected her thoughts, thinking of the disaster that had transpired. Coyotes had attacked her sheep, her elevator was badly damaged, rain would be coming very soon and the hay still wasn't all under roof. The sheep were lost and she had this man, nearly a stranger, involved in it all, and a dead neighbor to boot. The old horse started prancing around a little bit, anxious to be moving.

"What do you want me to do?"

As before, she couldn't believe his generosity, but now wasn't the time for polite chatter. Things were a mess. Still she decided to give him the chance to walk away.

"Adam," she spoke as she reined the horse around to a better position, "please don't misunderstand me. You've been a tremendous help, but don't you think you'd better get back to your life? You could call Harley. I know he'd give you a lift back into town. You could take my old pickup, but it's broke down right now."

He appeared hurt and turned to look back down the hill towards the farmstead. Instantly she felt bad.

"Or you could unload some more of the hay and keep an eye on Andrea." She thought he nodded but wasn't sure. She slapped Chief on the rump and the horse took off like an Olympic sprinter, jumping over the broken barbed wire fence and galloping across the CRP with Jamie locked on his back.

Hawkett stood there in amazement as Jamie and her horse disappeared across the tall grass field. He had began to disregard the notion that he had once had; that farm life was slow and boring. He decided to walk back to the barn and unload more hay. Right now that was the extent of his plans for the rest of his life.

CHAPTER
19

Benjamin sat in the idling car, air conditioning running at full blast, and smoked two cigars. He was at a crossroads. What to do now? He'd better tell Sheriff Spencer about his encounter with Denny Cordoe, but he didn't really want to. He should probably call Brightwall and report their, or rather his, progress, but he didn't really want to do that either. Who the hell, he wondered, had killed Doug Cordoe, if it hadn't been his son? Hell, he thought, this should be easy to figure out. Only five adults lived on Dead End Road, not counting Denny Cordoe: the Oldham sisters, the Wilsons, and Jamie. Thinking in terms of who would have the physical strength to drive a pitchfork clear through Cordoe's torsoe, would probably narrow it down to two suspects, Mike Wilson and Jamie. What about Jamie, he wondered. She seemed like a hell of a nice kid. Still, the murder had occurred closest to her home. She was sure attractive enough to draw unwanted physical attention from a guy who appeared to lean that way. She had experienced some sort of financial troubles in dealing with the bank, or had she? No, he couldn't recall that being said. They had established that her husband had killed himself, but no discussion had taken place as to the reason. He would need to ask for more information along those lines.

And yes, hell yes, he thought, he'd better see something from a local coroner or justice of the peace declaring an investigation had occurred and it had officially been ruled a suicide. So, for now, Jamie would remain on the list of suspects. Lord, he wondered, had they been helping the murderer load hay just that morning? She certainly had the strength to run a pitchfork through the victim's chest. Had Cordoe made sexual advances toward her? It wouldn't have surprised Benjamin.

So two main suspects stood out: Jamie and Mike Wilson. Were there any other unknown suspects? Not one word had been said about any strange people or strange vehicles. In such a small geographic area, and with so many witnesses, something was missing. These good people weren't telling the whole truth, he thought.

Though he despised the thought, he knew what had to be done. The investigation had to be started all over again and he was going to ask the hard questions that had seemed irrelevant when they'd been sure young Cordoe was the culprit. Damn right, and he'd better get going. If Jamie ended up being the murderer, he was going to have to get Hawkett the hell out of there, one way or another.

Benjamin tossed his cigar stub out the car window, shifted the car into gear and took off with new purpose and determination in his heart.

Mike Wilson stopped pounding down on the steel fence post to see who was driving up the lane. He grimaced. It was those damn detectives again, no only one, the fat one. He wondered where the other one was.

Benjamin spotted Wilson and drove right to him, shifted the car into park, shut off the ignition and climbed out.

"Mike, how're things going?"

"Okay, I guess."

"More questions, Mike, and please be honest with me. I've no interest in getting you all riled up, but we've, er, got to get to the bottom of this mess."

Mike nodded, a neutral expression on his face, seeming not as defiant as before. Good, thought Benjamin.

"Were you home all last weekend?"

"Yes, well, except for church Sunday morning."

"The whole family?"

"Yeah, our whole family goes to church together every Sunday."

Benjamin could see the defiant look creeping back onto Wilson's face.

"You or your wife saw no strangers or strange vehicles on Dead End Road the entire weekend?"

"No."

"Did you ever see Cordoe over the weekend?"

"Which one?"

"Either."

"No. Well I might have seen Denny. I was moving my heifers to a new paddock Saturday morning and I think I caught the movement of a human off to the west side of the north pasture, down by the stream. I guess maybe that's where they found his old man, right?"

"Yes, that's correct. Are you sure it was him? Could you see what he was doing?"

Mike shook his head, "No to both questions. I just thought I saw somebody and I figured it was Denny. It's not unusual to see him out roaming around."

"Has Denny ever stolen anything from you?"

"I've never caught him. My wife is sure he's stolen produce from our garden on several occasions. Could be raccoons or other critters too. We've never caught him red-handed."

Benjamin stared into the deeply-tanned, sweat-streaked face of Mike Wilson. He just didn't believe this guy was lying to him and he was a pretty good judge. Through his line of work, he had dealt with a great number of liars.

"Mike, you said the bank sold you out, specifically Cordoe, right?"

"That's right."

"How do you support your family now?"

"Still have my cows, still have my grass. We do the best job of rotating the cowherd to good pastures and only milk during the grass-growing season. I hire out when the snow comes, cut wood, help other farmers, that sort of stuff." He shrugged his shoulders.

"And you get by that way?"

"Starting to get ahead," Mike said. A smile actually began to

114

form on his face. "Our income's been reduced by nearly twenty-two percent, but our expense is down over 500 percent. Hell, the cows are happy; I'm happy."

Benjamin cocked an eyebrow in a look of astonishment.

"I got the records to show. Never kept any business records before the sale, should of I know, but...anyway in a few more months, we'll have enough saved up to buy a real nice car, nothing new, but something nice. And no borrowing from any damn bank."

"You like that, right, Mike?"

"Damn right."

"Good luck to you and your family, Mike." Benjamin shook the man's hand, turned and started to get into his car, then paused.

"Uh, Mike?"

"Yeah?"

"I guess you might say, even though you hated Cordoe, he did you a favor in a way."

"Yeah, well I guess, yeah."

Benjamin drove down the driveway and pulled onto Dead End heading towards Pigmy. If Mike Wilson wasn't the murderer and the victim's son hadn't killed his father, Benjamin knew who he was left with, three female suspects: the elderly Oldham sisters and Jamie. He just knew this mess was going to end up at Jamie's.

CHAPTER
20

Hawkett slowly walked back towards the hay rack. As he walked, he took inventory of all of the joints in his body that were radiating with pain. It seemed like all of the muscles running from the base of his neck down to the back of his legs were aching. He hated to think about what he would feel like when he quit working and his muscles started to tighten. He was beginning to feel that he needed a drink, then stopped in his tracks. Did he need a drink or did he want a drink? The psychiatrist had said there was a difference. He realized that it felt good to even be pondering the question. Maybe fate had placed him in a position to deal with some of his problems. Maybe the physical pain was the price. At any rate, he felt trapped. Pride would not allow him to walk into town to reconcile with Benjamin. He wasn't worried about his job. Hawkett had decided that part of his life was over, or at least he was pretty sure it was. He remained confused. Still, he wasn't drinking and that was good. Would it go on? He looked at the loaded wagon of hay and felt the pain burning in his back. Shit, he thought, and started to reach for the nearest bale.

"Hawkett," the squeaky young voice of Andrea startled him. She was sitting on top of the unloaded hay, her lamb, Junior, lying on one side, and the border collie, Jack, on the other. The three must have watched him walk all the way down the lane.

"Yeah?" he looked up at her innocent face.

"Where's Mom?"

"She went to find the rest of her flock. Rode that big black and white horse."

"His name is Chief."

"The horse, his name is Chief?"

"Yes, mom gives me rides on him, sometimes."

"Well, I bet that's fun."

"Do you have a horse, Hawkett?"

"Nope, never even ridden one my whole life."

Her eyes opened wide in disbelief, "Really, never in your whole life?"

"That's right." Hawkett shrugged his shoulders somewhat apologetically.

"And you're pretty old, right?"

"Well, yeah, I mean."

"How old are you?"

"I'm thirty-seven."

"Yep, that's pretty old, all right." A serious expression spread across her face as if she was in deep thought. Jack stood up and stretched.

"Mom's thirty-four, well almost thirty-four. Her birthday's in September. You gonna give her a present for her birthday?"

"Well," Hawkett was caught off guard by the little girl's frank question and sincere manner of speech, "I guess, if I'm here, I will." He realized this was the longest conversation he'd ever conducted with a child. She didn't irritate him, but he was nervous. Andrea climbed down off the top of the hay bales and stood on the floor of the hay rack, her eyes almost level with his.

With a very intense look, she stared straight into his eyes. It made Hawkett feel very uncomfortable, almost guilty, though he couldn't figure out why.

"My dad is in heaven you know."

"Yes, I'm sorry. I bet he was a good dad."

Tears began to swell in her eyes and he wondered if he'd said the wrong thing, wondered what the hell he should have said.

She said nothing, but nodded her head up and down slowly as if agreeing he was a good dad. A tear had trickled halfway down her cheek and stopped. Hawkett reached out and gently wiped it off with his index finger. Suddenly, the small child stepped forward and wrapped her arms around his neck and held tight. Not knowing what to do, he gently patted the little girl on the back and gave her frail body a gentle hug. Was this the right thing to do, he wondered. It felt right, but still, he didn't know anything about children. Andrea released her grip, stepped back, and smiled at Hawkett.

"Thanks for the hug, Hawkett. Mom says you might be dangerous cause you hunt killer guys, but I think you're a nice man, too." With that judgment having been issued, she turned and leaped off the other side of the hay rack with the lamb right behind. Her dog Jack also followed but stopped, turned, and looked Hawkett right in the eyes before doing so. The dog's look had sent a message to Hawkett, he knew. He just wasn't sure what the message had been.

Hawkett watched the trio sprint up to the house, and Andrea went inside. He climbed up on the hay rack and slowly began to roll bales off the side into the barn. He decided to roll five off, then get off the rack and carry them over to the stack. He had rolled the third bale off when he heard the screen door on the front porch bang and he looked up to see Andrea, sprinting across the farmyard, carrying a pail of some sort. She ran around to the edge of the garden to a small pen with a doghouse inside of it. Hawkett could hear her calling an animal's name as she unhooked the door of the pen. He had assumed the dog pen had belonged to Jack and was surprised to see yet another dog come slowly trotting out of the house. This dog appeared to be heavier and slower then Jack. It stopped at the gate to be petted by the small girl, then trotted over to the hay rack and watered the front right tire. Upon close inspection, Hawkett came to the conclusion that the dog was some sort of the bird hunting variety. Andrea and her gang followed the old dog to the hay rack.

"What's that dog's name?"

"Oh, this is old Britt. He was my dad's hunting dog. But mom and I never hunt and besides, he's getting too old to hunt much, so I just use him to gather eggs?"

"Gather eggs?"

"Yes, it's my chore. I do it every single day unless it's too cold or wet and then Mom does it."

Now Hawkett was curious. "How does this dog gather eggs?" he asked with a smile on his face. Had this been an adult he was talking to, he would have been sure he was being set up for some kind of practical joke.

"Well, see, our hens, well, we have five of them. They just run all over the place." She turned and swept her arm pointing around the farmstead, "So Britt he just finds them and...well, just watch, okay?"

Hawkett nodded.

Attempting to sound authoritative, Andrea in a deeper voice commanded, "Hunt on, Britt."

The fat, old Brittany turned and just looked at her, his mouth hanging open while he panted. Hawkett was fairly sure the old dog was just going to lie down under the wagon and rest in the shade. But to his surprise the animal began loping around the farmstead, actually giving the appearance of hunting. Suddenly, right at the edge of one of Jamie's flower beds, the dog stopped and froze into a rock solid point, his right front leg lifted slightly off the ground and his nose pointed straight into the flowers. If Hawkett didn't know better, he would have thought the dog was a statue, it was that still.

"Steady boy, steady," Andrea ordered as she trotted over to the flower beds and tiptoed past the dog. Hawkett watched her peaking down into the flowers, then saw a dark red chicken come sprinting out of the flowers, clucking a loud, distressed cry. The old dog started to move, but a repeated "steady" command from Andrea caused him to freeze in his tracks once again. Hawkett could see Andrea reaching down into the flower bed. She raised her hand to show him an egg.

"See?"

He waved in acknowledgment. He wished Benjamin could see this. Andrea placed the egg into her basket and turned to the Brittany.

"Hunt on, Britt."

Instantly the old dog was off again and, from the distance, Hawkett could see him pointing into another open door by the barn. Andrea tiptoed by him into the barn.

He chuckled. What next, he wondered.

As Hawkett was carrying a bale of hay into the barn, he was startled by a booming noise in the distance. He was surprised to see how dark the sky was off to the west and watched as some distant bolts of lightning crashed to the earth. The wind was starting to pick up and the air was definitely cooling. He was no meteorologist, but it was obvious that a major thunderstorm was fast approaching. He had better get Jamie's hay unloaded.

CHAPTER 21

Benjamin slowed down as he reached the Oldham residence and turned into their driveway. Thelma was, once again, working in her garden. No wonder it looked so spectacular. He got out of the car. The rows of vegetables reminded him of a fresh salad, and he realized he was getting hungry already. Thelma had her back to him, pretending, once again, to be unaware of his presence. That trick was beginning to irritate him.

"Thelma," he yelled, not wanting to walk across her garden, unsure of where to step.

"What ya want?" an irritated voice startled him from behind. Turning, he saw Pearl walking her antique bicycle around the house.

"Ah, Pearl, how's it going?"

"I'm suing the son of a bitch!"

Same pleasant attitude, thought Benjamin. "Uh, who are you going to sue?" He wondered as he spoke if she was referring to him in regards to running her off the road.

"That sons-a-bitch Wilson, big Mikey."

"Pearl, please don't use that kind of language! Mike is a fine young man, you know that," admonished Thelma as she joined them at the car.

"I'm suin' his ass anyway. I'm not putting up with it anymore, no siree."

"Uh, putting up with what?" Benjamin couldn't resist asking.

"Cow shit, that's what." She stood and stared at Benjamin, assuming he understood the full implications of her crude reply.

"I, er, uh, don't quite get your drift."

"All over my damn bicycle, can you imagine? I just got done hosin' the son of a bitch off out back," she turned and looked at her beloved bike.

"Pearl, really!" Thelma turned to Benjamin to explain, "Mike sometimes drives his cow herd up and down the road and lets them graze the road ditches, more often now that he's lost his machinery. Pearl was riding her bike into town this morning and she drove through some, well, you know, cow manure." Poor Thelma turned beat red at having to use what she considered graphic language.

"Fat boy, did you ever drive a bicycle through cow shit, huh? I'm talking about the fresh stuff, really picks up on the wheels and..."

"Pearl, shut up!" Thelma, her face redder than before, had had enough. "Take your...bike, and go get the mail or something, go, get!"

"Well, Big Mikey better have a damn good lawyer," Pearl fired her last shot as she wheeled the bicycle down the drive.

"Really, I apologize, Major. Such language."

Major, why had she called him Major? Had he heard her right? "Well, nevermind, I've heard a lot worse," and he knew that was no lie. "I sympathize with you having to deal with a relative having this kind of attitude."

"Yes, she wasn't always this bad. I mean, Pearl was always short-tempered, even when we were little girls. I've known her all my life. I don't know; it's her age I guess. Losing John made things worse, much worse." She slowly shook her head back and forth continuously as she talked, staring at the ground just beyond Benjamin's feet. "She rides out to the cemetery every day, did you know? Sometimes takes a lunch with her. Just sits there, right by his grave. Says she talks to him, can you imagine?" Thelma was still slowly shaking her head back and forth.

"Does she blame the bank for her husband's death? I mean the stress from the foreclosure. I think you said they lost their farm on account of co-signing a loan for a son, right?"

"Yes..." her voice faded when she couldn't remember his name.

"Benjamin," he reminded her.

"Yes, Benjamin, that's what happened. I don't think she really blames the bank. I mean she talks that way, but then Pearl always does. I think deep down inside she's just a very lonely, lost, senile woman."

"Even having you?"

"All I seem to be able to offer Pearl is a roof over her head. We don't seem to be able to communicate very well anymore. We just exist." Thelma took a deep breath.

"Thelma, did Pearl kill Doug Cordoe?" That ought to shake her loose, thought Benjamin, though it seemed cruel.

"No!" A defiant Thelma glared at him.

"Were you aware of her activities during the entire weekend past?"

"Yes!"

"Yes?"

"Yes." The glare died. Thelma turned and walked a few steps away, her back to Benjamin, wringing her hands.

"Can you keep this confidential, Benjamin? I mean if I tell you where we were, and then you'll know we didn't have anything to do with the murder. It's, you know, something personal."

"Only if it has nothing to do specifically with the case I'm investigating."

Thelma wrung her hands some more then sat down on the edge of a cement step leading into the house. She was quiet for nearly a minute, staring at the ground, her lips silently moving as she talked to herself.

"Well, this is delicate, Benjamin. You see, there's a person, I'm not saying who right now. This person, let's say, is a very old friend, been a very good friend, is becoming more and more emotionally unbalanced." She looked at Benjamin and he nodded his comprehension.

"This friend, well, could be dangerous, could hurt somebody with a personality like that. So, we uh, Pearl and I, took a trip to an institution we know of in Bakersfield, Minnesota—took the bus from Creston. A friend from church took us to Creston. Anyway, we left Saturday morning and spent the weekend at Bakersfield at a retreat they have that helps people make decisions, you know? We weren't going to jump into

123

this thing. Really, I just as soon wash my hands of the whole thing, but still, God is watching you know."

"When did you get back?"

"Monday just before dinner."

"Would it be possible for you to give me the names of your driver to Creston, the bus line, and the institution in Bakersfield?"

She looked up, hurt by his mistrust. "Yes." Then she got up from the step, straightened her skirt and retrieved the information for Benjamin.

Pulling away from the Oldham's house, Benjamin mused. So she was going to institutionalize her obnoxious sister-in-law. It surprised him the way Thelma had danced around telling him about "her friend." Thelma must be feeling pretty guilty about it. She probably feared that her church group would be critical. He shook his head, fickle people. Then hell, he thought, wait a minute. Their alibi would only be good from Saturday morning on. What about Friday night? He hoped that the lab boys had come up with a more realistic time of death. If it were proven that Cordoe had died sometime after Friday night, it would leave only one realistic suspect: Jamie. Well, he would check the Oldham sisters' alibi thoroughly, and he was confident that it would hold true.

Turning his thoughts to Jamie, who was quickly becoming the most likely suspect, he pondered another theory. Maybe Jamie had been doing something in one of her pastures along the road or scooping up a broken hay bale? Here comes Doug Cordoe, possibly in the beginning of a weekend drunk. He stops the car, makes a pass at her and she gets mad. Or maybe she had reacted in self defense. Yes, self defense, that's the way to play it, get the kid off as light as possible. Or maybe, he could drop it, get the reports so screwed up that nobody could solve it, throw in some rumors of unconfirmed strangers; yeah, he could do that. Cordoe had probably brought the murder upon himself, probably had it coming. Yeah. No, he couldn't. Benjamin couldn't do that. He knew he wasn't perfect, but a person had to draw the line somewhere. Hell, with Hawkett tangled up like this, it was really going to be a mess.

CHAPTER

22

Hawkett was stacking bales inside the dark barn when he heard Jamie calling for the dog. He stepped out the barn door and was nearly run over by Jack blazing up the hill toward Jamie, her horse and a large flock of woolly ewes. Still seated atop the black and white horse, Jamie yelled some commands at the dog and made signals with her arms. Hawkett couldn't understand what she had said, but evidently the border collie could. With amazing speed and agility, Jack swept back and forth behind the flock of sheep guiding them down the hill toward a gathering pen adjacent to the barn. One sheep attempted to break away from the flock and flee back to the hill pasture, but Jack would not have it. With incredible quickness and agility, he gracefully outpaced the ewe, turned her back into the flock and resumed his herding.

Hawkett was amazed at how dark the sky had become as he looked up at black churning clouds crashing into each other as they boiled through the heavens. Suddenly, thunder erupted nearby and a bolt of lightning struck something out beyond the hay field. Fat drops of cold rain began to fall. At an incredible speed, Jamie rode the big horse towards the barn and effortlessly descended from its back, shouting orders as she did.

"Chief, to your pen!" she shouted as she slapped the horse on his rump with her hand and watched the horse sprint toward some destination on the other side of the barn. Quickly she turned to the sheep nearing the barn, thanks to Jack's steady persuasion.

"Pen, pen!" she yelled at Jack, as the rain began falling much harder. She swung open a gate to a corral near the barn. The dog understood her command completely and began working the herd that direction. Again she yelled, "Andrea, to the house; take Junior and stay away from any windows." Watching the small girl run towards the house, she jumped up onto the hay rack and began throwing the remaining twenty some bales into the open door, not waiting for Hawkett to catch them. The rain was falling hard now, and the temperature had dropped a good twenty degrees in less than three minutes. The combination of the cool air and the excitement of the storm somehow recharged Hawkett's adrenaline and, with everything he could muster, he threw bales away from the doorway allowing space for a place to throw more in. When the rack was empty, Jamie jumped off and ran into the barn with him. She trotted to the side window and checked the house, feeling content only after she saw her daughter and the lamb staring back though the safety of the screen door.

"Anymore hurt?" Hawkett asked.

"One dead," replied Jamie. "And one ewe has part of an ear ripped off. They're all stressed, but other than that, they look okay. I'm going to keep them in this pen until I can figure out how to deal with the coyotes."

"You think they'll be back?"

"I've heard once they start, they don't stop until every ewe is dead. Of course I suppose it depends on how many coyotes are involved. Might just be one mother and her litter. I'll have to ride Chief back up to the pasture and bury that dead ewe."

Together, they watched the storm in silence, Hawkett thankful to be completely dry unlike Jamie who was soaked.

He was finding it increasingly difficult to avert his stare away from Jamie, standing before him, in her rain-soaked clothes. It had been a long time since he had been with a woman, and it was becoming increasingly difficult for him to deny the physical attraction that he felt towards her. He had thought that she was beautiful the first time that he saw her, but in the barn, at that very moment, he felt almost intoxicated by her presence.

A lightning bolt struck outside, lighting up the black sky and creating an electrifying background for the rain-soaked woman standing in the doorway. Hawkett could feel a charge of sexual energy vibrating through his body, a feeling that had been gone for a long, long time. It felt good. He smiled to himself, squared his shoulders and took a deep breath. Jamie turned, saw the smile and returned a puzzled smile. What was he smiling about? Was she safe? She felt safe. He didn't look like a maniac or anything like that, but what did the smile mean? Hell, she had thought the Cordoes were both perverted, but then, they had that look, a look you couldn't trust. This guy, this detective, sitting here in her barn, smiling, looked like somebody she could trust.

Yet, she still didn't know whether or not she should. He'd been in her life for only twenty-four hours. He'd forced his way in. She was confused by him. She didn't think that relationships were supposed to begin this way. Normally, two people were introduced to one another, maybe go out for dinner or to a movie. Slowly, things proceeded slowly, as each person learned about the other in bits and pieces. But, were they forming a relationship? She wasn't even sure. Surely, watching her endure hard physical labor hadn't been a turn-on for the man. She knew he was in poor physical condition though he had a good body. A good body, there I go again she thought. She shook her head back and forth. So he was a good-looking guy that she felt she could trust; well, that was something. Still, she felt trapped and nervous. What she really felt, she guessed, was confused, unsure of whether or not a relationship was what she wanted. What she really wanted, at that moment, was to have a friend that she could confide in, but she had no best friends except for Andrea and at times, Harley, and neither of them were of the maturity level to handle this type of discussion. She wasn't sure that she could either. She turned and glanced at Hawkett again. He gave her a warm smile. What did he have on his mind, she wondered again, only this time, her nervousness had subsided.

"Well, rain's letting up a little bit; 'spose I better go check Andrea, make sure she's not into anything. You want to come up to the house for some tea or anything?"

"Sure," Hawkett started to get up, but a fiery shot of pain traveled through his lower back and he dropped back down on the bale issuing an embarrassing moan of pain. He took a deep breath and opened his eyes. The effort increased the pounding sensation in the back of his skull. She was looking at him with a look of compassion in her eyes. He felt like a fool.

"Here, I'll give you a hand." She reached out her right hand and Hawkett painfully extended his. She started to grasp it, then recoiled at the feeling of a warm substance on his hands, blood. The guy had bloody hands from handling the bales. She grabbed a handful of loose hay and gently wiped off her hands. He felt even more foolish.

"Sorry, I didn't..."

"That's okay," she spoke so softly he barely heard her. "You just wait here; I'll be back in a little bit."

Hawkett nodded, and found even that motion to be painful.

Jamie dashed through the rain to the house, mud splashing on her. Andrea met her at the door with a towel and a hug. Jamie was glad to see that the pet lamb had not gone beyond the porch. However, she was irritated when she noticed that the lamb was wearing one of her sweatshirts; its two front feet protruding from the sleeves. She took a quick shower and put on clean, dry clothes. Lord did that shower make her feel better, lifted her spirits. Then, she spent some time taking care of her daughter's needs. She made a sandwich for Andrea and gave her an apple and a glass of milk. Andrea was ordered to eat it, all of it, before she could get out her paint set. She gathered a load of items from around the house into a picnic basket, pulled on her mud boots and headed back out to the barn, trying not to splash mud on her clean clothes. She was wearing a clean pair of bibs over a long sleeved flannel shirt. The passing storm had driven the temperature down substantially making the air much cooler but intoxicatingly fresh to breathe.

She found Hawkett, sitting on the same bale, staring out the barn door. She wondered, as he sat there, if he was wondering how he'd ever gotten himself into this mess. He didn't appear to be unhappy though. She was impressed that a pleasant look covered his face, even though he was feeling a lot of pain.

"Here, I brought you these." She pulled a bottle of pills from the basket and handed it to him. "They're pain pills from when I had Andrea. I think they're still okay to use, pretty strong. I used to have to take two, so I think you could probably handle maybe four." She felt guilty, dispensing drugs like that.

She pulled a thermos from the picnic basket and offered him a drink of iced tea to wash the pain pills down. She then brought a pailful of clean water from the barn hydrant to Hawkett and set it, along with some towels and soap, on the bale of hay next to him.

"Thought you might want to wash up, then eat something. Are you hungry?"

Surprisingly, he was. Despite a lot of physical pain, he could clearly detect his stomach signaling for sustenance. Seeing the sandwiches made with homemade bread, in her picnic basket helped to spur his appetite. He stood up, carefully walked over to the bucket, then very tenderly cleaned his hands and face with the cold water and soap. As he turned around, wiping with a towel, he was amazed at how quickly Jamie had set up eating arrangements. She had laid a cloth over a bale and had placed the food upon it. Then, she had drug a bale to either side for them to use as makeshift chairs. He wondered how many other gentlemen had joined a lady friend for supper in a barn, sitting upon bales of hay. Hell, he thought, after what he'd witnessed on this farm the last couple of days, maybe this was a common occurrence. Regardless, it sure didn't bother him.

The two adults shared a delicious meal of leftover roast lamb on homemade bread, cheese, apples picked from a tree on the farm, and cold cherry pie. Jamie even pulled a thermos full of hot coffee and two cups out of the basket. He wondered how she had managed to pack all of these supplies into the same picnic basket. He was certain that the Red Cross could use a person of her caliber.

She smiled at him; he smiled at her. "Did you get enough to eat?"

"Yes, I'm stuffed. It was excellent. Thank you."

"You earned it. I wouldn't have gotten even half the hay unloaded without your help."

He started to mention the broken elevator as being the start of her problems, but decided not to bring it up. It might spoil the mood. Mood? What mood? So they were enjoying each other's company. What did that mean? What did he want that to mean? He was going to have to sort out his emotions pretty quickly; he knew that. Still, he wanted this moment to last; he didn't want her to leave, didn't want Andrea to come sprinting through the door at that moment.

She started gathering up cups and containers. He reached over to help and was rewarded with a jolt of pain in his lower back. The pain was distinctly duller than before. The pain pills were working. In fact, he was starting to feel genuinely mellow, in a sort of pleasant buzz. She broke the mood.

"What now, Adam?" Jamie asked with a very serious expression on her face.

"What now, what?"

"Tonight. The rest of your life?" She shrugged with perplexity in her face.

"Oh." The last two days he had been living only in the present, no worries about tomorrow. She had a right to know what his plans were, and he would tell her just as soon as he had the foggiest notion of what those plans might be. He shrugged. A shrug wasn't good enough. She deserved more. She was waiting for it.

He cleared his throat. This wasn't going to be easy. Benjamin hadn't hung around to bail him out. He had no transportation. She had none, unless he could repair her pickup, and he didn't even know what was wrong with it. Well, he would continue to take things as they came. Doing that had worked well for the last two days. They had been two of the most memorable days of his life.

He cleared his throat again, "Well, I, uh, need to take a shower or something, then find a place to sleep." He shrugged his shoulders anxiously, looking into her eyes, trying to interpret her feelings, her response.

She had a serious expression on her face. She picked up the pail, walked to the barn door and tossed the water out.

"You need some clean clothes, too?"

He nodded.

"I've got some of Bud's old stuff, probably a little small, but it might work for you."

He nodded again.

She looked out the barn door; the rain was again falling, though much more gently now. The air smelled fresh and wonderful. He saw her take a deep breath and turn to him, as if she'd made a decision.

"There's a rain spout that drains onto the cement behind the barn. Right now some clean rainwater will be running out through it. You can stand under that and take a shower, it may be a little cool, but clean water. You've still got some soap and towels. I'll get the clothes from the house. You'll have to sleep out here. I'm sorry, but I've only known you two days and maybe it seems silly." Now she was shrugging her shoulders.

He was still in shock thinking about taking a cold shower under

130

a rain gutter spout. Sleep in the barn, on what? He was about to protest, but the look in her eyes told him that wouldn't be wise.

"I'm gonna' go get the clothes. Don't be runnin' around here naked when I get back, okay?"

CHAPTER
23

Hawkett watched the steady stream of clear water run out of a hole in the rain gutter. It splattered onto the cement floor below, leaving an area on the pavement incredibly clean. The water felt cold, really cold, but he had no other alternative. Every part of his body had been soaked with sweat during the day, and he could feel bits of hay and chaff itching him under his clothes. He had a definite desire to be clean, but the water looked so cold. Hawkett looked around to make sure no one could see him. The leaky rain gutter was on the back side of the barn, opposite the house and the road, but still he felt odd. He wondered if this was how entering a nudist camp for the first time would feel.

What the hell, he was feeling good now, really good. The pain pills had temporarily released him from pain. Hawkett stripped off his clothes, took a deep breath, walked forward and boldly stood directly underneath the rain water tumbling down from the barn roof. The shock that he felt from the temperature of the water nearly caused him to black out, and he momentarily lost his breath. He stood there, hoping no one could hear the string of obscenities he issued. Soon, the frigid shower became bearable and, with more time, it became damn near enjoyable. The water had an incredibly-fresh smell and feel to it. No wonder, he thought, considering its short history on Earth before cleansing his body.

Jamie had provided him with soap, towels and even a razor to shave. He wondered if the razor had belonged to her deceased husband or if it was hers. He hoped the latter and felt yet another jolt of sexual awareness, as he imagined her using it to shave her legs. He found himself stepping into the cold shower once again.

Hawkett, now shaved, showered and dressed in clean blue jeans and a tee-shirt, felt a whole lot better. The rain had stopped and the sky was clearing in the west. The sun had peeked out, but as the day was coming to a close, it was starting to drop behind the horizon.

Hawkett leaned on the barn door and stared out across the farm. It was beautiful. The grass and flowers, refreshed by the late summer rain, radiated their colors. The animals out in the small pasture lots grazed peacefully. The sheep seemed incredibly content, especially considering their ordeal with the coyotes. He took a deep breath. He wished he could freeze his life in that very moment; stop time, stop change, stop life from running away from him. How had this happened, he wondered. Had God planned this? Probably not, thought Hawkett, remembering how his life had continuously lacked religion. Was it fate or just plain dumb luck? He didn't know. Would it last? Probably not.

Was he falling in love with this farm woman? He felt very perplexed. He knew there was an attraction. He knew there was physical attraction, and he also knew he respected her. Respected her for her courage, her intelligence, and her compassion. Did she respect him? He shrugged. She probably thought he was a fool, maybe a pervert as well. Sleep in the barn, he thought, hell... His train of thought was broken when he heard the screen door bang at the house, startling him. He turned to see Jamie, walking across the barnyard, dodging rain puddles, carrying some blankets toward him. He reached out to take the blankets from her, feeling a little guilty, thinking of all of the trouble that she had gone through to accommodate an intruder of sorts.

"Thanks,"

"Careful, there's a radio inside the big blanket."

He laid them down on some bales. She unrolled the biggest blanket and pulled out a transistor radio.

She carried it over to an open barn window. "You'll probably have to fiddle with it to get a station you like. Sometimes it doesn't work very well, but I thought you'd enjoy it." Jamie clicked the radio on and stood with her back to Hawkett, fiddling with the controls. Suddenly from the static, a disc jockey's voice announced "And here's Roy Orbison and Linda Ronstadt singing 'Rainy Day Feeling Again.'"

Jamie backed up, still looking at the radio, "An appropriate song for today, don't you think?"

Hawkett, who was standing almost directly behind her, replied "Yeah, I like that song."

She turned, almost bumping into him. They stood face to face, merely inches between them. He didn't back away. Lord, she smells great, he thought.

She felt extremely nervous, maybe a little scared. Still, she could feel the attraction between them, and it felt good.

"Want to dance?" Hawkett asked softly and hesitantly.

"What?"

Embarrassed, he replied, "Oh nothing, I..."

"Sure."

"Sure?" Awkwardly he reached out, took her hands in his and realized that she was trembling slightly. The trembling soon subsided as their bodies came together and moved slowly to the beat of the music. The burned-out homicide detective and the struggling farm widow suddenly were part of a different world. As they slowly danced around the barn floor, each knew their life would never be the same.

"Squawk, squawk!" Both Hawkett and Jamie jumped apart startled by the loud, foreign noise. Through the barn door ran Andrea, with her lamb and dog in tow, blowing on something that sounded like a party horn from a New Year's Eve party.

"Andrea, stop! Give me that!"

The small girl stopped. The lamb walked between her legs and turned his head up to peek at the two adults. "I found that call in Dad's stuff. You know, Mom, his hunting things. I thought maybe Hawkett could use it like Dad used to when he was hunting coyotes. You know, Mom, when he took his big gun out."

"Yes, Andrea, I know. But you almost scared us to death, running in here blowing on that thing. Where are your boots?"

The small girl looked down at her mud-splattered tennis shoes, then back at her mother. Guilt was written all over her face.

"To the house, now, young lady! Get those shoes washed and

don't track in. You know better. And don't let Jack or Junior in the house."

"I didn't let them in."

"Good, but just don't forget. Now get going. Here, give me that."

The little girl handed her the coyote call that she'd been blowing and took off for the house. The two adults stood there, awkwardly, as the child sprinted across the barnyard, intentionally running through every mud puddle on her route.

Hawkett, wanting to break the awkward silence, asked, "What is that, that thing Andrea was blowing on?"

"Oh," Jamie handed it to him, "It's a coyote call. You're supposed to hide out in the brush and blow on it. It's supposed to sound like an injured rabbit and attract the coyotes. Bud used it. He'd get a coyote every once in a while."

Hawkett turned the hard plastic instrument over in his hands and examined it.

"Could this be used to get the coyotes that attacked your sheep?"

"Probably, but I'd have to use Bud's gun and I don't feel comfortable with guns. I'm not sure I really even know how to load it." She shrugged her shoulders, a little uncomfortable with this lie, trying to justify it in her conscience, telling herself, okay, you've just lied to him, how do you justify that?

Hawkett thought for a while, "Want me to try?"

"I don't care. I suppose you know how to handle guns. Well, of course you do."

He lifted the coyote call to his mouth and gave a couple quick blasts. He wondered if an injured rabbit actually sounded like that. He had no idea that rabbits could even make a noise.

"What time of day is best to try this thing?"

"I think Bud used to go out really early, just before daybreak, before he did any chores."

"Do you care if I use his gun?"

"No."

"Do you have any idea what kind of gun he used?"

"Only that it's a shotgun. I should know more. I gave it to him as a Christmas present, but he picked it out."

"Sure."

135

"I'll go get the gun. I think there's a box of bullets with it." She returned after a while, carrying a gun case in one hand and a box of shells in the other. She placed both just inside the door of the barn, then paused for an awkward moment in Hawkett's presence.

"Well, there it is then," she said nervously.

He wanted to hold her again. She wanted to be held. But somehow the awkwardness of the situation would not allow it. "Look, make yourself comfortable, okay?"

"Yeah, sure," he smiled.

"I've got to get into town before dark and pick up some more allergy medicine for Andrea. We'll ride Chief. I'll probably drop Andrea off at the Oldham residence. They seem to enjoy her company." She started to walk away.

"Hey, Jamie."

"Yes?" She turned to face him.

"Thanks."

She didn't reply, just smiled at him and walked toward the house.

CHAPTER
24

Benjamin parked the Escort along the curb in front of a red brick building called Dave's Place. A neon sign in the front window declared "PABST On Tap." The cardboard sign that hung below it, read "Fresh Pizza."

Outside, the air was muggy. Dark, threatening clouds were gathering above Pigmy. Inside, the tavern's air conditioner was keeping the building pleasantly cool, and Benjamin took a seat on a bar stool. A bald-headed, heavy man with tattoos on both arms walked toward him.

"Yes, sir, what'll it be?"

"Oh, how about a draft beer?"

"Sure thing."

The bartender pulled a heavy glass out of the cooler, filled it from a tap and placed it on a napkin in front of Benjamin.

"Thanks," said Benjamin and he immediately picked up the mug and took a deep draw. The cold beer tasted good. Damn-hot, muggy Iowa summer, nearly drained a man of all his fluids, he thought as he put the mug back down on the bar.

Suddenly, a large explosion crashed outside and a flash of lightning that struck nearby illuminated the street. Benjamin shuddered. It was followed by the patter of raindrops and then Mother Nature dumped the whole bucket. Benjamin sat on the bar stool watching the heavy rain pelt sheets of water on the street outside.

He wondered what Hawkett was doing. Stupid shit. He wondered what he should be doing to straighten things out. Well, solving the murder would do for a start.

"You a lawman?"

The question startled him as he turned on his bar stool to face the tattooed bartender.

"Yes, yes I am. DCI."

"Working on the murder, huh? Our friendly banker, Cordoe?"

"Yeah, that's what I'm up to." Never knowing where interesting bits of information might turn up, Benjamin asked, "You know anything about it? I mean, a man with your job hears a lot of gossip, right?"

The bartender smiled and pulled a pack of cigarettes out from under the bar. He made a theatrical production of lighting one, then took his first draw.

"Yeah, I hear things." Another draw was followed by another artistic blow of smoke. "Hear you guys kind of took care of Deputy Dog."

"Deputy Dog?"

"Yeah, well his real name is Homer Cog. But Deputy Cog got changed to Deputy Dog, know what I mean?" The bartender smiled, displaying his nicotine-stained teeth. "Anyways, Deputy Dog, he's a piece of shit, doesn't belong in no lawman uniform, that's for damn sure. He's Sheriff Spencer's shirttail relation or else he'd be working somewhere else. Yeah, ol' Deputy Dog, real piece of dog shit."

Benjamin nodded politely, a slight smile on his face, but made no reply. Within a few moments, the bartender continued, telling him what the public thought had transpired at Cordoe's town residence.

"What the hell happened anyway? I mean, I heard Deputy Dog got beat up by his neighbor, that muscle-bound Bobby Bowers, but somebody said one of you guys worked him over."

Benjamin shook his head. "One of us guys? DCI you mean? Hell, we're lovers not fighters. We investigate things. Amazing, isn't it, the way these stories get started?"

"Yeah, amazing," said the bartender with a questioning look on his face, wondering if this overweight detective was bullshitting him. He squashed the cigarette into an ashtray and got Benjamin another draft.

"Well, tell you somethin'. Ain't gonna be too many tears shed for Cordoe. Son-of-a-bitchin' vulture that guy was."

"He come in here much?"

"Hell no; no banker drinks in a local bar, be a fool to. Too much potential for violence. No, he'd pick up a case of beer and spend the weekends out at his farm, working around the farm and drinking with his boy. You saw the boy, his son Denny?"

Benjamin lied, "No, can't say I have yet."

"Neither have I, but I guess he's strange, I mean really strange."

"So when Cordoe wasn't working, he spent most of his free time out there, at his farm that is?"

"Yeah, that's if he wasn't chasin' women. Guy thought he was a real stud. Some of the stories I hear in here about women he's hit on, well, it's pretty disgusting. I think most of his love life involved the exchange of twenty dollar bills if you know what I mean?"

Benjamin nodded with a knowing smile. He finished his second beer but refused the bartender's offer for another. He pulled out a cigar and lit it.

Looking out the window, he noted that the heavy rain had stopped and a beam of sunlight was trying to peek through the fast-moving clouds above. Not much of a storm; that was good anyway. Benjamin looked at his watch. It was nearing 7:30 PM, no wonder he was so hungry. Where to eat? He wondered if he should have a pizza there at the bar. No, he was going back to June's restaurant.

Benjamin paid the bartender, deposited his cigar stub in an ashtray and stepped out on the rain-washed sidewalk. The brief rainfall had removed the stifling humidity and replaced it with beautifully-tasting post-summer rain air. Benjamin took a deep breath hoping it would give a little relief to his smoke-weary lungs. The air tasted clean, good.

He turned and started to walk up to the street towards June's Cafe. No use driving; it was only a couple of blocks away. Hell, he thought everything in this town was only a couple of blocks away.

Walking around the corner, he was surprised to meet Jamie Chambers. She was just coming out of the Pigmy Drug Store, a small white sack in her hand.

"Jamie, we meet again." Benjamin greeted her with one of his

139

warmer smiles. He really liked the kid. Good mom, hard worker. Traits that he admired. Good looking too, he thought once again.

"Oh, hi, Benjamin, how's things going? I mean with the investigation." She felt guilty, his partner being stuck out on her farm, but hell she thought, it hadn't been her idea. Still...

"Where's Andrea?" he asked. He had wanted to say, "Where's Hawkett?"

"She's at the Oldham sisters' place. I dropped her off there while I came to town to pick up her allergy medicine." She lifted up the small bag as if to confirm her intentions.

"Oh, I see. Uh, get the hay unloaded okay?"

"Oh yeah, sure, just beat the rain, what a relief,"

"Good, good, I, uh really feel bad about that elevator, Jamie."

"Hey, no, don't worry, I'll get it repaired."

"Yeah, well, uh, did Hawkett come back into town with you?"

She paused before answering. Why the hell did she feel so guilty? "No, he uh is, or was when I left that is, still resting in the barn."

"Resting in the barn, is he?" A frown had replaced the jovial smile on Benjamin's face.

"Yes, I made him some supper. He was feeling pretty sore. I assume he's not in very good condition for the kind of physical labor he did this afternoon." Was she defending him now, she wondered. How the hell had she gotten stuck in between these two detectives? Just minding her own business and in...

"Had dinner yet?" asked Benjamin disrupting her train of thought.

"Well, yes, just a sandwich," she replied. He didn't need to know she'd shared an enjoyable little meal in her barn with his partner.

He took her tone of voice to mean she hadn't really eaten at all. "Well, good, join me for supper. My treat. I hate to eat alone. I'm just heading for June's Cafe now."

"Oh, no, I have to get back to the farm and..."

"No, I insist." With that he pointed toward June's just up the street.

"Well, okay, but I'm just going to have a quick bite...gotta get back and pick up Andrea before it gets too dark."

Hawkett, meanwhile, was enjoying a slow tour of the farmyard and adjacent fields taking in the views. The combination of Jamie's pain pills and the freshness of the rain-washed air had him in sort of a gentle high. He watched the sheep grazing in the small pasture lot. The woolly animals seemed to have overcome the coyote trauma and were contentedly eating. In another pen, he observed two big, black and white sows with small piglets nearby. The sows each had their own bedded hut where they lay on their sides, grunting comfortably while piglets alongside nursed with zest. Hawkett could see a wooden, low-profile tank filled with water, almost like a small, muddy swimming pool. He'd seen the sows lounging in it earlier during the heat. He could also see their feeding floor, an automatic waterer and evidence of where they'd grazed alfalfa in their small paddock. No wonder these animals look so content, he thought, they have their own little paradise here.

His wife, former wife that is, had been an activist for many causes, one of them, some sort of an animal rights movement. The local chapter had met in their apartment several times and, although Hawkett hadn't participated, he could hear them carrying on in the next room. At times their conversations had become quite emotional. He remembered overhearing time and time again how all the farm animals were being locked in small metal cages and treated inhumanely. He'd gathered that this was the main reason the group was protesting meat consumption, and Ann had gone right along with them, but she'd been a vegetarian for years anyway. That in itself had been another source of conflict in their marriage. He could care less what she ate, that was her choice. The rub lay in her constant criticism of his choice of diet. Her moral tone, taking the "high road" as she always did—fit right in with her career.

Where the hell were all these caged animals anyway? He remembered the cattle they'd seen in the many pastures on the trip here from Des Moines. He remembered the calves racing across the pasture. Her horse, the sheep, these pigs, chickens and maybe other animals he hadn't even seen walking around the farm. Well these animals sure weren't suffering. Hell, he'd seen a lot of people, adults and children both, living in poorer environments. He'd have to ask Jamie about it.

Benjamin ordered a steak, a potato and a salad. Jamie ordered only a salad.

They visited about the farm, about Andrea and about Benjamin's life. They avoided talking about the murder investigation although it weighed heavily on both adults' minds.

Benjamin ordered some cherry pie for dessert, but Jamie de-

141

clined. The waitress brought Benjamin his pie and a third cup of coffee and gave Jamie a cup of hot tea.

Jamie decided they'd been dodging the issue long enough and asked, "Benjamin, Adam made the comment to me today that his life hasn't been going very good lately. What'd he mean?"

Benjamin took a sip of coffee. He felt like smoking a cigar, but refrained. "Well, his divorce for one thing."

"Recent?"

"Yes."

"Any children?"

Benjamin snorted, "No, no, not from Ann. She, well, Ann's a professional activist you know. Green Peace, Save the Whales, I don't know, several others. Anyway, I remember Hawkett saying she'd joined a group called Zero Population Growth. They believed the key to saving the world from people was to produce no more people I guess. She refused to get pregnant. Told him the world was in such terrible shape, she didn't want to bring a child into it anyway."

"Did he want to have children?"

"Well, the older he got, the more he talked about it. Yeah, I think he wanted to."

"I see. And this divorce is the main reason for his depression?"

"Well," Benjamin grimaced, "No, there's more." He told her about the Bennett family murders, the children, and its effect on Hawkett. He told her about Hawkett's personal involvement in recent murder investigations, the drinking and the depression.

Then he told her about earlier times before Hawkett's problems, and about their success in the DCI. Hell, he bragged, but was that so bad? He told her a couple of humorous stories involving pranks he had pulled on Hawkett. The one involving a baby alligator in Hawkett's bathtub made her laugh until tears ran out of her eyes.

Jamie's initial opinion of Benjamin had been one of positive acceptance and he'd done nothing to change her opinion, but, her neighbor was dead. This investigation would not go away. Could she confide in him, tell him what had happened? What would happen to her? What would happen to Andrea? And that thought overpowered all other thoughts. Her life was her child. Everything she did, everything she said from here on out was ruled by her love for her child.

She finished the last of her tea and looked at her watch. Damn, it was nearing 9 PM already. She couldn't believe how quickly the time

142

had passed.

"Benjamin, I've got to be going; it's getting late. Thank you so much for the meal. I enjoyed it and the conversation as well."

"Hey, we'll do it again sometime. Next time bring Andrea and... Where's your car? I'll walk you to it."

"No car. I have a pickup but can't get the darn thing started. I had to ride my horse. He's parked in a barn on the edge of town, just two blocks away."

Benjamin was taken aback by her statement. "Sure you'll be okay? Hell, I can drive you home."

"No, really, I'll be fine. Thanks again."

Jamie saddled her horse, swung onto its back, and started down Dead End wondering what Hawkett was doing out at her farm. He was, in fact, at that very instant, wondering where she was while he lay on a pile of hay and stared out through the barn door at the stars in the darkening blue above.

The night temperature had cooled down to a perfect 70 degrees and the air was dead still. Jamie rode slowly along on her trusted old horse. Silly, she thought, commuting on a horse like this. She wished she could get the darn pickup to start. Still, she enjoyed riding her horse. It provided her quiet time to collect her thoughts, a time to contemplate problems that had arisen in her life. A bunch of them had been dropped on her the last two days. She sighed aloud, and Chief cocked his ears back, checking for a command of some sort from his master.

Jamie reached down, patted his neck and reined him into the Oldhams' driveway. Pearl sat on the front porch, slowly rocking back and forth, with Andrea sleeping on her lap. Jamie marveled, as she always did, at the tranquil effect Andrea seemed to have on the normally cantankerous Pearl. Pearl carefully arose from her chair and carried the sleeping Andrea to Jamie, still mounted on the horse. As Pearl lifted the sleeping child up to her, Jamie whispered her thanks. The old horse stood perfectly still while, with some effort, Jamie balanced the sleeping Andrea, in the saddle in front of her.

Jamie gently kicked the horse in his side, and he turned and headed out the driveway toward her farm. Both of her hands were needed to hold the sleeping child, so the horse walked along with no reining. Chief knew the way home and seemed comfortable going on his own.

The moon was full and bathed the Iowa countryside with an undiscriminating layer of light. Still, the shadows fought back and cast their eerie darkness wherever possible, especially at the approaching bridge, the bridge under which the body of Doug Cordoe had been found. Jamie felt goosebumps building and suddenly felt cool. Abruptly, not twenty yards from the bridge, Chief stopped, lifted his head and snorted. Both of his ears turned forward listening; he lifted his head once again, smelling. Jamie's heart started to race. Maybe she should turn around, go back to the Oldham house. They'd put her up for the night. Then, just as quickly as he stopped, Chief started to walk ahead again, and Jamie, fear subsiding, suddenly felt foolish. What had she been afraid of anyway? Denny? Denny had never bothered her before. Doug had been the problem. But no more, she thought, thinking of his dead body lying under the bridge.

Suddenly, a fast-moving bank of clouds intersected the moon above and the bridge darkened almost as if somebody had turned the lights out. Jamie's heart began to pound again. Alright, she admitted to herself, she was scared of Denny. She felt very vulnerable holding onto her daughter as the horse's footsteps made loud, clopping noises on the wooden floor of the bridge. Chief jumped a little, startled by a small raccoon which raced across the bridge floor and dropped out of sight under the railing on the opposite side.

"Easy boy," she spoke, calming the horse while rebalancing Andrea in her arms. She gently kneed Chief in the side and commanded him to move forward. She wanted to get across this damn bridge. She turned her head toward a rustling sound that she heard coming from the bottom side of the bridge railing, thinking it was the raccoon again and wondering if the animal could be rabid, but it was no raccoon. She cried out in fright as two hands appeared on the bridge railing and Denny Cordoe's angry face appeared. He screamed an inhuman sound as he pulled himself over the edge of the railing and lunged toward her.

The scream startled the already-jittery Chief who broke hard to his right. Jamie felt Andrea slip from her grip and nearly drop off of the horse, barely catching her as she fell to Jamie's right. At the same time, she felt Denny's hands grabbing her left leg. Incredibly, it was the two forces, pulling in opposite directions that prevented her from falling off of Chief. Chief broke into a gallop with Jamie desperately trying to hold onto Andrea, while Denny, having lost his balance, clung to her foot and drug along. Summoning all of her strength, Jamie returned Andrea to her position in the saddle. She felt her left tennis shoe slip off as Denny lost his grip and thumped to the bridge floor. Once more, she lost her balance as his grip broke loose, nearly losing her daughter again, but the horse shifted his gait in such a manner that she was able to regain her balance. She locked one arm around Andrea and the other to the saddle horn as the horse, reins dragging on the ground, raced down the dead end road. Denny screamed at her from the bridge behind.

Jamie brought the horse to an abrupt stop right by her yard gate. Andrea was awake and upset. She set the small child by the picket fence, then pulled the saddle, saddle blanket and bridle off Chief. She gave the horse a light swat on the rump and he trotted on out to a pasture lot behind the barn. She dumped the saddle and bridle right there for the night. She turned and looked back up the road. No sign of him.

Still shaking, she carried Andrea into the house and locked both doors behind her. In light of the encounters at the bridge and her state of fright, Jamie decided to put Andrea in her bed rather than in the little girl's own. She pulled Andrea's shoes and socks off, but opted against trying to change her into her pajamas. She tucked Andrea in, kissed her on the forehead and tiptoed back out to the kitchen.

She cautiously peeked out the kitchen window and her heart skipped a beat when she saw movement by the barn, until she remembered it was Hawkett. What was he doing out walking around? She wondered if she should call out to him; tell him about her encounter on the bridge. No, it'd wait until morning. The doors and windows were locked and she had Bud's shotgun. No! Shit, she thought, Hawkett has the shotgun! She desperately looked around the kitchen for a weapon of some kind, eyeing plenty of knives and a rolling pin. She'd be safe enough. Also, she thought, she should be safer from Denny with Hawkett around, or was she? She remembered Benjamin's words: "nervous breakdown," "drinking problem," "divorce."

145

CHAPTER 25

Hawkett had decided to sleep in the haymow. He liked the idea of being up, off of the barn floor. He had originally considered sleeping on hay bales, but experimentation had proven it to be a bad idea, the prickly hay kept poking through the blankets. So, he ended up making a bed near a barn door on the floor of the haymow. He opened up the small door and moonlight poured in, along with the sounds and smells of the farm.

From this vantage point, he had a moonlit view of both the farmstead and much of the surrounding countryside as well. Again, he marveled at the incredible contrast in his life, not only environmentally, but emotionally as well. He wondered what tomorrow would bring. Who could tell? Why worry?

He lay his head down on a rolled-up blanket and relaxed. He was bone-tired and could feel his eyelids getting heavy. The sounds of the farm, crickets chirping and frogs croaking drifted through the barn door. It was peaceful, so very peaceful. No traffic, no domestic violence, no stinking polluted air. He drifted off into a peaceful sleep.

Later, he was awakened by a loud noise in the barnyard below and looked out to see Jamie's horse run by without its rider. He looked toward the house and saw lights come on. She must be home, he thought to himself. He sighed, laid back down on his bed and was starting to drift off again, when nature called.

He arose from his blankets, climbed down the mow ladder and started to exit the barn, but hesitated. He was wearing nothing but his boxer shorts and wondered if he'd be spotted. He probably should climb back up to the loft and get his jeans. But hell, it was dark, who would see? The females were probably asleep anyway. Having decided to risk it, he padded, barefooted, out the main barn door into the moonlight where he quickly slipped into the shadows and walked around to the back side of the barn.

Having completed his mission, Hawkett started back toward the barn door and was about to enter it, when movement registered in the corner of his right eye and caught his attention. For a moment, he thought maybe it had been his imagination. Then he saw it again, somebody by the back fence of Jamie's yard. He slipped into the shadows of the barn, instantly fearing that Jamie would see him in his underwear. He peeked around the corner of the barn. The figure by the fence was now crawling over it. As Hawkett realized it wasn't Jamie, the hair on the back of his neck stood up. Who? The son? Cordoe's boy, Denny? The guy they called crazy? Hawkett's heart was pounding. He took a deep breath, steadied his nerves and began quietly edging toward the house, staying in the shadows.

Jamie was restless and had not yet fallen asleep. The stranger, well, he was still basically a stranger she thought, was hopefully asleep in her barn. He had upset her life. Or maybe, she thought, Cordoe's death had upset her life, and Hawkett was just more trouble. She lay there, trying to force all thoughts out of her mind, trying to force herself to relax and fall asleep, but each time that she closed her eyes, he'd slip into her thoughts again. She was trying hard to drift off when she heard an unusual noise. She opened her eyes. Had she been dreaming? Then she heard it again. Someone was fiddling with her bedroom window. Who? Denny? No, it couldn't be Denny, could it? He'd never come near her house. Hawkett, why? No time to sort it out but her instincts told her it was Hawkett and she feared she was about to discover things about him she didn't want to know.

Hawkett moved more quickly now, his instincts taking over; he was back in his element. The hunter. Stalking a killer. Trying to prevent further harm.

Jamie, half scared, half mad, quickly slid out of the bed and quietly crossed the bedroom floor to her closet. She reached up to the top shelf for Bud's shotgun but, with horror, remembered again it wasn't there. She'd given the gun to the very man who was breaking into her bedroom. As the screen window was removed, she ran to the kitchen in panic. She could grab a butcher knife, but what good would it do her if he had the shotgun? She grabbed a knife anyway from the rack over her stove, then left the kitchen, ran back into her bedroom and lifted the small child from her bed. As she stumbled out of her bedroom, carrying the disoriented child in one arm and the knife in the other, she prayed for enough time to get out the front door and run.

By the time Denny had the screen window off, Hawkett was standing behind him. "Stop right there!"

Startled by Hawkett's voice, Denny almost jumped clear off the ground. He spun around, and in the light of the moon, saw the larger man standing there in his boxer shorts highlighted by the moon beyond him. Denny decided to run. He took off like a rabbit, screaming some sort of a high-pitched moan as he went.

Hawkett was surprised when Denny went racing around the corner of the house. He'd thought Denny would want to retreat in the same direction that he'd come, and Hawkett would have been able to cut him off. Not so, he discovered, and he took up the chase, running around the house after the wild man. Denny was heading for the open garden gate in the far corner of the yard and Hawkett, picking up speed as he went, raced straight through the large flower bed in an attempt to stop Denny. His plan would have worked had it not been for the clothesline strung across the far edge of the flower bed, a taut, steel-wire clothesline that Hawkett couldn't see in the dark. He hit it at full stride and was thrown backward, as if by a slingshot, and landed spread-eagle on his back right in the middle of a bed of begonias. He was slightly dazed, as he laid there, looking up at the Big Dipper, feeling the moist vegetation and soil on his bare back.

The screen door banged and the next thing he knew, the beam from a flashlight was blinding him. He moaned and started to get up.

"Stay right there, I, I've got a knife!" It was Jamie. Her voice was threatening and he could tell that she was trembling. She turned the flashlight and quickly pointed it toward the carving knife in her left hand as if to accentuate her threat.

Hawkett was speechless. How the hell had he gotten into this mess? He rolled over and started to get up, suddenly remembering he was wearing nothing but a pair of boxer shorts.

"What's with the knife? He's gone now!"

"Stay back or I'll use this thing!" Jamie threatened, "Who's gone?"

Hawkett shrugged, "The guy who was messing with your window. I thought maybe it was young Cordoe. Whoever the hell it was needed a bath. I could smell him ten feet away."

Now Jamie was confused as well as angry and frightened.

"Where are your clothes?"

"In the barn," he retorted with a hint of irritation entering his voice. He self-consciously tried to move out of the beam of her flashlight. Then he understood. He realized why she had been confused. "Hey, that wasn't me messing around with your window. I chased the son of a bitch. Would have caught him too if it hadn't been for that damn wire."

Jamie was more bewildered than ever; it had all happened so fast. She quickly turned and flashed her light onto the front porch. Andrea had miraculously fallen asleep again where Jamie had laid her on the porch swing. She turned the light back to Hawkett again, blinding him.

"Get the damn flashlight out of my face, okay?" Hawkett was getting really irritated now.

Confused, she lowered the light from his face only to have it shine directly upon his boxers. Embarrassed, she lowered the flashlight further yet and took a few steps back, the knife still in a defensive position. He was irritated as hell, but was trying to understand her fear, wondering how to resolve this standoff of sorts.

"Look, I wasn't trying to get into your house; it was somebody else. Probably young Cordoe, I don't know. I didn't get a good look at his face. I was just out taking a...well I spotted the guy and snuck up behind him. Didn't you hear me yell?"

Yes, she'd heard a yell but couldn't make out what it was. She'd been too damn scared to care.

"You were outside the barn, dressed like that?" The flashlight's beam jumped once again to his midriff and then quickly away.

"Well, yes, I mean, I was just taking a leak. Well hell, there's no toilet in the damn barn." Hawkett was growing more embarrassed and frustrated. They stood quietly in the dark for nearly thirty seconds, neither one able to see the expression on the other's face.

Hawkett, thinking of nothing else to do or say, turned and walked toward the barn. He probably should have said, "If you need me, I'll be in the barn."

She probably should have said "Thank you."

Neither of them said anything, however, but returned to their respective beds.

Nearly a mile away, Denny stopped by a walnut tree and tried to listen over his heavy breathing. He looked back across the landscape. No one appeared to be following; he could hear no sirens coming from town. Shit, he thought, shaking his head. "That guy scared the hell out of me. Didn't even know he was there," Denny muttered to himself repeatedly.

Denny was still badly shaken, but now his fear was giving way to anger. The stranger had ruined his plans, ruined his chance with the woman. He wanted to have the woman before he died, and he somehow sensed that his death was nearing. Tonight he had gathered his courage. How had that man known? Had he been lying in wait, ready to ambush him? Where the hell were his clothes? Had he already been in bed with her? Denny's anger grew. Shit! Suddenly his stomach rolled and he bent over and threw up the wild plums he'd eaten earlier. He dropped down on his knees and pulled wet grass from the earth, using it to clean himself. He crawled on all fours over to a moonlit spot near the base of his favorite tree. Tomorrow he would take action. He would get revenge. He was scared, but he knew what to do. He'd watched his father die; he would get revenge for that death. The killer would pay. And there would be payback for the stranger chasing him away from Jamie's window. Oh yeah, he could taste the anger it was so intense. Then maybe things would be better. Maybe. Shit, he didn't know. He dropped down on his side and cried himself to sleep.

CHAPTER
26

What now? Benjamin sat in his car parked on Main Street of Pigmy and smoked a cigar. He was wondering if Jamie had arrived home safely. Probably should give her a call he thought. He'd do that as soon as he got back to the motel. He could drive out to her farm, confront Hawkett. No, he was still pissed at that guy. Leave him out there. He wondered what the hell was going on between Hawkett and Jamie. This whole investigation had taken a strange turn.

Lord this small town was peaceful, he thought. He'd sat there for nearly ten minutes and not one vehicle had passed. This place kind of reminded him of Mayberry and the old *Andy Griffith Show*. He smiled to himself remembering Barney Fife and the single bullet he carried in his pocket. Yeah, he had really loved that old show. Another era, maybe a happier time. Glumly he thought of the cop shows on TV today. Blood, violence. He shook his head, yeah he'd take Mayberry RFD anytime over the big city crap.

Maybe he ought to quit the DCI and get a job in law enforcement in some little burg, like Pigmy. Hell, Sheriff Spencer had said he was retiring. It was something to think about. Nice quiet evenings like this, listening to the crickets chirp. Yeah, definitely something to think about.

Well, best be getting back to the motel, make a couple of calls, read a little, he thought. He tossed the cigar stub out the window, then guiltily opened the car door and retrieved it. This wasn't the city; this was a place to respect. This little town was still a place with some hope of remaining clean and decent.

He started the Escort, shifted into gear and eased out into the street. Only two blocks to the motel, no hurry. A pair of headlights came around the corner, and as he met the oncoming vehicle, he could tell it was a city patrol car.

The patrol car spun around in the street behind him, squealing its tires as it did. In his rearview mirror, Benjamin could see the patrol car accelerating, nearing his rear bumper until it almost made contact.

His initial thought was that it could be Sheriff Spencer wanting to talk to him. Maybe they'd captured young Cordoe. Then the patrol car swerved around the Escort and cut Benjamin off, forcing him to brake hard and veer into the curb.

What the hell, he wondered, his anger rising as he put the car into park and climbed out. Oh, crap, he thought as he recognized the bald head, the big, bulky shape of Deputy Dog or rather Cog, who was already out of his car, smiling. It was not a pleasant smile, but a smile which silently spoke of revenge. Even in the darkened street, illuminated by only an occasional street lamp, Benjamin could see the bruises on Deputy Cog's face. The irate neighbors must have worked him over pretty good.

Cog never said a word, just stood there and stared at Benjamin. Finally he spoke, "Where's your buddy?"

Benjamin didn't reply, he just sat there with a cold stare aimed at Cog. This nut could be bad business. What to do? The escort was pinned in. He couldn't drive away without causing severe body damage to the car. There was a time when whipping this bastard would have been easy, Benjamin thought, but that time had passed.

Hawkett's .38 was still in the glove compartment, but he hated like hell to go for it. He'd never pulled a gun on another cop, and he sure as hell didn't want to shoot this guy. He'd probably do everybody a favor if he did, but he wasn't going to let the situation get any worse. Should he try to run away? Hell no, he still had his pride. Suddenly Benjamin felt old, vulnerable, like he hadn't felt for years.

"I asked you, Mister Detective, where the hell is your partner?" His menacing voice had a slur to it, and Benjamin wondered if he'd been drinking. There was nothing worse than a drunk cop.

"Where my partner went is none of your business. I suggest you move that son-of-a-bitching patrol car and get back to your business."

Cog snorted, extended himself slightly over his front hood and spit across onto Benjamin's Escort. Benjamin could see a stream of tobacco juice running down his fender.

"Listen, you jackass," yelled Benjamin, his anger intensifying, thinking maybe he ought to go for the .38 after all.

"No, you listen piss ant. You listen to this little club here." Having said that, Cog pulled a baseball bat out of his car and started sauntering around the front of his car. "You listen to the sound of this little club going rat-a-tat-tat alongside your head." He moved closer as he talked.

Go for the gun, thought Benjamin, and he reached for the door handle wondering if he still had time.

"All units, attention all units. Code red, code red, officer down, I repeat officer down," a voice spoke over Cog's radio. Both law enforcement officers froze when they heard the two most dreaded words in their vocabulary, "Officer down." Cog stopped and listened for more.

"This is Polly, dispatcher in Page County. We have a highway patrolman down, out on Highway 2. Wounded, gunshot, but able to make radio contact." She paused, then her voice came over the radio again. "Suspects have escaped. Two males, one black, one white, in newer Cadillac. Last seen heading east of Clarinda on Highway 2. All units please respond."

And respond they would. Nothing brought on the law like an officer shot.

East of Clarinda heading east. Hell, thought Benjamin, they could be heading right by Pigmy. They had probably detoured to the sideroads, but still...

Another voice came over the radio, "Who the hell's out there? Cog are you awake?"

Cog trotted around to his door, tossed the baseball bat in and reached for his radio. "Yeah, Sheriff, I'm here, up on Main Street."

"You hear the call, officer shot?"

"Yeah, I heard it."

"Get your ass out to the highway and keep your eyes open. If

153

they're heading this way, they may already have passed. Hurry up! I'll be there shortly."

"Gotcha." Cog jumped into his car, backed away from Benjamin's car, laid a patch of rubber on the street and flew out of Pigmy with his lights flashing.

Benjamin stood there watching him race away, wondering what to do. He didn't idle long though before climbing into the Escort and following Cog. Probably a wild goose chase, but still, one of his fellow officers was losing blood somewhere, and he damn sure couldn't ignore that, Cog or no Cog.

Highway 2 lay just on the north side of Pigmy and as Benjamin came to the edge of town, he could see Deputy Cog's car already parked at the intersection.

Benjamin veered to the side of the road and turned off his lights. He was positioned roughly two blocks up the hill from Cog's patrol car. From that vantage point, he could see not only the intersection but also had a clear view of Highway 2 stretching almost a mile to the west. If the bad guys were coming this way, he'd have some advance warning unlike Cog parked below.

Benjamin flicked on his radio and listened to the communication firing back and forth over the airways. Patrolmen of all sorts were converging on the area at breakneck speed. The Life Flight helicopter was already en route from Des Moines.

Benjamin wondered what was detaining Sheriff Spencer. He should have been here by now he thought. They needed at least two cars to set up a road block. The Cadillac was probably busy sneaking down backroads by now. It would be stupid to stay on a major highway. Still, thought Benjamin, they'd shot a cop. It could mean they were high on something, or it could mean they were just plain rotten, or both.

Suddenly a set of headlights popped over the hill coming from the west. The vehicle appeared to be moving at a high rate of speed. Benjamin's pulse quickened and instinctively he reached across the car and removed Hawkett's .38 from the glove compartment.

The car was approaching quickly and Cog was delayed in spotting it. Benjamin could see the deputy's headlights come on, then his flashers. He glanced in his rearview mirror. Where the hell was Spencer?

He started the Escort's motor and pulled out onto the road. Odds were probable that the car belonged to some harmless soul, but nothing was certain. Benjamin wondered what Cog would do. What he should do was turn his damn flashers off, let the car go by and tail it. Then if the plate numbers and description were a match, he could easily call for help and pursue the criminals. With just one car and by himself, he damned sure didn't need to try to be a hero. But with dread, Benjamin could see exactly what Cog was attempting to do as he pulled right out onto the highway trying to block the oncoming vehicle.

Fool, damn fool, thought Benjamin. He accelerated down the hill thinking of all the things that were about to go wrong.

The approaching vehicle started to slow, then sped up. It appeared as if the driver was going to detour around the front of the patrol car and Cog gunned his vehicle forward in an attempt to block it. Just as Benjamin had foreseen it happening, the car, which he could clearly see was a Cadillac, swerved to its right and flew past Cog's rear bumper.

Benjamin took the corner as fast as possible and pulled in behind the accelerating Cadillac. Benjamin knew the Escort wouldn't be able to keep up with the Cadillac for long. His goal was to get a reading on the plates and keep the car in sight for as long as possible. Over his car radio, he gave his location and a complete description of the Cadillac. He managed to get a reading on the plates before the Cadillac started to pull away. Benjamin couldn't believe they'd stayed on a main highway. They should have run the backroads. They probably thought the patrolman they'd shot wouldn't be able to call for help.

Benjamin could see help was on the way as flashing red lights appeared in his rearview mirror. The high-powered patrol cars would be able to outrun the Cadillac which was quickly leaving Benjamin far behind. "Shit," Benjamin cursed to himself as he recognized the Pigmy patrol car as it passed. Cog. Deputy Cog, in a rush to err again. Benjamin's speedometer read somewhere over 90 mph as Deputy Cog flew by. Must be doing nearly 110 mph, thought Benjamin. Bastard will probably kill himself.

Whatever Cog's car had for an engine must have been damn powerful, because Benjamin could see that he was gaining on the Cadillac.

Benjamin got on the radio again and added Deputy Cog's pursuit and his estimate of their location. The dispatcher reported that at least twelve county and state patrol cars were closing in from different directions. This chase will soon be over, thought Benjamin, but he wondered if it would come to a completion before Cog got himself killed.

He watched in horror as Cog overtook the Cadillac and appeared to be trying to run it off the road.

"Wait for help, you jackass!" Benjamin shouted though no one could hear him. Just then, Cog rammed the Cadillac and both cars skidded out of control. Benjamin could see brake lights come on as the two drivers fought to keep their cars under control. Both cars veered off their respective sides of the road but stayed upright bouncing down into wide, shallow, grassy ditches.

Cog brought his patrol car back up onto the road, accelerated and rammed the Cadillac as it tried to reenter the roadway. Benjamin, still maintaining a high rate of speed, flew by the two cars which had finally skidded to a halt. He ducked as he went by, hoping to avoid being shot, and yelled the situation into his car radio. He braked the car fifty yards beyond the others and turned to look back. It was dark, but in the flashing lights, he could see Cog's large frame standing outside of his patrol car.

Fool, damn fool thought Benjamin as he shoved the car's transmission into reverse and accelerated backwards toward the two cars. He heard gunfire and saw Cog go down. With no time to plan, Benjamin reacted on instinct. The Cadillac was already trying to pull away from the patrol car wedged against it.

Benjamin had one hope as he backed up. He knew the Cadillac was equipped with driver and passenger side air bags. Benjamin mashed the accelerator and backed his Escort into the Cadillac. Just before the cars made contact, he threw himself down onto the seat and gripped hard on the .38, not wanting to lose track of it in the collision. The crash was harder than Benjamin had anticipated and the Escort's seat almost gave way, but Benjamin was able to keep his senses and was out of the Escort immediately, the .38 pointed, ready to kill.

With his heart pounding, he thanked God and the GM corporation as he saw that the exploded air bags had stunned the two criminals long enough for him to get a jump on the situation.

Keeping one eye on the Cadillac, he reached back into the Escort, felt for the radio, steadied his voice and reported the situation. Grimly he reported that another officer was down as he looked at Cog's motionless body laying near his patrol car, the front of his shirt soaked in a dark liquid.

Movement in the Cadillac caught Benjamin's attention. "You

bastards make one move and I'll blow you away! Hear me?" he shouted.

The only reply was a mumbled, "Shit."

From his position Benjamin could see flashing lights coming from three directions. If only Cog would have waited a few more minutes.

CHAPTER
27

Benjamin, back in his motel room, took off his shoes, loosened his tie, sat down on the bed and reached for the telephone. He had to report to the bastard. Hated it, but what the hell. What to say? The truth. Well, yes, hell he had nothing to hide. But still, he hated to call. Deputy Cog was on his way to the undertaker and Hawkett was staying with the prime suspect of the murder investigation. Not the kind of things one likes to report to a superior.

It was that stupid bastard Hawkett who'd screwed everything up. Dumb shit! He shook his head back and forth, then dialed Brightwall's home number.

"Hello," answered Brightwall.

"Willoughby here."

"What have you got for me?"

"Some progress."

"Like?"

Benjamin sighed. Honesty to a point, he decided. "We're thinking the most likely suspect is a widow lady who lived neighbors to the victim. I've, er we've spent quite a bit of time interviewing the other neighbors and checking motives, alibis, you know."

No reply.

Benjamin cleared his voice, "Anyway, it appears to have been committed by someone local. We can't find anyone who saw any strangers over the weekend, and the sheriff's inquiries lead the same way. I just spent the last two hours with him and his staff. There's been another death." He filled Brightwall in on the incident that led to Cog's death and his role in it.

"So you're in the clear on this Cog deal?"

"Sheriff Spencer seemed satisfied with my report. Most of what happened can be documented by tapes of the radio transmissions."

"Good. How's this Spencer been to work with? Cooperative?"

"He helped me check and verify alibis. Yeah, Spencer's a real good fellow to work with. Not terribly bright, but real cooperative."

"What makes you think the widow did it?"

Benjamin grimaced. He wished he hadn't referred to her as a widow. He could see the headlines now: "Widow Wipes Out Wanton Womanizer."

"Her name's Jamie, Jamie Chambers. About 35-36 years old. Has a real cute little girl. Husband killed himself a couple years back. His suicide could have had something to do with problems at the bank. She's a pretty good-looking lady. This Cordoe, Sheriff tells me, was a real womanizer, you know the type, fifty-year-old stud horse."

"Like you?"

Asshole! thought Benjamin. "Gimme a break."

"Any witnesses?"

"No."

"Can you tie her to the pitchfork?"

"Yeah, but it might hurt."

Brightwall didn't laugh, didn't reply at all.

"Sheriff Spencer said the lab boys were here for a couple of hours this afternoon looking at the car. I guess they examined the pitchfork and the body too. They come up with anything yet?"

"Nothing had come across my desk before I left."

"Have somebody fill me in if you get anything exciting, okay?"

"Sure. You think she did it? Are you going to be able to pin it down?"

159

"I'm going after a confession. Put a little pressure on her. She's the soft type. It's going to be a self defense kind of deal. I can feel it."

"Otherwise, you haven't got shit? No witnesses, no motive, no confession. Enjoying your vacation, Willoughby?"

Benjamin almost slammed the phone down. He sat there and stared at his stocking feet, so mad he couldn't articulate.

"Where's Hawkett? At the local pub? Or is he already shit drunk in your hotel room?"

Benjamin pulled himself together. Years of dealing with bureaucratic bastards had given him experience. He took a deep breath and collected his thoughts.

"Hawkett's out doing surveillance. Right now he's standing in a cold, wet cornfield, mosquitoes eating him alive, keeping an eye on the Chamber gal's residence. He hasn't had a drink since we left Des Moines. I think the guy's getting his shit together. He's been working like a damn beaver trying to solve this case. We'll have it sewed up within twenty-four hours and hand it to you on a platter, so you can go brag to the press. Okay?" He'd almost said, "Okay, asshole?"

"That's what I like to hear; see you tomorrow night." Click, the line went dead.

Shit, thought Benjamin, I should have been a farmer. He thought about the next day's agenda. It wasn't going to be fun. Only one way to get the mess cleaned up. Wade right in and pick up the pieces.

160

CHAPTER 28

Hawkett woke with a start. Had he heard a noise? His eyes focused, in the still partial darkness, on the barn roof above. Where the hell was he? Oh yeah, he remembered. He slid back the covers and started to sit up. "Shit," he grimaced, pain shooting down the lower part of his hip. He braced himself with his hands, both of which were raw and painful, blisters where callouses should have been. He laid back down, ever so gently, on his back and looked at his watch, 5:30 AM. His hand bumped into a foreign object, and he slowly turned his head to see what it was. Setting on the barn floor was a thermos, a plastic food container, and the bottle of pain pills. She'd been there. A folded sheet of paper was under the thermos. He picked it up. The note read: *I'm going out. Please keep an eye on Andrea. She's still asleep in the house. Sorry about last night, I misunderstood your intentions. -Jamie*

He wondered how stupid he had looked. He had probably been lying with his mouth open, snoring like a chain saw. Anyway, her visit explained the extra blanket lying on top of him. He felt good, content somehow. Then he frowned, remembering the encounter that he'd had with Cordoe the night before, the confrontation with Jamie. She'd apparently sorted things out, forgiven him. But forgiven him for what?

He reached over for the thermos and the pain pills. The thermos had hot coffee in it and he sipped some of it in order to wash the pills down. Having done that, he lay down once again, rolled over and stared out the barn door. It was still dark out, but not too dark to see somewhat. He heard a clomping noise to his right and peeked further out the door. She was leaving on her horse. In the dark, he could barely see, but the white color of the horse glowed through the darkness. He heard her gallop out of the farmyard. He wondered where she was going.

Hawkett pulled the covers up around his neck, surprised at how toasty it felt, snuggled there on the floor of her haymow. Aside from the back pain, he felt pretty good, especially considering the fact he'd done more physical labor the day before, than he had done the previous ten years of his life and had slept on a barn floor all night to top it off. Slept, that was it, he'd actually slept for almost eight hours. And, no nightmares, no dreams at all. How long had it been since he'd gone through a night without the nightmares about death, somebody dying. Had he been released from the guilt? Would the nightmares be back?

He smiled to himself thinking of the time and money people spent trying to deal with depression. The different psychiatrists, specialists, drugs, hell he'd even met twice with a depression encounter group. All had failed. Then, he landed on a farm, worked until he was about to drop, slept hard for a night in cool, fresh air and bang, suddenly he felt like a different person, somebody with a future. The whole issue made his head start spinning.

And then, another surprising fact came to light. He'd not had a drink of alcohol for almost forty-eight hours. Unbelievable! Was he drying out? He was excited and happy, and he wished he could share his thoughts for the moment with someone, but nobody was there, so he closed his eyes and just basked in the moment instead.

He laid there for almost half of an hour, staring at the barn rafters, contemplating his thoughts. Finally, he tried to sit up again, slower this time. The pain was still there, but duller. He smiled at the little bottle of pain pills. He shifted around and sat with his back against a large twelve by twelve inch beam which originated in the barn floor, traveled through a hole cut out of the hay mow floor and ended at the barn roof. He hooked his foot around the plastic container left by Jamie and slid it toward him. Opening it up, he discovered two thick, caramel-covered cinnamon rolls. Their fresh fragrance rose to his nose. He poured a cup of coffee and devoured the cinnamon rolls.

Probably should plan my day, he thought, then chuckled at the thought. Nothing had gone as planned since he'd arrived in the country. Hell, he'd just wait and see what happened. Take things minute by minute. Strangely, that had seemed to work pretty well the last couple of days, damn well in fact. His clothes, which had been soiled the day before, lay, washed and dried, in a neat pile on a bale near the wall. He wondered if Jamie ever slept. He recalled their experience the night before, on the ground floor of the barn below, right after the storm, dancing with her. What could he do to bring back that moment when he'd held her close? Then he remembered the incident that had followed at her house with Denny, and frowned. Where did he stand with her now he wondered. He pushed that worry out of his mind, put on his clean clothes and slowly descended the ladder to the barn floor below.

Near the barn door set the shotgun and coyote call reminding him of the prior night's promise. It seemed kind of silly now, he thought, blowing on that little obnoxious horn, expecting a cunning coyote to come trotting. Ah well, he had promised to give it a try. What the hell, he had nothing else to do, didn't feel like going back to sleep, wasn't hungry. He slid the shotgun from its case, a 870 Remington twelve-gauge pump. It was clean and in good condition, almost identical to Benjamin's, only with a longer barrel, not intended for the close-up encounters that Benjamin was prepared to deal with.

He loaded five shells, no. 2 buckshot, into the gun, stuck a few in his pocket and picked up the plastic coyote call. He walked out of the barn and stared across the farmyard. Seeing the farmhouse reminded him of Jamie's request to keep an eye on Andrea. Well, he thought, he sure as heck couldn't go off and leave her alone with that animal Denny wondering around the neighborhood. A chill ran down his spine as he stared across the horizon into the neighboring fields and pastures, wondering if Denny was staring back at him, that wicked little smile on his face. He was about to cancel the coyote hunting expedition entirely when he heard the sound of an approaching car. It was Harley in his battered-up pickup truck. He rolled the pickup to a stop in front of the barn.

"Good morning Harley. Not delivering mail today?"

"No, still taking some medical leave. Probably could work but I got so much leave built up, if I don't use it, I'm gonna lose it so..." He shrugged and smiled. "Thought I'd pick some of Jamie's late sweetcorn, take it to the farmers' market tonight, see if I could sell it for her." He smiled and shrugged again.

"What you doin' with that gun?"

"Oh, yeah, well, I was going to try and take care of some of those coyotes for her, but, she's taken off on her horse and left a note asking me to keep an eye on Andrea, so guess I better stay around. Especially after last night's ordeal," he said, once again remembering the encounter with Denny. He informed the ever-attentive Harley of the prior night's events, everything from the incident outside of Jamie's house to the point where he collided with the clothes line and Denny escaped.

As to be expected, the normally-jovial Harley was visibly upset and angered by the story. He shook his head back and forth, "that damn maggot, I'm tellin' you..." but he couldn't finish the statement, overcome by emotion. He turned and stared towards the house and didn't speak for several moments. Hawkett was shocked upon seeing a side of Harley he didn't know existed. He looked towards the house as well and then had a thought. "Hey, Harley, how long you going to be around? Any chance you could keep an eye on Andrea for a while?"

Harley appeared to wipe tears from his eyes. Hawkett wondered if they were tears of anger.

"Sure, I'll watch the little tike for a while. Maybe she'll want to help pick sweetcorn; she usually does anyway."

"Hey thanks, I'll go give the coyotes a go. I don't think Denny will be snooping around here in the daylight, but I feel a lot better knowing you're around."

Harley interrupted Hawkett with anger in his voice, "Ain't nobody gonna be hurting Jamie or her daughter while I'm around, and you can damn sure take that to the bank!"

Hawkett, caught off guard by Harley's forceful remark wasn't quite sure how to reply but said, "Yeah, okay, well I'll be off. See you later."

Where should he go? Up into the hills somewhere? Maybe near the sheep pasture? He'd have to be careful, not knowing his way around the farm. He didn't want to be shooting any of Jamie's livestock. He started walking up the hill, the cold steel of the shotgun felt good against his tender hands. He was feeling good all over now, full of purpose. Take it one minute at a time, he thought.

164

By 6:30 AM, Benjamin was up and around also. He was troubled. Today was the day. He had promised Brightwall. There'd be no stonewalling now. He'd eaten breakfast already at the cafe, surprised by the number of people who were already there, already on the move. He climbed into the Escort and hit the key. No use screwing around, he thought. He dropped the car into gear and headed to Dead End Road. What would he find? Would they be in bed together; would Hawkett be gone or what? He didn't know, but he did know that there was only one way to get this mess cleaned up. She'd confess, he knew. He could feel it. He wasn't optimistic about it though. It didn't feel good. He wished he was someone else, doing some other work, at least for a day. He turned onto Dead End Road and headed for her farm.

Hawkett, seated behind a stunted cedar tree, continued to blow on the coyote call. He was starting to feel silly. He'd been puffing on the damn thing for nearly ten minutes. The morning air was dead still and the sun was just peeping over the horizon. All in all, it was really a very beautiful, peaceful beginning to the day and Hawkett felt guilty squawking away on the foreign-sounding instrument. Did this racket really sound like a rabbit in distress, he wondered again. Jamie had assured him that that was what it was designed to do. She wouldn't deceive him, would she, he thought. Suddenly, Hawkett froze.

Over his shoulder he'd caught sight of some movement. He turned around ever so slowly until he was facing back toward the direction from which he'd come. Jamie's buildings lay down the hill and across the field in front of him. Then he saw it again, a brownish-red coyote moving silently from tree to brush, peeking at him. His heart started pumping harder; he'd not anticipated the excitement of the hunt. Now what? The coyote was still well out of range of his shotgun, and it wasn't coming any closer. Well hell, it finally hit him; in the excitement, he'd stopped blowing on the call. He placed the call in his mouth and began blowing again, not feeling nearly as silly about it now.

Again the coyote advanced toward Hawkett, seeming to readily respond to the renewed calling. But suddenly, still well out of gun range, it froze and dropped to its belly. Hawkett watched the coyote cock its head to the left and realized that it was watching something else. What the hell, he wondered, again halting his efforts at blowing on the call. What had captured the coyote's attention? And then he saw what

165

the coyote had spotted and his excitement turned to panic. Actually, he heard it before he saw it and probably the coyote had smelled it before that.

In the quiet morning air, Hawkett heard a soft, bleating sound he recognized immediately as Andrea's pet lamb, Junior. And sure enough, out from the brush at the side of the pasture, appeared Junior, bouncing and twisting his plump little wool-covered body as he frolicked up the hillside above the farmstead.

The squeaking noise emitted from Hawkett's coyote call was not actually foreign to Junior. He'd heard Andrea, blowing on it different times around the farmyard and, therefore, assumed he would find her where the noise originated.

The coyote, a three-year-old bitch who was very thin from a summer of nursing four pups, saw breakfast. She abandoned the thought of an unknown rabbit and started sneaking down the hill intent on taking the lamb quickly.

What Hawkett saw unfolding, before his very eyes, was disaster. Even though he'd stopped blowing on the call, the little lamb continued to gallop along merrily in his direction. The coyote was now moving quickly in Junior's direction, and it was evident that Junior had no knowledge at all of his impending fate.

What Hawkett should have done, he readily admitted later, was fire the shotgun in the air and the coyote would have aborted her mission and headed for parts unknown, pronto. But Hawkett screwed up, big time. A flashback took him right back to the living room of the prior murder investigation, those small children, their mangled bodies. He had to move and move fast. His immediate instinct was to save the lamb by beating the coyote to it. He jumped up from under the cedar tree where he'd been hiding and started to sprint down the hill, immediately he tripped over a thorny multi-flora bush and went flying, head over heals. The shotgun broke loose from his hands and bounced down the slope, fortunately not discharging any shells as it did. Hawkett, unhurt, but slightly disorientated, jumped up, spun around and watched with horror as the coyote attacked the lamb. The old bitch was running dead out now and Junior spotted her at only the very last fraction of a second. Junior's immediate response was to jump straight up in the air just as the coyote reached him, causing the killer teeth to miss his neck. The little lamb had avoided death for a few seconds, but her attack had thrown Junior off balance causing him to land on his back. The bitch spun around

166

and moved in to finish the job. Hawkett, still a hundred yards away with no gun, started to yell, realizing he was too late. A yell might scare the coyote, but the lamb would already be dead.

But his yell was drowned out. Drowned out by a gunshot that, in the quiet country hillside, sounded like a cannon. As the gunshot exploded, so did the coyote, blood streaming from her neck as she dropped to the ground only three feet from Junior, quivered, then lay dead. The small lamb, back on its feet again, looked at the coyote, then quickly turned and hobbled back toward the buildings, carrying its right front leg off the ground.

Like they always say, "Everything happened so fast." And so it had been with this situation. Hawkett scanned the hillside to see where the gunshot had originated, just now beginning to worry if he, himself, was in danger. He thought of young Cordoe. Then he heard a yell and turned around, spotting Benjamin's parked Escort on the road across the pasture. Both doors were open on the driver's side, and Hawkett could see Benjamin's high-powered rifle lying across the front hood. He shook his head in disbelief as he tried to estimate the distance the bullet had traveled. Benjamin was a marksman alright, but that shot had been almost superhuman. He wondered how his partner had shown up just in the nick of time. His partner, he thought with a sinking feeling. Well, he'd better go thank him anyway.

167

CHAPTER
29

"Nice shot."

Benjamin shrugged, "Sheep okay?"

"I think so. It was carrying one leg, but it hobbled all the way back to the house. Jamie will probably be able to take care of it."

Silence set in as Benjamin wiped his rifle off, zipped it back into its case, and laid it in the backseat of the Escort.

Hawkett, leaning on a fence post along the road, marveled, "How'd you get that gun out of there so fast?"

Benjamin snorted, "Speed, my friend, pure speed. No actually, I think I saw the coyote before you or that sheep did. I stopped and shut the car off to watch the coyote and I damn near died of fright when you started making that infernal noise. What the hell was that anyway?"

Hawkett pulled the plastic coyote call out of his pocket and gave a couple of quick toots. "S'posed to sound like a rabbit in distress. You could hear it all the way down here?"

"Damn right, I could."

Benjamin eyed the small plastic instrument. "Must work huh,

anyway the whole drama unfolded in front of my very eyes. Standing here I could see the coyote, the lamb and the top of your head. Lord, I would have loved to have had my camera and gotten a shot of you rolling down the hillside," Benjamin chuckled softly. "Anyway I, though not being the great white hunter that you are, never-the-less quickly saw everything was going to hell and went for my rifle. I'd moved it from the trunk to the rear seat this morning thinking I might use the scope to try and spot young Cordoe up on one of these hillsides. Anyway, if the coyote would have gotten the lamb... that was a lamb wasn't it?"

"Yeah, Andrea's pet lamb."

"Yes, well, if the coyote would have gotten the lamb on its first attack, I'd have been too late, I was still trying to get a shell into the chamber when she knocked him down the first time."

Again an awkward period of silence developed. Hawkett was still leaning on the fence post, Benjamin against the car.

"So, Hawk, what now?" No anger in his voice, no impatience, just an open, honest question.

No answer.

"Brightwall's on my ass. Wants this thing wrapped up, today."

"Anybody seen young Cordoe yet?"

"Yeah, I had a little run in with him yesterday. Creepy little bastard, I can tell you." Benjamin shook his head remembering the sad state of the guy and the smell. "Guy needs a bath, some food, and a doctor; I can guarantee you that."

"You had a run in with him? Where?"

"Half a mile back up the road there toward town. Spotted the idiot sittin' up in a tree. Pulled my gun on him and we chatted a little."

"He murder his father?"

"I don't think so. But I think he knows who did."

"Where's he at now?"

"Beats me."

"You let him go?"

"Yeah, sickly little fart could run a hell of a lot faster than me."

"But you said you had a gun on him."

Irritated, Benjamin replied, "Yeah, but it wasn't the place to shoot somebody in the back, you know what I mean?"

And Hawkett knew exactly what Benjamin meant. He'd seen Benjamin kill, without hesitation.

Hawkett told him of his own run-in with Denny.

"So we've both let him get away. Well, that's about par for our performance so far involving this investigation," Benjamin retorted.

"What else is going on, any other leads. What have you been doing?" He knew he was going to get an angry reply. He had it coming.

"Well hell, I've been carrying on with my job. Uh, that's the detection business, in case you've forgotten, and I've been eliminating suspects right and left. Alibis, witness collaboration, that sort of thing, remember?" There was no mistaking his deeply-sarcastic tone. And then in a more somber tone, he recanted the story of the previous evening that led to the death of Deputy Cog.

Hawkett knew that Benjamin was leading up to something, something that had been troubling Hawkett, hanging around the back of his mind, nagging at him.

"Anyway, I've only got one suspect left." Benjamin turned to look Hawkett right in the eye. "Your lady friend."

Hawkett said nothing, feeling a flush of anger.

Both men stood there, staring at each other, saying nothing. An impasse.

Then Benjamin lost his temper and began to yell "Well help me out here, I'm trying to solve a murder! I'm trying to do my job. No, I'm trying to do our job by myself, while you screw around. Did she murder him? Has she said anything? Have you seen anything?"

Hawkett challenged him. "Why the hell would Jamie kill him? What motive could you possibly..."

"Oh, for pete's sake. They had financial problems with the bank. Her husband kills himself. The banker has a farm next to hers that he keeps his deranged son on. The banker's a drinker and a lady's man. She's a good lookin' lady. There's a motive in there somewhere. Right? She know how to handle that gun you're carrying?"

"No, she said she..."

"Yeah, she kills him with a pitchfork instead. She's strong enough; you saw her handling those bales. Son of a bitch stops her on the road, he's half drunk. Makes a pass at her. Had her on his mind for a long time, probably. Gets too aggressive, I don't know, and all the hate and frustration ignites and suddenly our banker, Cordoe, has a chestful of pitchfork! Hell, this is not a complicated case, Hawkett. We've seen this kind of thing dozens of times, you know that."

Hawkett's shoulders dropped. A sickening feeling was coming over him. He felt speechless, dread sinking into his soul.

170

"Has she got a pitchfork? Have you seen one lying around the barn or her house?"

"Well, no, but..."

"Yeah," Benjamin interrupted again. "You know why? Cause the son-of-a-bitchin' one she owned is now tagged and classified as evidence. We can probably figure out a way to link it to her. Then we're talking motive and weapon and that, my friend, is murder one!"

"Still..." Hawkett started to raise his hands in a gesture of rebellion.

"Still what?" Benjamin retorted.

No reply. Hawkett stared down the road at Jamie's farmstead wondering.

Benjamin took a deep breath, his anger temporarily vented. He lit his cigar and puffed on it for a few moments, trying to collect his thoughts.

The silence once again hung in the air.

"Well, this is a damn mess, alright, and it's gonna have to end now, today. You go talk to her. If it's self defense, we'll fix it that way. If you want to warn her and let her run, okay. But Hawk, don't run with her, okay? You hear me, Hawkett?" His voice rose again.

Hawkett replied, "Yeah, I hear you." No animosity in his voice. "I'll take care of things. I'll talk to her, try to sort things out."

"Yeah, sure." Benjamin suddenly felt a different rush of emotion. Seeing his partner deflated, he cleared his voice. "Hawk, I'm sorry it turned out this way but...well, hell, I'll give you twenty-four hours, okay? Tomorrow morning we'll finish this thing. I feel as bad as you do about arresting her."

"Yeah, I know." Hawkett turned and walked toward Jamie's farmstead, his heart full of dread.

CHAPTER
30

Benjamin squeezed into the little Escort, started the engine and headed back toward Pigmy. It suddenly dawned on him that he was at loose ends. He had run out of suspects. At first, he'd believed that the murderer was the banker's son, Denny. Not now. Then the Wilson kid, maybe. No, not him either. The Oldham sisters? Preposterous. It just had to be Jamie Chambers, the good-looking, soft-hearted woman who might just offer some salvation for Hawkett's miserable life. Just had to be her. Who else? Nobody, unless a new suspect popped out of thin air. So now what?

Oh, shit! Grimly he remembered the previous night's conversation with Brightwall. His promise to wrap it up today. Now what? Go back and force Hawkett to confront Jamie right now? Get it over with right now? He could just visualize it, arresting her in front of the child.

"Shit," he muttered out loud to himself.

No, not today. I'll stall for another twenty-four hours, he thought, just like I told Hawkett I would. Put Brightwall off. But tomorrow, definitely by tomorrow, this thing's got to be wrapped up.

Having made this decision, he drove into Pigmy and stopped to visit with Sheriff Spencer. Spencer had nothing new to offer. He was busy making funeral arrangements for Deputy Cog, the first law officer in the county who had lost his life in the line of duty. He had hoped Benjamin was making progress but really seemed to be uninterested in the banker's murder. He started making references to retirement again. No help there.

Benjamin decided to head back to Des Moines, check his apartment, loaf around a while and try to figure out how to stall Brightwall another day.

By the time Hawkett got back to Jamie's farmstead, she and Andrea were already tending to the injured lamb. The lamb struggled, not wanting to be held down, not understanding that their intentions were to help him. Jamie was thankful that it was still small enough that she could control him with one arm while inspecting the wound.

"How's he doing?"

She looked up, startled. "What happened?"

He recounted what had transpired, leaving out the part where he had jumped up from his hiding place, tripped and pretty much made a complete fool out of himself. Hell, he thought, she already knew he was a fool.

She listened, patiently, while examining the lamb's injured leg, prodding and determining the extent of the wound.

"Don't think anything's broke, but he's got a pretty good rip in his hide. Andrea, get my vet box out of the back porch and bring some penicillin from the fridge."

"Peni' what?" replied Andrea.

"Those bottles down in the bottom compartment, you know?"

"Yes."

"Bring one that is filled with white stuff. Okay?"

"Sure, Mom." Andrea raced from the barn. "Well," she looked up at Hawkett. "Darn good thing your partner, Benjamin, was around. He must be a pretty good shot."

"Yeah, he's a marksman. Always wins the best marksmanship awards at the annual DCI shooting tournaments—has for years."

"Is the coyote still up there? I mean did you move it or anything? It is definitely dead, right?"

173

"Oh it's dead alright."

"I suppose I should go up and bury it. I buried that dead ewe this morning. I'm getting to be a regular grave-digger, huh?"

This statement puzzled Hawkett. "How come you're going to bury the dead coyote? I mean, after all, it could be the one that killed your ewe, right?"

"Probably was, yes."

"Then why not leave the damn thing alone, let the environment take care of it for you?"

"Environment," she thought, remembering he'd been married to an animal rights activist. "Oh, I don't think that would be the right thing to do. Heck, the coyote has just as much right to live on this farm as I do, and killing my ewe was just part of its job. That is, I mean, part of its job as a coyote sees life."

He stood there, with a puzzled look on his face, thinking, well hell, it's her farm, her life, but this is just silly.

"Are you upset because we, well Benjamin, killed the coyote?" Hawkett asked.

"No, not at all, I'm very grateful."

"But, well then, why are you making it a point to furnish your enemy with a decent burial so to speak?"

"The coyote wasn't my enemy. Well, coyotes in general are not my enemies. They do a lot of things around this farm that are beneficial, like keeping the rabbit and rodent populations in check for example," explained Jamie.

"I guess I see," Hawkett shrugged.

She knew he didn't. She explained, "To live on a farm, Adam, to be part of its everyday operation, puts farmers in a position where they must deal directly with Mother Nature, usually on her terms. Nothing is black and white. It's a live and let live situation with the farmer always having to do a juggling act. And most farmers are good at it."

He had inadvertently hit on one of her pet peeves, and she could almost feel herself climbing up on a soap box. These damn activists! What the hell did they think farmers were anyway?

The lamb struggled. She tightened her grip.

"Most farmers have to make daily decisions in their operations to help balance their business of food production with the stewardship of the land. Windbreaks, erosion control, water quality, wildlife habitat and other things. These have to be balanced with farm debt, cost of living

174

expenses, government regulations."

"I didn't mean to..."

She interrupted him, a full head of steam going now. "And most farmers do a damn good job of balancing things with Mother Nature despite what you may hear from all those damn environmentalists and damn tree hugging groups and..."

Andrea came running through the door with the items her mother had requested.

Jamie went to work on the lamb, cleaning its wound, applying iodine, much to the lamb's displeasure, and finally, stitching it shut.

Hawkett watched quietly, thinking maybe he should find a shovel and get up there and bury that damn coyote himself. He heard a vehicle coming down the road from beyond Jamie's farmstead and watched as Harley drove by with a load of sweetcorn. He wondered why Harley had come from that direction. Was there sweetcorn to be picked at Cordoe's? Hadn't he said he was going to pick Jamie's sweetcorn? He started to ask Jamie but decided to let it go. Better let her concentrate on the lamb.

Jamie gently handed the lamb to Andrea. The small girl carried her lamb out the barn door talking reassuringly to it all the while.

Jamie turned to Hawkett. "Hey, I'm sorry I got so wound up there about the coyote. All these environmental issues...I don't know. We've been farming this old earth for thousands of years and suddenly everything the farmers do is environmentally questionable. People eat higher-quality, lower-cost food than ever before in history and then after having stuffed themselves at a local fast food joint, they march up and down the street protesting how their food is produced. Those damn vegetarian animal rights groups are the worst. They really get under my skin."

Hawkett remained speechless. He didn't want to get into a debate with her on a subject he knew nothing about. Actually, he didn't want to get into a debate with her period. He was wishing he'd kept quiet in the first place. "Well I'm sorry I brought it up. I didn't mean to upset you."

She looked at him again, searching his eyes. The surprising thing about all of this was that she was starting to get used to him being around. Now that had to be really crazy, but, hell, her whole world had turned crazy. The murder just down the road and her role in that, the coyote, her dead ewe, the injured lamb, this man standing in her barn.

She sighed, wondering if she'd be able to hold up under the pressure of it all. She had to though, there was nowhere to run, no one to turn to.

"Well, do you want me to go bury the coyote?" Hawkett asked.

"No, I'll ride up later."

"Okay, but can I help with anything else?"

"You still want to help?"

"Yes, I want to."

She sighed, trying to clear her head, find a path towards sanity somehow. "Okay, come on."

She led him to a shed west of the barn with a large sliding door in front. She unhooked the door and slid it wide open. Setting inside was a dust-covered, red Chevy pickup. Hawkett reckoned it to be a '69 or '70 model.

"Are you a mechanic?" Jamie questioned.

"Well, somewhat, but not really. What's the matter with it?"

"Beats me, won't start. It's got oil and gas. I can charge the battery up and it turns over good, but it just won't start."

Hawkett lifted the hood apprehensively. He guessed he could at least take a look.

"Have you got any tools?" Hawkett asked.

"On the shelf behind the pickup."

"Well, I can play around a little, give it a try anyway."

"Can't do any better than that. If you need me, give a yell." Having said that, she turned and walked towards the house.

Hawkett spent the next two hours cleaning the spark plugs, adjusting the points and cleaning out filters. After each adjustment, he climbed into the truck, turned the motor over and found that his attempts were unsuccessful. Sometime around midmorning, deciding to make one last attempt before declaring defeat, he crawled into the pickup, pumped the gas pedal twice and hit the switch. It startled him when the motor roared to life. He let it idle for a little while, got out, picked up the tools that he had been using and closed the hood. As the old pickup continued to purr pleasantly, he got in, shifted it into low gear and drove it out into sunlight. He steered the pickup across the barnyard and up to the house and shut off the ignition.

Feeling pretty good about his accomplishment, he climbed from the cab as Jamie and Andrea came trotting out of the house with smiles on their faces.

"You did it; you got the old beast going! How'd you do it?"

Trying to suppress his pride and be modest in the face of her praise was not easy for Hawkett. Getting the pickup started was not that big of a deal, he thought, and yet it seemed to be a big deal for her.

"Oh man, Adam, you can't believe how much easier things will be with the pickup running. Right Andrea?"

The little girl, who by now was seated in the back of the pickup with her dog and lamb, nodded and smiled.

"Well, come on, you guys. I've made some fresh cookies. Let's take a break," Jamie prodded.

He was still basking in the glow of her praise and had to admit he was feeling pretty good about himself.

Benjamin arrived in Des Moines just before noon and stopped at a local fast-food joint to get something to eat. The food proved to be disappointing in comparison to what he had eaten the previous two days.

From there he stopped at his apartment, sorted through his mail then took a two-hour nap. Following the nap, he took a shower, shaved and put on a freshly-cleaned suit. Feeling really top notch, he climbed into the Escort and headed for DCI headquarters, prepared to lock horns with Brightwall.

It took a while to get to Brightwall's office. He had to stop and chat with so many people. Benjamin liked the people he worked with and they liked him, except for Brightwall, of course.

As he traveled the last hallway leading to Brightwall's office, Benjamin began to feel anxious about confronting his boss directly. He had concocted a sort of half-ass story to justify their delay in making an arrest. Brightwall would see the obvious holes in it, and the two men would trade insults, probably loud ones, but that would be okay if it stopped at that. What worried Benjamin was that Brightwall, in his fury, might decide to send other agents to Pigmy to take over. Then things would go to hell. There would be no cover up then. There would be hard, disciplinary action taken against him and Hawkett. Careers would be ended.

With a dark cloud of worry and anger following him, Benjamin entered Brightwall's outer staff office and stopped at his secretary's desk.

"Benjamin," she smiled cheerfully. "Good to see you back! Where's Hawkett?"

"Uh, he's still working the case. We haven't got it quite wrapped up yet. Loose ends...you know? Is the big chief busy? I need to visit with him."

"Sorry, the superintendent's gone for the rest of the day. Doctor's appointment in Omaha. Ulcers. Gone to see his ulcer specialist, I guess. Won't be back in until tomorrow morning."

"Oh, too bad," said Benjamin sarcastically, when in reality, he felt tremendously relieved.

"Want to leave a message in case he calls in?"

"Yeah, uh sure, tell him we need another twenty-four hours to wrap up this little problem down on the farm. He'll understand."

"No problem. I'll give him the message. Hey, you guys having fun playing cops and robbers down on old McDonald's farm?"

He just winked at her. Oh, the stories he could tell.

Benjamin spent the next hour roaming the halls of the DCI building, visiting with several friends. He stopped at his desk, read the daily paper, and worked on the crossword puzzle.

He stopped by the forensic lab for results on the banker's autopsy and his car, but Jenkins, who had been assigned to both jobs, was in court testifying.

Having accomplished almost nothing, and feeling quite good about it, he left the DCI at 5:30 and drove to the nearest shopping center. There he located the toy department and bought a doll for Andrea. He paid for the doll, returned to the Escort and headed to a bar, he had frequented for years, on the east side of Des Moines. It had become almost his home away from home. Benjamin spent several hours drinking beer, playing pool and watching the big screen TV with old friends. Every old friend except for Hawkett, he kept remembering. That thought nagged at him the entire evening. He wondered what was happening down on the farm and hoped they could finalize things tomorrow, try to keep their jobs, and keep Jamie out of jail. He shook his head and set his last empty bottle on the bar as he yelled good night to everyone.

He slept restlessly.

After dinner, inspired by his mechanical success with the pickup, Hawkett offered himself for further work detail.

Jamie decided to take a chance and let him try to mow the rest of her standing alfalfa. Yeah, she thought, this guy who's supposed to be

178

investigating a murder, mowing my hay. That damn Cordoe.

She spent an hour showing him how to operate the old John Deere, reminding him again and again how careful one had to be working around machinery. Reminding him that farming was, in fact, the most dangerous occupation in the United States.

She was impressed by how fast he got the hang of running the tractor and stood watching as he drove around the perimeter of the hay field, the mower cutting down swathes of alfalfa as the tractor popped along.

After a dinner of fried chicken, deviled eggs and iced tea, Hawkett returned to the pasture to mow more hay. Allowing him to mow hay, left Jamie time to tend to the other things that needed attention around the farm. She spent the afternoon weeding her garden, doing laundry and fixing a hole in the fence around the chicken pen. She continued to keep an eye on Hawkett and Andrea and that proved to be a challenge, but an enjoyable one. It reminded her of when Bud had been alive and that sobered her thoughts.

At mid-afternoon she sent Andrea out to deliver a thermos of iced tea and some cookies to Hawkett who was still mowing in the hay field. The girl was warned to stay well away from the tractor and wait until Hawkett stopped the machine, stepped down from it and came to her, and that is exactly what she did. Hawkett spotted the little girl from a distance. He pulled the hand clutch back on the tractor, locked the brakes and shut the machine off. He stretched, checked his sunburn and waved at Andrea. With Junior at her heels, she trotted toward him with the tea and cookies.

Hawkett's throat was dry and the tea tasted wonderful. He gulped down a couple of the cookies while Andrea chatted about her dog, the tractor and her life in general.

"How's your lamb doing? His leg okay?"

"Well, it sure hurts I think, but he can limp on the other three. See he has four legs, okay?"

Hawkett shook his head up and down trying not to smile.

"Anyway, Mom says he's gonna be okay, but he'll have to take it easy for a while, and Hawkett?"

"What?"

"You did kill that coyote, right?"

"Well, no, I didn't actually; my friend Benjamin did."

"But it's dead; it won't come after Junior anymore, right?"

"That's right. You keep Junior in around the buildings, and he'll be safe."

"Good! Because if that coyote comes to our house to get Junior, I'm gonna take Dad's gun and shoot it the way Mom did that guy..." She stopped, the anger in her eyes was replaced with anxiety. She quickly covered her mouth and stared at Hawkett nervously.

Hawkett's facial expression had changed as well. His pleasant smile was replaced with an expression of concern.

"Shot what guy, kiddo?"

"I wasn't s'pose to say nothing about it. Don't tell Mom, okay? She swore me to not say anything."

Now what's this all about wondered Hawkett. Who the hell had been shot? The banker had been stabbed. There had been no mention of any gunshot wounds. Denny? Could she have shot Denny? When? Where?

He decided to carefully question the little girl some more.

"Andrea..."

"I gotta go. See ya." The little girl and her dog took off, running across the freshly-mowed hay toward the house.

Hawkett stood there, his hands resting on his hips, wondering who the hell had been shot.

CHAPTER

31

Hawkett helped Jamie finish the supper dishes. Only three days prior, he hadn't even known that she existed and now they stood next to each other, him washing, her drying. From the window over the sink they could see Andrea playing with Jack and Junior in the front yard. Andrea had a frisbee. When she threw it, Jack would sprint after it and leap in the air to retrieve it in his mouth, ascending nearly four feet in the air to perform the feat. The small lamb, despite his injured leg, sprinted back and forth across the green lawn, leaping, kicking and twisting in the air. Then he trotted around behind Andrea, lowered his head and playfully butted her in the back of her leg. Surprised, she spun around and grabbed the lamb by his midsection; then the lamb and girl rolled across the grass, her laughter filling the air.

Hawkett watched, in disbelief. He was astonished by the activities that this little girl found in her limited environment, and the joy that they brought her. Afterall, she had no brothers or sisters. She didn't rely on a TV set or video games, or a mall loaded with thousands of other items that she didn't really need. Limited environment? Maybe he had it all backwards.

He couldn't help wishing he'd grown up on a farm. Not that his parents and home life had been inadequate. Just the opposite. He'd had two devoted parents and a home in which to grow and enjoy a nurturing childhood. Still, city life seemed choked and constrained in comparison to the life here on the farm. Somehow tenser, faster...yet.

She nudged his shoulder. "Hey, wake up. What are you day-dreaming about?"

He smiled. He'd been standing there, dumbstruck, staring out her window. "Oh, just watching her play, I guess, I don't know, soaking in her happiness. I think you must be a very good mother."

The last statement he'd made with more feeling than he'd planned. As had been his experience the last few days, many times, the words flowing from his mouth had seemed to be coming from a stranger.

Apparently, the statement, or his tone, or maybe both, had touched her, because a tear appeared in the corner of her eye and Hawkett had the notion that she might just give him a hug. That wouldn't have bothered him at all, but she didn't. Instead, she involuntarily dabbed her dish towel across her eye and turned and moved across the kitchen to put away the rest of the silverware.

And momentarily, once again, the awkward silence lingered. Two adults, unsure of themselves, unsure of their relationship to each other. Always the unspoken question: Where from here?

And the controversy, thought Hawkett, me being a detective, her being, well he had to admit it, probably the most-likely suspect in a brutal murder. That thought sure took the smile off of his face. How could he tell a woman that he thinks she's a great mother but might also be guilty of a violent murder. He knew nothing would ever really be clear between them until the cloud of this murder investigation had lifted. He knew that she knew it too. Depression once again started to seep into his feelings as he thought about this woman who attracted him deeply, both physically and emotionally, possibly being a murderess. If so, it would be consistent with the way his life had gone so far. Maybe he was just meant to be a loser.

"Adam," she broke his depressing train of thought.

He turned. She was leaning against the counter, her arms crossed and locked. She had a "let's get down to business" look on her face. Tension in her eyes, apparent in her body language.

182

"There are some things about my relationship with Doug Cordoe..." she stopped. "I'm afraid I probably haven't been as frank as I should, but I had my reasons. You see..."

She was interrupted by a banging screen door as Andrea, always full of energy, sprinted into the kitchen. Hawkett was greatly relieved. He didn't want to hear, didn't want to know the truth.

"Hey, let's go fishing. Hawkett, you a fisher guy? We got a pond with bluegills and bullheads, and it's really fun, so let's go okay?" Andrea pleaded.

Jamie looked at Hawkett. Hawkett looked at Andrea's eager face.

"Yeah, sure, I mean..." he stopped and turned to Jamie again, "Is that okay with you?"

Jamie, who had prepared herself for a serious conversation just moments before, was now melting, unable to complete a dreaded task. She decided to put it off. They would have this talk later. It could wait. Still, she felt guilty for so easily giving into procrastination.

"Sure, let's do it. But hey, you got any worms?"

"No, but I know where to dig some if Hawkett could maybe help me, okay?"

And so Hawkett did, accompanying Andrea to a shady spot on the backside of the chicken house. There, using a pitchfork with a broken handle, he turned up rich chunks of soil and Andrea snatched fat worms, until they had captured a dozen.

The pond lay in a draw up the hill from the house. Hawkett and Andrea, equipped with two bamboo fishing poles, a can of worms and a small tackle box walked up to the pond, Andrea, jabbering constantly, Hawkett enjoying her stories and observations. Jamie had promised she would join them shortly after checking her ewes.

The pond had a small dock made out of heavy wooden poles and planks which traveled nearly twenty feet out from the dam. Andrea led Hawkett out onto the dock explaining as they walked that she was only allowed to be on it with an adult.

The little girl patiently showed him how to unwind his line from the pole, attach a fat red and white bobber and secure the bait on the hook.

Both Andrea and Hawkett, seated with their legs dangling over the side of the dock, watched quietly as their bobbers floated motionlessly on the water's surface. Andrea had become quiet, and Hawkett wondered if something was bothering her or if she was just a quiet fisher.

Watching the bobber gently roll on the water was therapeutic for Hawkett. He could almost feel some of his sore muscles start to relax. He tried to think of a question to ask the little girl, get her talking, enjoy her chatter, tease her a little.

He turned and looked at her once again. She sat there, rigid, quietly staring out at the bobber on her line as it silently rolled on the pond's placid surface. He turned to look at his bobber, but it was gone.

"Where?"

"What?"

"My bobber's gone," and as he said that, his line tightened and the end of his pole bent deeply downward.

"Pull! Pull! Yank your pole, hook him!" the little girl yelled excitedly.

And Hawkett pulled, feeling resistance as the underwater bandit pulled back, now hooked.

"Pull him toward us and stand up," ordered Andrea, now standing beside him.

Hawkett clumsily stood up and pulled the fishing line up out of the water watching as the bobber appeared, followed by a fat, yellow and black fish.

He brought the line around to where Andrea could reach it. She grabbed it and finished retrieving the fish. She held the fish carefully so as to avoid getting jabbed by its fins and tried to remove the hook. After a few minutes of unsuccessful manipulation, she handed the fish to Hawkett who, with some difficulty, removed the hook from the fish's gill.

"What now?"

"Throw it back in."

"We're not going to keep any?"

"Not unless they get hurt bad by the hook. We got plenty in the freezer and Mom says not to keep anymore till we get them eaten up."

So Hawkett dropped the fish back into the pond water where it immediately swam away.

Within an hour, the two fishermen had caught four more bullheads and three bluegills, Andrea keeping close track of who was catching the most fish, and Hawkett playfully kidding her about it.

Finally, Jamie came walking up the hill carrying something

around her neck, and Hawkett could tell as she got closer that it was a camera.

"Catching any?"

"We sure did, Mom, I've caught five and Hawkett's caught two, but I told him not to feel bad cuz I've been fishing longer and kinda know how. You know?"

"Oh, I think you're probably just lucky tonight."

She looked at Hawkett. "Been getting quite a bit of advice from Chatty Kathy here?"

"Oh, yeah. We've been having a good time."

"Well, good."

"What are you doing with the camera, Mom?"

"I wanted to take a picture of you with your fishing pole, okay? Something to show my grandchildren twenty or thirty years from now. Okay?"

Andrea smiled sheepishly, "Sure, Mom."

She sat back down on the dock and posed with her fishing pole while Jamie took a couple of shots.

"Hey, Mom, how about a picture of me and Hawkett? Huh?"

"Sure, sounds great to me."

The little girl got up, went over to where Hawkett sat and stood beside him.

"Smile, you two."

They smiled and Jamie took their picture. "Okay, Mom, now I'll take one of you and Hawkett, okay?"

"Well sure, if it's okay with Adam."

"Sure," he replied awkwardly.

Jamie set the camera, gave Andrea her orders, then handed the camera to her daughter. She turned and walked back to pose by Hawkett who was now standing.

"Closer," the little girl ordered.

Jamie smiled at Hawkett and sidestepped a little closer, until their bodies just touched.

Hawkett could feel her, could smell her, wanted to hold her.

"Smile!"

The camera clicked.

Andrea handed the camera to her mother, then turned and looked at the pond. "I'm gonna skip some rocks, okay Mom?"

"Sure, but you remember the rule."

185

"Yeah, I know, ten steps away from the edge of the water."

"Don't forget."

"Okay, Mother," a tone of resentment rang in her voice.

Well, thought Hawkett, there's no such thing as a perfect child, though this kid had to be close.

Andrea worked along the pond bank, picking up flat rocks and tossing them across the pond surface, trying to make them skip.

Hawkett and Jamie sat on the dock, their feet dangling above the pond surface.

They visited about the pond, fishing, eating fish and fish in general. He kept trying to think of more questions, keep her talking about anything other than what they should be talking about. He dreaded the truth. It would come eventually, but until it did, he wanted to enjoy being with her. Just being with her was one of the most enjoyable things he'd ever done in his whole life.

Andrea had ventured nearly halfway around the pond. She was near a rocky spot just where the pond's edge butted against the rising hillside.

Up over the bank, in a dense thicket of scrub cedar trees, a solitary figure lay flat on his belly, barely moving. Denny's eyes followed the little girl's movements below, darkness in his heart. He was remembering last night, how this man, sitting with Jamie now, had ruined his plans, chased him off. His anger grew. He tried to estimate the time it would take for Hawkett to get around to this side of the pond. He carefully fingered the heavy club lying on the ground beside him. He knew he could leap down the bank, club the girl in the head and be gone. Show the big-shot just how he, Denny, could get revenge. Yeah, a mean smile creased into his dirty face. Yeah, he'd show that smart ass. Slowly, ever so slowly, he started to rise to his knees.

Jack had fallen asleep on the dock between Jamie and Hawkett. He was a very loyal dog, but even a loyal dog grew tired once in a while. He was lying there, peacefully dreaming about herding a flock of sheep, his favorite job on the farm, when the wind changed directions. The wind brought with it a smell that brought the dream to a halt and woke him.

The smell was laced with danger. He stood up and growled, his hair bristling. His nose, like radar, tracked the odor in the direction of Andrea and he sprinted away.

Hawkett and Jamie stood up, surprised by the dog's actions.

"Something's wrong," was all Jamie said and she trotted up the dock and around the pond's edge. Hawkett, though perplexed, followed after her slowly.

Shit, thought Denny, the damn dog. He spun and ran swiftly and quietly up the hillside, staying in dense cover.

Jack ran beyond Andrea, stared up the hillside and released a few threatening barks. Then, he turned and trotted back to Andrea where she scratched his ears and he licked at her fingers.

"What's wrong, boy?" asked Andrea as she stared up the hillside.

By that time, Jamie had reached the child and was calming down. Probably she thought, some animal, a coyote perhaps, that the dog had smelled.

Hawkett joined the two, still not quite sure what to make of the situation. "What's up?"

"I don't know. Jack doesn't usually act like that unless he's seriously upset. Probably a raccoon or something up there in the brush. He can sure smell it." She looked at the dog who was still staring up the hillside, anger in his eyes.

"I'll take a look." Hawkett began to work his way up the slope, the heavy thicket dragging at his body.

"Be careful, sometimes animals can have rabies."

Rabies, hell he thought, that'd just be his luck. Get bit in the ass by some rabid squirrel and...he froze. He was no great tracker, but he knew human imprints when he saw them. A chill went down his backbone as his eyes carefully searched the area in the direction of the footprints. It was scary. They were being stalked by a madman. That this madman might attempt to hurt Andrea and Jamie made his blood boil. Anger consumed him. He carefully scanned the horizon but saw nothing.

He turned and walked back down to the pond.

She could see the change in his face, his mood, immediately.

"Nothing," he said, trying to sound lighthearted but failing miserably.

She gave him a puzzled look.

"Later," he replied quietly.

She nodded, her face losing some of its color.

"Hey," he said, trying to be upbeat, "let's walk back down to the house and have some of that apple pie. What do ya say?"

"Yeah," chirped Andrea, "with ice cream on top."

"Sounds great," Jamie said with apprehension in her voice. The three started back toward the dock.

Hawkett stopped, kneeled down and called softly to the border collie. The dog trotted over and was rewarded by Hawkett stroking and petting him.

"Good boy," he whispered quietly.

Jack knew exactly why he had been rewarded, and proudly trotted ahead to catch up with Andrea. It was a dog's life, but he loved it.

They retrieved the poles and the tackle box and released the remaining worms. Together they walked down the hillside as shadows were beginning to darken the landscape, creeping across the valley floor. Andrea, walking next to her mother, reached up, and they joined their free hands. Jamie smiled down at her daughter, then turned and with her other hand reached out and grasped Hawkett's. She smiled and glanced, almost inquiringly, into his eyes and he smiled back. Silently they walked to the house, Hawkett, feeling strong, emotional waves flow through his body. Love he guessed. It was, almost, he thought, like they were a family. Something pure and strong and forever. Something to hold onto.

CHAPTER

32

Back at the house, Jamie busied herself with the task of getting Andrea to take a bath. The little girl was tired and grouchy but soon found herself bathed, dressed and in her bed. Hawkett, sitting on the porch swing, could hear Jamie reading a book to her child. He closed his eyes and took a deep breath of the fresh air. His head felt clear, his mind focused. Action had to be taken. The shroud of mystery hanging over this whole situation had to be lifted. The potential danger imposed by this crazy bastard Denny Cordoe must be ended. He could clear this up, he knew it. If Cordoc had to bc killed, so be it. IIe would do anything to protect Jamie and the child. If he should find that she was involved in the murder of the older Cordoe, he'd stand by her. It would be some sort of self defense. He knew it. Get a good lawyer. That'd be the first thing. Then he'd...

She walked out the screen door and stared up into the star-filled sky.

"Andrea in slumberland?"

"Yeah. Up by the pond, what did you see?"

189

"Footprints, human."

"Denny?"

"Probably. Barefoot, adult, who else?"

"Damn," she was upset now. Anger in her eyes. "To think that crazy animal was that close to my child." She shivered and wrapped her arms around herself.

Neither person spoke for nearly a minute. The silence grew uncomfortable. She turned, walked over to the swing and sat down by Hawkett. He wrapped an arm around her shoulder and they rocked back and forth silently for a few moments, staring out at the farmyard, bathed in moonlight.

"Adam?"

"Yeah?"

"Tell me about your life."

"Where do I start?"

"From the beginning."

So Hawkett, feeling more open and relaxed than he felt in years, gave her a brief narrative of his childhood, school days, his marriage to Ann and his decision to join the DCI. She listened intently, interrupting frequently, wanting further information, questioning often. She was especially interested in his relationship with Ann, their marriage, what went wrong.

They talked for nearly two hours, sometimes Hawkett, quieting, would be egged on by Jamie's prodding questions.

He held nothing back from her. His rotten relationship with Ann, the divorce, her career, their last confrontation.

And it felt good, damn good to talk it out, share it with her. She seemed to soak up his pain like a sponge. She acted like his past failures belonged to her, gently prying, wanting to understand, no guilt assigned.

A coyote screamed in the distance, breaking their dialogue.

"Hey" Jamie said.

"What?"

"Want something to drink?"

"Sure, all this gabbing makes a guy thirsty."

She got up, went in the house and returned with two tall glasses of chilled apple juice. The flavor was wonderful and Hawkett enjoyed it immensely.

"So, how about you?"

She smiled, "What about me?"

"Hey, this is the night of true confessions, let's hear it."

She searched his eyes for a little bit looking for something, then seemed to make a decision. "Okay, but this isn't going to be easy for me, okay?"

He hugged her. "I understand."

And as Hawkett had done, she gave a sketch of her life, her marriage to Bud, the birth of Andrea. When she got to the part about the problems with the farm, how Bud dealt with it, her tone changed and she spoke in broken sentences. One tear after another seeped from her eyes, but she continued on, almost forcing herself to speak. Finding Bud hanging in the barn, trying to cut him down. The ambulance, trying to revive him. Explaining it to two-year-old Andrea. The guilt, the frustration.

"We had an auction and sold all the machinery. That and life insurance benefits helped free us of any debt. I thought about moving away, but I love the animals, and it seems like a good place to raise Andrea." She stopped talking, but only momentarily.

"So now, we just take it one day at a time. Try to find all the joy we can. I'm not getting rich, but we're doing pretty well. Some money is being saved for a rainy day or Andrea's college education. I don't know, maybe we should move to the city, try to find a higher paying occupation. What do you think?"

Hawkett smiled to himself. There was no doubt in his mind what the answer to that question should be. He could spend an hour listing all of the reasons that she had for staying on the farm and continuing to raise her child there.

"No," he kept it short, "you belong here; Andrea belongs here. This farm, these animals, they need you, your care. This is your place in the world. Don't ever leave it."

He stood up and reached for her hand. She stood up as well. They came together, entwined in each other's arms, eagerly finding each other. He kissed her. It was a long, trusting kiss.

"Well, do we know each other now?"

She smiled, "We're getting there."

"It's getting late."

He looked at her inquiringly. She knew what the unspoken question was.

"Nope."

"Nope what?"

"You're not sleeping in my bed tonight."

He looked hurt. "I didn't..."

"I know, but you were thinking it, right?"

He couldn't lie to her.

"I like you, Adam. Maybe I like you a lot. Maybe more than just like. Maybe a seed has been planted that could grow into something really special. But things are moving pretty fast, wouldn't you agree?"

He nodded ever so slightly.

"I'm not complaining, but..." The sentence went unfinished as if she couldn't quite find the right words. "Well, one thing I know. Any man who shares my bed with me will be one committed to sharing his entire life with me." She stretched up on her toes and kissed him gently on the cheek then turned and walked through the screen porch door. She spun around to make one last remark. "And believe me, I'm worth it. Good night, Adam."

Hawkett had a hard time getting to sleep that night, the barn floor somehow seeming harder than the night before. His mind was completely consumed by thoughts of Jamie, what had been, what might be.

CHAPTER
33

Hawkett was interrupted from deep sleep by one of Jamie's roosters crowing his version of "Reveille." Actually, it was the second awakening for Hawkett. He'd been roused earlier by the sound of Jamie riding away on her horse. He wondered if that was how she started each day. He peeked out the barn's haymow window, trying to spot the rooster. Worse than a damn alarm clock. He lay back down on his make-shift bed and stared at the barn roof above, content, feeling rested. Life was good.

But the mood died as he came back to reality. The precious time he'd spent with Jamie, time when they'd ignored his real reason for coming here in the first place, was past. Today, they must deal with the harsh reality of the situation. A man had been murdered. Somehow she'd been involved. Their relationship could go no further until she came clean with him as to just what her role in this death had been. Thinking about it made him heartsick.

He rose from his bed, put his clothes on and climbed down to the barn floor below. As Hawkett walked toward the house, he spotted

Jamie. She was riding the horse back down the trail from the hill where Benjamin had shot the coyote not twenty-four hours earlier. She'd been true to her pledge of burying the coyote. She had something bouncing over her left shoulder and as she came closer, he realized it was a shovel. He stood there watching the lady gallop toward him, the big black and white paint horse floating over the green pasture. With the blue sky and rising sun in the background, he couldn't help but think of it all as a beautiful picture. A beautiful, living picture.

He was smiling at first, but then he returned to reality and frowned. Murderer. He remembered her gently handling the new baby lambs he'd helped deliver. He remembered her hugging her daughter. He remembered the pain in her face when she'd found the dead ewe. He remembered when they'd danced in the barn. Could this woman be a killer? Could she thrust a pitchfork through a man's chest. It'd been an accident, yeah it had to be. Hell, he thought, maybe she didn't do it. But if she didn't, then who did? Was Benjamin sure? Benjamin was never very fast, but he was generally pretty accurate. His thoughts darkened even more thinking of Benjamin, his promise to give Hawkett twenty-four hours to solve things. The twenty-four hours were up.

She cantered the horse right up to where he stood and just as he was about to leap out of the way, she braked the horse on a dime. She could see the look of deep concern on his face as she jumped off the horse and headed toward the barn, leaning the shovel against it. Now what, she wondered.

"Good morning, Adam," she said in a cheery, upbeat voice. "How's the back this morning?"

Benjamin, puffing on his second cigar of the morning, sat quietly in his car and carefully observed the Cordoe farmstead once again. He'd had a restless night, troubled by what he knew was going to transpire the next day. He'd left Des Moines at 5:00 AM. Breakfast had been at June's. He'd intended to go directly to Jamie's farm but had bypassed it and had driven to the end of the dead end road, thinking maybe he could get one last try at Denny Cordoe, maybe catch him. Try to tie the murder to that helpless bastard. He'd be better off in some institution anyway. But, of course, he knew that wouldn't do. The truth was the truth, and he just knew Jamie was tied to this murder somehow. Most likely she'd committed it. He glanced at his watch; Hawkett's twenty-four hours were over. He sighed. No sign of Denny. He wasn't really sure why he'd come back here. Even if Denny was around, even if he could catch the guy again, what would he tell him? Could he trust the maniac?

He climbed out of the car, stretched, and decided to snoop around. Kill time until Hawkett got his act together. It was going to be tough arresting her; he wasn't looking forward to it. A painful grimace came over his face as he remembered her daughter, Andrea. Something would have to be done with the child. "Damn," he swore out loud to nobody, shook his head back and forth, and ground his cigar out on the gravel beneath his feet.

He carefully worked his way through the tall weeds and garbage toward the trailer house. Benjamin peeked in some of the windows but could barely see through the filthy glass. He really didn't think Denny was in there anyway. Crazy bastard was probably out in the timber somewhere, slithering around. Probably watching me right now, he thought, and that thought sent a shiver up his spine. For some reason, Benjamin wished he had his shotgun in hand. He shook his head again as he carefully studied the terrain around him, the run-down farmstead. Silly. The crazy guy was just that, crazy. Not dangerous. Still he had this feeling.

Benjamin walked around to the back of the trailer and was surprised to find a well-worn trail. It started at the back door of the trailer and extended out through the tall weeds, so tall he couldn't tell where it led. Just for the hell of it, he decided to see where it went, and when he found the short trail's destination, he chuckled out loud. An outhouse, an old wooden outhouse. So the poor bastard hadn't even had an indoor toilet. Benjamin reminisced. It had been probably forty years since he'd seen a real outhouse, the toilets of early rural Americans. He could remember as a child staying at his grandfather's farm one Christmas vacation. He recalled feeling utterly shocked, as a child, upon being told where the bathroom was. He remembered sprinting out there on cold mornings. You didn't fool around, he thought, no sir.

The door on this outhouse even had a half moon cut out of it. He'd heard most of them didn't. So this, he mused, must be a first-rate outhouse or had been at one time. Actually, it was probably the only structure in fairly good repair on the Cordoe farmstead, with one exception, the door. It hung just slightly ajar, and for some reason that bothered Benjamin. Like a crooked picture hanging on a wall, he felt a compelling urge to straighten it. He walked up to the small building and took hold of the door handle, planning to lift and push, thereby placing the door squarely into its frame. But that didn't happen. Instead when he lifted up on the door handle, the door flew towards him, propelled from the other side. Propelled by the weight of Denny Cordoe's body leaning on the other side.

Benjamin jumped back, cursing out loud, his heart pumping. He stared in disbelief at the corpse laying on the ground at his feet. He checked for a pulse in Cordoe's neck, but he knew that was a waste of time. This guy was dead. Somebody had beaten the hell out of him. His head was a bloody mess, one ear cut nearly clear off, the skull badly bludgeoned. Both eyeballs were slightly popped out of their sockets indicating that he'd endured a powerful blow to the head.

He cursed again, this time not from surprise, but rather from disgust. Hells bells, he thought, now what? Two dead bodies. And shit, he thought, this body hasn't been dead long. Pretty damn quick he had his shotgun in hand and was working his way around the buildings, peeking through the weeds. He kicked the door open on the trailer house and searched it as well. Satisfied that nobody was around, Benjamin walked back to the car, laid the shotgun gently on the hood and lit a cigar. He puffed on the cigar while observing the surrounding landscape, trying to piece things together. Was Hawkett in on this? Had he helped her? Why would she have killed the son as well? Hell yes, the son had seen her kill his father. Denny had said something like that after Benjamin had flushed him out of the tree. Probably blackmailed her, stupid shit. Man, oh man, what a mess. It'd be damn hard to keep Hawkett out of it now.

Benjamin was disgusted, but more than that he was heartbroken. Hawkett had been more than a partner. He'd been Benjamin's family, the son he'd never had. Now the scenario lying ahead looked bad, real bad. Hawkett, some sort of accessory to murder, Jamie two counts murder, Andrea in a foster family. He shook his head and wiped the tears of anger and hurt from his eyes. And his own career, he knew, would be finished. Brightwall had him now, there was no way out. He couldn't ever remember being in this bad of a jam. And no way out that he could think of. He blamed himself. He should have drug Hawk off of her farm. My fault, yes, he thought.

He threw the cigar on the gravel and smashed it with his wing tip. He was surprised to notice a strong aroma of wildflowers, wafting from somewhere nearby. He took a deep breath and inhaled the fragrant, fresh air. Birds were singing, the scenery was gorgeous, and a beautiful blue sky lay overhead. How could things have gone to such hell in a place as beautiful as this little farming community?

CHAPTER
34

Hawkett walked out onto the front porch carrying a cup of coffee with him. The aroma of curing hay he'd mowed the day before filled the air. He stared out across the mowed hay field, proud of his work, feeling a strong sense of accomplishment. That felt good. He felt good. Jamie looked beautiful. He and Jamie had shared a quiet breakfast of poached eggs and toast. It was going to be another beautiful day. Still, the knowledge of what had to be dealt with that day weighed heavily on his mind. They must end their fantasy, deal with reality. He would have to confront her about the death of this banker. That was very depressing. So much for the beautiful day ahead.

He saw Jamie and Andrea walking into the barn, Andrea lugging her injured lamb. He finished the coffee, set the cup down on the porch railing and walked toward the barn to see what they were doing. Inside the barn, Andrea sat on a bale of hay while her mother examined the lamb's injured leg. Seeing the mother and daughter working together in a cooperative manner was an enjoyable experience for Hawkett. Where the idea came from he had no idea. It just popped into his head. Hawkett, still on an emotional roller coaster, suddenly had a wish. He wished he could tear down all the cities, their suburbs, their ghettos; tear them down and move all those desperate boxed-in people out to farm country. Smash the video games the kids sat glued in front of. Starve the drug dealers who sold the kids drugs. Break up all the gangs and spread them out over the countryside. Give them fresh air to breath, endless fields to roam and play. Give them chores, responsibility, effort, purpose. Yes, that was it. Purpose.

That's what society was losing. Purpose. The mind couldn't exist in a healthy state without it, and society was steadily destroying purpose in its children. Society was on the brink of becoming completely computerized, destroying any need for people to think, only to analyze. Analyze endless printouts, endless statistics, endless despair. People didn't need that, no. What they needed was purpose, hope too, maybe. Goals, work, good physical work.

He thought again of the millions upon millions of overweight American children plopped on their couches glued to television sets. For many, the TV had become their surrogate parents. It filled them up with children's shows in the daytime, then polluted them with red hot sex and violent murder in the evening. "Damn," he cursed under his breath, but evidently loud enough that the two females working on the lamb both immediately looked at him.

He was embarrassed, looking into their inquisitive eyes, hell the lamb was even looking at him. "Nothing, I'm sorry. Talking to myself again."

"That coyote's dead, isn't it, Adam?" Andrea asked again.

"Yep, it's dead alright." He turned and walked out of the barn and into the light of the warm, mid-morning sun.

"Well, now what?" he asked himself. He moved back from the sun into the shade of the barn and sat down on a sawhorse. The old Brittany bird dog appeared from around the corner of the barn and trotted up to Hawkett. It stood squarely in front of him, looked up inquiringly, then sat on its haunches. Hawkett reached down and scratched the dog behind its ears. The old dog's mouth dropped open in a smile. The animals, all these animals, he thought, if she goes to prison, who will take care of them? Besides Andrea, she'd said, they were all she had, her animals. Then he had an idea. Maybe he could take care of them until she... He stopped. He felt guilty for assuming that she was guilty. But Benjamin had seemed so damn sure. He tried to remember a case in which Ben had been that positive of the guilt of anybody. Had he been wrong before? Sadly as he looked back over the years, he couldn't recall an instance of that type. When Benjamin was sure, he was dead sure.

Benjamin spotted Hawkett and drove right up to the barn. He rolled down his window and poked his head out.

"You alone?"

Hawkett motioned towards the barn door beside him. Benjamin understood.

"Hop in the car, would you?"

Hawkett rose, brushed off his backside, walked around and climbed into the car, its air conditioner already on high. He shivered.

"What's up?"

"I just found young Cordoe, beaten to death."

Hawkett's heart sank with the implication. The only other possible suspect was now a victim and Jamie's position looked even worse.

"Where?"

"Right down the road there." Benjamin pointed towards the Cordoe farmstead. "He was shoved into an old outhouse. I don't know for sure if he was killed in there or if somebody moved his body there."

"Stiff? Any idea when..."

"Son of a bitch was still slightly warm. He's been killed this morning. You been out hunting more coyotes?"

"Hey, I didn't..."

"I know!" Benjamin snapped back. "But somebody killed the miserable son of a bitch!"

The two men sat in silence for nearly a minute as they stared out the front window of the car, trying to collect their thoughts, make some sense of this mess.

"Well?" Benjamin broke the silence.

"Well, what?"

"Well, where the hell has your girlfriend been all morning?" he snarled, patience gone.

"I don't...well, she left early. Rode that horse." He pointed at the Paint gelding standing in a lot adjacent to the barn. "She went to bury the coyote you shot yesterday."

"Took a shovel, I suppose?"

"Yeah, sure..." Hawkett stopped. His voice dropped. "You think

200

she attacked him with a shovel?"

"Well, hell, somebody sure as hell attacked him with something and I suppose a shovel would do the job. How long was she gone?"

"I don't know, she left early. I was kind of groggy, still half asleep, lying up there in the haymow."

Benjamin turned to look at Hawkett, one eyebrow cocked upwards. "You spent the night in the barn?"

"Yeah, she well, I mean, there's been no hanky panky. She uh," Hawkett shrugged and said no more.

Benjamin thinking to himself, that's good, no sex entanglement. "Okay, okay, where's the shovel now?"

Hawkett turned his eyes toward the barn, and Benjamin followed his gaze towards the shovel propped there.

"You gonna get it or shall I?"

Hawkett didn't respond but opened the car door, stepped out and walked to the shovel leaning against the barn. He peeked through a nearby window and could see Andrea and Jamie still working with the injured lamb.

He heard Benjamin's door open as he started to reach for the shovel.

"Fingerprints," Benjamin hissed and Hawkett stopped.

Benjamin walked up, drew a handkerchief from his pocket and grasped the handle. It was awkward carrying it that way, but he managed to carefully lift and place it into the backseat of the Escort. Still, Jamie was oblivious to what was going on outside her barn. Hawkett felt like a traitor.

Benjamin dusted off his hands and looked at his partner. "Okay, let's go."

Hawkett didn't reply, just stood there staring at Benjamin.

Benjamin turned, looked the other way and raised his hands to the sky, "Hells, bells, you idiot," he turned to Hawkett again. "Hawk, we've screwed up this whole investigation. There's going to be hell to pay. Come on, let's get the hell out of here now. She's killed twice now. Probably the little bastard tried to blackmail her, saw her murder his father. You can't help her. I can't help her."

And then for the first time, in a long time, Hawkett regained his feeling of purpose. The haze of befuddlement clouding his mind evaporated. His tense muscles relaxed, shoulders dropped slightly. He took a deep breath. Suddenly the maze that had been formed by his thoughts and feelings became clear. He took another deep breath and turned back towards Benjamin.

"Okay, I'm sorry, I've been a real jackass."

"Damn right, you have," replied Benjamin, but felt his anger drop with the utter of each word. "So let's get the hell out of here..."

"No," interrupted Hawkett. Before Benjamin could fire back, he held up a hand. "I'll stay here and talk to her, reason with her, straighten out what happened. I don't think she'll lie to me. Come back in a couple of hours, say about eleven, eleven thirty. I'll get her to confess, turn herself in to Sheriff Spencer. We'll keep an eye on her. I'll go with her if she wants, stay with Andrea if she wants, I don't know."

Benjamin was running the scenario through his mind. Her confession. His reporting to Brightwall. Keep the mechanics of the investigation hazy, he thought, but leave an image that they played a strong role in its success. Well, hell they had. Except they'd probably broken half the department's regulations. There would still be the damn reports to fill out, but hell, that'd never been a problem before. Benjamin was a pro at report doctoring. Still things could get messy. Interrogating her might reveal some embarrassing facts. Lord, he grimaced, remembering they'd helped a murderess bale hay. Still, maybe he could conjure reasons for their bizarre actions. Undercover work, that sort of thing. Yeah, he could do that. He pulled a cigar out, lit it, and took a draw.

"Okay Hawk," he said as he looked at his watch. "See you at noon. I'll be in town, probably at the sheriff's office. I'll hold off on reporting the death of young Cordoe; he isn't going anywhere. I'll call Brightwall and tell him we're wrapping this thing up. Okay?"

With that said, Benjamin climbed back into the Escort, turned around, and drove up Dead End Road toward Pigmy.

CHAPTER
35

Hawkett watched Benjamin drive away, a trail of dust rolled out from behind the car. He felt beads of sweat trekking down the side of his forehead and his armpits were soaked. It was turning into another hot, humid day, but that wasn't the primary reason he was sweating. He knew that. But still, his perception of what lay ahead remained clear and his resolution of seeing it through was solid. Rock solid. He would stick with her, fight for her every step of the way. Her defense, her child, her farm. Whatever it took. Why? Out of love, he decided. He turned back toward the barn, walked through the door, and almost ran right into Jamie coming out.

"Who was in the car?"

"Benjamin."

"Oh," she sensed something in the tone of his voice, saw something in his eyes. Suddenly she felt very apprehensive, felt like he had some really bad news to tell her. She almost shuddered.

Softly he said to Andrea, "Hey kiddo, how about going to the house for a little bit? I want to visit with your mom."

"Sure, Adam." Surprisingly she replied with no argument, no questions. She grunted as she picked up the injured lamb, his leg now rewrapped with fresh tape and smelling of iodine, and lugged the pet out the barn door.

Both adults watched her go.

Jamie looked back at Hawkett. The two stood less then a foot apart. Hawkett stepped forward, reached around her and hugged her to his body. She gave no resistance and returned the embrace. They stood there, in each other's arms for several moments, then she pulled back slightly and looked up into Hawkett's eyes.

"What, Adam, what do we need to talk about?" She knew the answer to that question. She just didn't want to face the issue. Not now, not ever.

He looked into her eyes. Brown, deep brown eyes. Hawkett took a deep breath; this was going to be tough.

"Benjamin and I were just talking. He had some bad news. He, uh, found young Cordoe, Denny that is, dead."

She gasped, put one hand over her mouth. Hawkett could see her turning paler.

"How?"

"Murdered."

Now she was trembling. Fear, but fear of what? Fear of prison? She stepped forward into his arms once again. He could feel her trembling body.

Hawkett took another deep breath. This was going to be real tough.

"Jamie?"

"Yes?"

"Before I say anything more about these murders, I just wanted to thank you."

"Thank me? For what?"

"I don't know, I guess for putting up with me the last few days, allowing me to waltz right into your life. I know I've seemed a little strange, disoriented maybe, but I don't know, my life just kind of wandered this way."

"I know what you mean; I understand."

"You do?"

"Sure, Adam, I could see it in your eyes the first time we met, right here in this barn. The look in your eyes reminded me of the face I saw in the mirror, that empty look I had for weeks after Bud died."

She pulled back and looked up into his eyes once again. "Best get on with our lives, huh?"

"Yeah, they're so short. Our lives I mean. Listen, Jamie, we've got to talk about these murders. Talk to me okay, I'm your friend, I want to help."

The look on her face immediately turned to one of puzzlement. "Talk about what?"

Oh shit, he thought, there goes any hope for any easy confession.

He made a quick decision and decided to take the easy way out. Blame Benjamin. "While I've been helping you, Benjamin's been up and down the road here investigating, eliminating suspects, looking for motives, you know?"

She didn't reply but stood there like a statue, those dark brown eyes locked on him.

Glancing away he continued, "Anyway, he thinks there's a good reason to suspect you. Thinks maybe the older Cordoe came onto you, got too friendly maybe and you..."

"And I murdered him?" she finished his sentence, speaking quietly.

"Yes, well uh, that's what..."

"And what about Denny?"

"He thinks, well Denny said earlier he knew who'd killed his father. So Benjamin's thinking..."

Once again she interrupted. "So I had to kill him too? Blackmail?"

"Yes, that's what he thinks and..."

"And what do you think Adam?" She was no longer pale. Her complexion was turning red and she looked as if she was about to explode.

"Well I..." he cleared his throat.

"You bastard, you dirty rotten bastard! And I thought you were something special. Yes, well I guess you're something special alright. A special bastard shot straight from hell. Well let me tell you..."

"Jamie!" he tried to interrupt, but to no avail. Her wrath flowed on unheeded.

"You've been sneaking around this farm as some kind of undercover agent, right? Pretending to be my friend, hell that's what really

205

hurts." Tears were running down her face now and she suddenly felt cold, remembering this man, this stranger had held her only moments earlier. "What a fool, what a damn fool," she began muttering to herself as she marched back into the barn, Hawkett following right behind her.

"Jamie, it isn't like that, honest. I didn't believe it was you."

"And now you do, right?"

Hawkett's heart was somewhere near his ankles. The purpose he'd found only moments earlier left him, and presently, he was feeling confused, hopeless.

"Jamie," he held his hands out toward her, then dropped them to his sides. He couldn't find the words.

She spun around, marched toward the corral, swung the gate open and grabbed Chief by his halter, startling the horse. She led the horse toward the barn door, snapped a lead to his halter and tied him there. She slammed the tack room door open, stepped in and grabbed the horse's saddle and blanket.

Hawkett, dumbfounded, just stood there and watched her, knowing anything he said would be the wrong thing to say.

"What? Where are you going?" he stuttered.

"None of your damn business, Hawkett. Why? Are you going to arrest me? Got your handcuffs in your back pocket? Gonna read me my rights, are you, good buddy?" She was almost yelling at him, tears still streaming down her face as she slipped the bridle onto Chief's head. Even the old horse pranced around nervously, sensing its master's anxiety.

With one easy movement, she swung up and onto the saddle and spun the horse around to face Hawkett, sending dirt spraying from the horse's hooves right into his face.

"Buster, get out now! There's the road. Start walkin' and don't come back, understand?"

"Jamie," he tried to yell, "I wanna help, I'm not..." but she wasn't listening. She spun the horse around, dug her heels into his side and left the barnyard in high gear, heading across the bottom towards the surrounding hills. Hawkett couldn't believe how fast she pulled away from him, the horse's hooves pounding on the ground in a machine-like rhythm.

Jamie laid her head down near the horse's neck and edged him on at full speed, the wind drying her tears as she went.

Benjamin stopped the car at the beginning of Dead End Road,

right at the intersection that ran into Pigmy. He was feeling better, but still nervous. Would Hawk come through? He had to. That was all there was to it. Was there anything else he, Benjamin, could do before going to the sheriff's office? Nothing came to mind. He tossed his cigar out the window and restarted the Escort, but then shut it off again as he saw a familiar pickup approaching. Harley again. Benjamin had a quick thought, an inspiration of sorts and immediately decided to act on it.

Harley stopped his pickup next to Benjamin's and attempted to roll his window down. After three attempts, he managed to accomplish the task. Harley started to say something, but then his pickup started rolling ahead as he realized he'd forgotten to take it out of gear. Harley backed the vehicle up, shoved the lever into park and shut it off. He turned and smiled at Benjamin, mission accomplished.

How did this man manage to deliver mail, Benjamin wondered again.

"How's Harley?"

"Can't complain," Harley chuckled. Suddenly the little rat terrier appeared from somewhere and looked out the open window to see what was going on.

"So inspector, how's the investigation going, any hot clues?" Harley chuckled again, this time a little nervously.

"Going good. In fact, I'd say an arrest is eminent."

"Oh really?" For the first time Benjamin could remember, the half smile seemed to disappear from the mailman's face.

Benjamin knew he was about to commit an unbelievable sin, but he had his motives. Tell Harley what had transpired, send him to help Hawkett, get her confession. Jamie trusted Harley. He was like a father to her. She'd said that, he thought. He decided to go ahead with it.

"Harley, we know who killed Doug Cordoe and who has now killed his son as well. You do too, right?"

Harley didn't reply, but a sickening look embedded itself upon his face.

"Look, Harley, Doug Cordoe probably deserved to be murdered, probably asked for it. We all know he sure as hell was no sweetheart, but still, the laws the law, right?"

Harley still didn't reply.

"Anyway, I left Hawkett out at Jamie's. He's waiting for a confession. He knows more about all this than I do. In fact, most of the questions I have are still unanswered, but that will come later. Why don't you go out to Jamie's right now and help him straighten things out, okay?"

Harley nodded his head up and down, very slowly.

"We need a confession, Harley. That would help a lot, make things easier on everybody, you know?"

Again Harley nodded his head up and down. Benjamin hated having to dump on the old man like this, but it'd happen sooner or later anyway.

"Right, then see you in a little while." Benjamin started the Escort and continued into Pigmy. He'd head for the sheriff's office. Finish this mess.

CHAPTER 36

Andrea peeked out from the bushes under which she, Junior and Jack were hiding. Actually the animals didn't know they were hiding, just obeying their master. Any movement by either brought a stern look from Andrea and the whispered command to "hush up." Jack could sense her nervousness and lay on his belly, ears cocked forward and nose on full alert. Junior on the other hand, being more laid back, settled down for a little nap in the cool shade. Andrea was upset. She had witnessed the argument between her mother and Hawkett. It upset her vision. Her vision of Hawkett and her mom getting married. Her vision of having a dad. She liked Hawkett. He was kind to her. And she thought her mom liked him too, but she wasn't sure. The night before, when her mom had tucked her in, she'd asked, "Mom do you like Hawkett?" Her mother hadn't replied immediately. She had folded her arms and stood there in thought, a smile on her face.

"Yes, I like him. Do you?"

"Yes, I think he's very kind. What I mean Mom is do you like him a whole lot? You know like maybe you and him..."

Her mother had stepped forward, laid a finger on Andrea's lips, "Hush, kiddo, I think I know what you're leading up to and I don't want to discuss it."

"But, what..."

"Hush," her mother interrupted her once again. "Let's just take one day at a time, okay?"

"Okay, Mom."

"Love ya."

"Love ya too, night."

As she watched her mother fly off across the pasture on Chief, a tear trickled from her eye. Ever alert Jack turned quickly and licked it off. He was quietly scolded.

Hawkett stood there and watched Jamie race away. He felt empty. He felt useless. He felt like a traitor. His feet were leaden and his body numb. A turning point in history had come and gone for Adam Hawkett, and he had come up empty. She was gone, the fragile relationship built in the last few crazy, unpredictable days had collapsed. It wouldn't, couldn't be rebuilt. In another hour or so Benjamin would show up with some deputies and they'd read her rights, haul her off. Some social worker would take Andrea as well. He shook his head sadly. He felt so sorry for her and the child. As for himself, he just felt empty, ready to die. Give up on a failed life. Let someone else fill his useless role in the scheme of things.

He stood in such a trance that he didn't hear the pickup coming until it had nearly driven right up to him. Turning, he saw Harley sitting behind the wheel of the pickup. The question popped into his head: could Harley take care of the child? But a father-like instinct dismissed that idea. Harley was too old, too befuddled. The look on Harley's normally-jovial face seemed to support his doubt. Not the half smile, but rather a half stare, a cold hard stare. Had he witnessed their argument, sensed Jamie's anger?

Harley slowly climbed out of the pickup, never taking his eyes off Hawkett. Daniel raced out the door and took a whiz on the front tire, but today the comical dog did not capture Hawkett's attention. His attention was on Harley. Befuddled Harley. Harley who always seemed to be around. Just how the hell did Harley really fit into all this? Was that innocent-looking, simple-faced grin really a mask that disguised other emotions? Had Benjamin questioned Harley further, questioned him enough? He remembered seeing Harley's pickup coming from the direction of Cordoe's farmstead just the day before. Why? Alarms were starting to go off in Hawkett's mind. Something just wasn't right.

Harley slowly climbed out of his pickup truck, closed the door and stood quietly facing Hawkett. Stood there with the same unchanging, cold stare, saying nothing.

"Hi Harley," Hawkett spoke the greeting almost in a questioning tone.

"What's up?"

"What do you mean?"

Harley turned and pointed back up the road. "Your partner says you're about to make an arrest."

Hawkett frowned wondering why the hell Benjamin would give such information to Harley. This just didn't make sense. Something was wrong. This case was not being finalized, a part of the puzzle hadn't been examined yet. Harley was that piece; Hawkett suddenly was more sure of that than he was about any other part of the mess.

"Harley, who killed Cordoe?"

Harley chuckled nervously, "Beats me. That's your job, right? To find out who murdered him? Hell, I'm the mailman. I just deliver mail."

He was lying; Hawkett knew it. The man had guilt written all over his face. He had guilt resonating in his voice. But what did he know? More evidence that would only be used to incriminate Jamie? Would he go so far as to lie for her?

Little Daniel trotted up to Harley's feet and pawed his master's leg. Harley quickly bent over, picked up the small dog and stroked him affectionately.

If only that little dog could talk, thought Hawkett, he'd probably seen something, probably could unscramble this whole mess.

Suddenly an idea popped into Hawkett's head. As he thought of the animal...and then in his desire to obtain the truth, he remembered an ancient form of lie detection used in the Orient hundreds of years earlier. Would it work today under these circumstances he wondered.

"Harley, you wouldn't be lying to me, would you?"

Still no smile. "Told you once, I don't know anything about it."

"Would you be willing to take a lie detector test to verify that for me?"

"Where, at Des Moines? Hell, I've got my mail route to take care of. I can't be runnin' off."

"No, here, today. Right now. We can go do it right in the barn."

"In the barn?" Harley's stare turned into a look of disbelief. "You got a lie detector tester in that barn?"

"Don't need one, we'll use Daniel."

"What?" Harley asked incredulously. "Are you crazy or..."

"It's common knowledge that animals, especially pets, can sense emotion much more effectively than humans. Perhaps it's their sense of smell. Whatever it is, you just can't lie to an animal without them knowing it. For example, when you get ready to take your dog here to the vet, he senses it, right? Immediately becomes more nervous than usual, right?"

Harley nodded his head up and down slowly, still stroking the small dog's back.

"Well, Harley, here's what I'd like to do, and I know it sounds crazy, but bear with me, okay?"

No reply.

"I'm going to take your dog into the barn and tie him up in the empty grain storage room. With the door shut, it'll be dark in there, but he'll be okay."

Harley started to protest, but Hawkett interrupted him. "You'll be with him shortly. I'll put a bale of hay by him that you can sit on."

"But why in the hell...? What's this got to do with lie detection?"

"Because, Harley, when you enter the darkened room and sit on that bale of hay by your dog, I'm going to ask you to lay your right hand on Daniel's back. Okay?"

Harley nodded.

"Then, I'm going to ask you some questions about this murder investigation. If you answer truthfully, the dog will sit there quietly. If you lie, however, the dog will howl loud and long."

"Hell, you're crazy, I'm not gonna..."

"Hey, it's either here or Des Moines, Harley. We can subpoena you."

Harley glanced at the small dog in his arms then back at Hawkett. Then, after he'd made up his mind, he stepped forward and handed the dog to Hawkett. "Hurry up, let's get this over with; I got more mail to deliver."

"Good, you wait here while I set it up. Won't take long." Hawkett quickly carried the rat terrier into the barn, found an unused piece of baling twine and opened the door into the empty grain storage room. It was pitch black. He found some more items around the barn with which to prepare for the lie detection test. When he was done, the small dog sat, almost hidden, deep inside the dark room tied to the wall near a bale of hay.

"Okay, I'm ready for you," Hawkett yelled out the door. Harley ambled toward the barn. Hawkett knew his plan would either work extremely well or he'd look like a complete ass, and either way, it damn sure would never be admissible evidence in a court of law.

Harley, apprehensively, entered the barn and Hawkett led him to the opened grain room door.

"Okay, Harley, Daniel is already in there. See him, tied by that bale of hay?"

Harley peered into the darkened space and nodded his head.

"Okay, what I want you to do, Harley, is walk in there, and sit down on that bale of hay by your dog, okay?"

Harley didn't reply as he cautiously eased his way along the wall and sat down on the bale by his dog.

"Okay, Harley, I'm gonna shut this door before I question you. I'll be right outside here. It's going to be pitch black in there, but that's necessary for the proper effect."

Harley started to object, but Hawkett was already closing the door.

"Now, Harley," Hawkett raised his voice a little louder so Harley could hear him through the wooden door. "I'm going to ask you a question, just one question. You lay your right hand firmly on Daniel's back. Be sure to make good contact. If you answer truthfully, the dog will remain silent. If you lie, he'll howl. Okay?"

"Yep, I understand. Hurry up, okay?"

"Okay, hand on the dog? Good contact, Harley?"

"Yep."

"Okay, here's your question Harley. Did you have anything to do with the murder of Doug Cordoe or his son Denny?" A few moments of silence passed before Hawkett heard a reply.

"Nope."

No other noise traveled through the closed door. No howling, no whimpering, nothing but silence.

Hawkett let a few more moments of silence pass, then opened the door. Harley stood up and walked right past Hawkett.

"I'm glad that's over with. Gawd, I felt like a damn fool sitting in there. Let that dog loose and I'm getting the hell out of here. Lie detector, bullshit!"

Hawkett entered the darkened room and untied the twine from Daniel's collar. The small dog immediately exited and followed his master out of the barn. Hawkett followed them to Harley's pickup.

"Harley, hey I'm sorry, but it's my business not to trust people. I'm really sorry I put you through this little trial." He raised his hand to Harley for a reconciliation hand shake.

Harley didn't accept the hand immediately, but then with a half smile shook Hawkett's hand.

"Didn't hear no howlin' from my dog, did you? Proves I'm innocent, right?"

"Yes, I guess your dog proved your innocence. He deserves a good pat on the back, huh?"

"Yup" as he answered, Harley bent down and stroked the dog's back but recoiled his hand immediately. He turned the palm of his hand towards his face to examine a dirty, greasy substance on it. "What the hell...?"

Hawkett, no longer apologetic, replied. "It's a mixture of grease and dirt I smeared on Daniel's back before I tied him up in the room. It's impossible to touch the dog on his back or head without getting it on your hand. There wasn't any on your right hand when we shook a minute ago. How could that be, Harley?"

A brighter or more devious man might have found some plausible lie or at least just turned and left, but not Harley. His face registered shame. He hadn't touched the dog in the darkened room. That had been his way of beating the ridiculous lie detection scheme.

"You murdered them both, didn't you, Harley?"

Harley appeared confused. Tears of anger, anger from being tricked, seeped from the corners of his eyes. He didn't reply.

"Jamie had nothing to do with it? Either murder?"

Harley looked at the ground and shook his head back and forth.

Hawkett had found the murderer, but his evidence was laughable. He needed a confession. He needed a witness to the confession. He needed to move fast, before it dawned on Harley that he had no proof. He needed Jamie to convince Harley to spill his guts, to confess. He needed, also, to apologize to her, to hold her.

Hawkett turned, shaded his eyes with his hand and scanned the treeline above. Should he try to yell to her, he wondered.

CHAPTER
37

Benjamin steered the Escort into a parking spot next to a county patrol car and got out. Glancing up at the courthouse, he noticed that Thelma and Pearl Oldham were entering the building. What the hell are they up to, he wondered, but then he remembered that there were several other county offices stationed in the courthouse. They were probably renewing their drivers' licenses, he assumed. He smiled to himself as he thought of the cantankerous Pearl. He hoped they wouldn't cross paths again; the woman was hard on his ego. Harmless old biddy though, he thought.

Benjamin noticed his stomach grumbling and looked at his watch. Nearly ten o'clock. Too early for dinner. He decided to go wrap some things up with the sheriff, then stop for a couple of cinnamon rolls at the restaurant.

Inside the courthouse, just before reaching the sheriff's office, Benjamin pulled up short. Sitting outside Sheriff Spencer's office were the Oldham sisters, both staring at him as he approached. What were they up to? Yes, he knew. The old girls had been lying to him. Confession time, right girls? They'd seen her, seen Jamie run the fork into Cordoe's chest. This angered him. They could've saved everyone a lot of trouble if they'd only confessed earlier. Stupid old bags. He walked right up to Thelma's chair as she drew her purse defensively up in front of her. What the hell, he thought, does she think I'm going to belt her one? But the guilt was in her eyes, he could see it.

"Good day, ladies," he said, having to force the pleasant words from his mouth.

No reply.

"Come to visit the sheriff, have we?"

Thelma replied weakly, "Yes, yes, we have."

His anger began to subside, and he felt a tinge of guilt radiate into his soul. After all, they were old, lonely, vulnerable. And there had been no malice in their silence. Still, young Cordoe's life might have been saved if they'd spoken earlier. He decided a slight reprimand was not out of order. He wouldn't have to be mean about it.

In a neutral, controlled voice, "Ladies, had you come in earlier, it sure would have helped everybody out." He looked each lady squarely in the eyes, waiting for a reply. None came. They were both beet-red. Benjamin shook his head and started to walk into the sheriff's office. Just as he had stepped through the door, Pearl uttered a loud, barking cough, and, for some reason, he stepped back through the door to see if it had, in fact, been uttered to get his attention. Sure enough it had. Holding her hand behind a handkerchief, where Thelma couldn't see, Pearl was very vividly giving Benjamin the finger. He backed into the office, laughing out loud as he did. Cantankerous, yes.

Jan, turned from her typewriter and greeted him with a smile. She pointed at the sheriff who was talking on the telephone, then pointed at a coffee pot in the corner and went back to her typing.

He started to pour some coffee when the sheriff spotted him.

"Yeah, wait a minute, he's just walked in, I'll let you talk to him." He laid the phone down and motioned at Benjamin. "It's your supervisor, Brightwall. You can use that phone over there on Jan's desk."

Shit, thought Benjamin, his mood darkening. He walked over and picked up the phone.

"Yeah, Willoughby here. What's up?"

"What's up with you? Case wrapped up?"

Benjamin looked at his watch, "Will be within the hour."

"Widow do it?"

217

"Yes, she's coming in to confess," he lied.

"Good, 'bout time. You boys have had too long a vacation. Can I leak it to the press yet?"

"Hell no." Stupid bastard, playing politics as usual, turning a potential murderer over to the press, so she could be put on trial by the public before she actually made it to any court of law.

"Keep those bastards from the press out of here. They'll screw everything up."

"Sure, no problem. Mum's the word."

Lying son of a bitch, thought Benjamin. He'd begin leaking the news within the hour.

"Oh, by the way, have you nabbed the local dog killer yet?"

Benjamin was momentarily confused, then replied, "What the hell are you talking about?"

Brightwall snorted on the other end. "Got a report here from the lab boys. They went over the victim's car, remember? The blood on the steering wheel, remember Sherlock?"

"Yeah."

"It's dog blood, not human blood."

"Dog blood?" Benjamin replied unbelievably.

"Yeah, you know, Fido, Spot, woof woof? Does that fit into the facts of your carefully-plotted murder report?"

Benjamin was nothing but confused. Dog blood. How the hell did that fit in? What did it mean? Did it mean anything?

"Well?"

Benjamin came out of his trance, and remembered that he was still on the phone. "I uh, can't say. Listen, I'll visit with the sheriff here and call you back by one, okay?"

"Excellent, don't be late, okay?"

"Yeah." With that, Benjamin hung up the phone. Dog blood on the steering wheel of Cordoe's car. What did that mean? Suddenly, he was feeling very uneasy. Something wasn't right. The picture had suddenly gone out of focus. But what? He poured himself yet another cup of coffee, forgetting the cup he'd already filled, found a chair in the corner, and sat down to think, almost oblivious to the entrance of the Oldham sisters.

"Yes, sit here, ladies. Cup of coffee? Okay, what's up?" The sheriff guided the Oldham sisters to two chairs near his desk. Thelma repositioned her purse on her lap, straightened her hair, and glanced nervously around the room. In doing so, she caught Benjamin's eyes and brought him out of his trance. She cleared her voice for the second time and started to shuffle her purse again.

Pearl motioned toward Benjamin. "Better start talking, else fat boy over there will probably take us into one of the back cells and give us the rubber hose treatment."

It was her sincerity that made these outrageous statements so hilarious. Benjamin noticed that Sheriff Spencer had covered his mouth with one hand and was pretending to be looking at something outside his window, but it was obvious that he'd found the comment humorous. His body shook as he tried to contain his laughter. Deputy Secretary Tenton made no attempt to control her emotions and heartily laughed out loud.

All this just made Pearl grow angrier still. She glared, menacingly, at both Benjamin and Jan. Her mouth moved slowly as she silently uttered a series of obscene oaths in their direction.

"Thelma, get on with it or I'm leaving."

Summoning courage from Pearl, Thelma once again cleared her voice. "Well, you see, Sheriff, I seemed to have told a lie. Only one mind you and it's the first one since the spring of 1963."

Benjamin was sure that he knew what her most recent lie had been, but he found himself wondering what lie the woman could have possibly been harboring since the spring of 1963. What kind of person went decades without lying, he wondered.

"Lied about what, Thelma?" the Sheriff asked politely after regaining his composure.

"It was to Detective Willoughby, the gentleman sitting over there." She nodded in Benjamin's direction without looking at him.

"Fat boy," Pearl added, as if that nickname would clarify for the sheriff, the individual in question.

"Yes," Spencer replied, smiling in Benjamin's direction. "And what would the lie have been, Thelma?"

"Well, it was not actually a lie, you know; it was more of an incomplete answer. You know the kind that..."

"Thelma!" Pearl raised her voice once again.

"Okay, okay!" Thelma replied irritably. "Anyway Detective Willoughby asked me if I'd seen any stranger on Dead End last weekend?"

Oh shit, thought Benjamin, she's gonna dump another suspect in our laps. Hell no, and just when he'd told Brightwall they had the case

219

sewed up. Time to start planning for early retirement.

"And did you see a stranger, Thelma?" Again the sheriff patiently coaxed her to continue.

"Oh no, no Sheriff, not a stranger. More like a situation. Oh, how can I explain it? A strange situation, yes."

Pearl lost what little patience she had, and abruptly interjected, "She saw Harley walking up and down the road last Friday night crying his eyes out, talking like a crazy bastard. I seen him too. Told her he was probably drunk. Stupid shit interrupted me watching Friday night wrestling!"

"Harley? Harley our local mailman?" Now Sheriff Spencer was neither amused nor polite. He'd become stoic and intent. "Did you talk to him?"

"I stepped out on the porch and tried to get his attention, find out what was wrong. And Pearl yelled some, well, some unpleasant statements in his direction, but he wouldn't respond."

"What time of the night was this?"

"Oh, maybe nine, nine thirty, it must have been, because Pearl's wrestling show doesn't come on until after *Murder She Wrote* and that's on from eight to nine."

"Yeah, the idiot interrupted a tag team match between the Macho Mikey twins and the Rat and Cat brothers. Pissed me off, I tell you!"

"Pearl, please," pleaded her sister-in-law.

"He was crying, you say?" the sheriff continued to interrogate.

"Yes, well crying and sort of moaning."

"Moaning like he was hurt?"

"Yes, but emotionally, you know, not physically."

"Sounded like his balls were caught in his bicycle chain," Pearl added, a sly smile on her face.

"Pearl, enough! Hear me? Clean your mouth or get out of here now!" Thelma was genuinely mad now and Pearl shrunk back into her chair, thoroughly chastened.

"So you, neither of you, have any idea what was wrong with him?"

"Not for certain, but it might be..."

"Yes?" The Sheriff continued to prod her.

"Well, you know, Harley had his two dogs and he loved them like they were his own kids."

Spencer remembered seeing two dogs bouncing around in the

mailman's car sometime in the past, but that was all he knew of them. "And?"

"Well, one of them has disappeared and nobody knows what happened to it. I called Jamie and she says she thinks he probably ran over it. We've known Harley for over sixty years, Sheriff. He stopped by on his mail route each day, since his wife died, to have a cup of coffee with us. And Harley, well you know what he's like, he's just...I don't know, he's just Harley." She shrugged her shoulders. The sheriff nodded his head as if to indicate he understood what she was trying to say.

She continued, "Anyway, Harley's changed Sheriff; he's been acting pretty strange lately. Frankly Sheriff, he's become a little bit scary. Pearl thinks he's getting Alzheimer's Disease." She shook her head, "I just don't know. Anyway..."

Benjamin interrupted, "Wait a minute. Was Harley the mysterious friend you were thinking of when you took that trip last Saturday? I believe you went to some type of care-facility, in Minnesota or somewhere. Was that done with Harley in mind?"

Thelma slowly nodded her head up and down. "He hasn't got any other family. A person has to be responsible for their friends."

Sheriff Spencer quickly digested the new information. He was about to patiently reassure the Oldham sisters that he'd look into Harley's problem. He'd tell them that, more than likely, this all had nothing to do with the murder, but he never got the chance. He was rudely interrupted. Interrupted by Benjamin's coffee cup dropping to the floor as the DCI agent leaped from his chair.

"Get your boys out to Jamie's now," he ordered as he ran out the door. Benjamin's heart was pounding. He was scared. My God, what have I done, he thought, as he ran down the courthouse steps. He'd sent a mentally-unstable, brutal murderer to confess to unarmed, unaware Hawkett, the lady and the child. He didn't know what had happened, but instinct told him there was no time to spare. He knew that it was possible that his error could cause more deaths. Knew more deaths would occur. He remembered the picture of the banker with a pitchfork stuck in his chest. He remembered the dead son, his head bashed in and his eyes popped out. Their assailant was at Jamie's, and there was no telling what his next move would be.

He backed the Escort into the street, mashed the accelerator to the floor and raced for the edge of Pigmy. Once again, he turned onto

Dead End Road. Only this time, he was traveling fast, with one thought in his head: to save lives, as many as possible.

CHAPTER
38

Jamie reined the horse to a stop beneath a shady maple tree at the top of the hill. The old horse was breathing hard and sweating. Guilt joined her other emotional pain and she jumped off the horse to begin stripping the sweat off his neck and shoulders. She'd had no business pushing the old horse like that. The old fellow could still run though. She loosened his saddle girth and patted him on the head. She turned and looked back down the hill toward her farmstead. She was surprised to realize that he was still standing there, still staring up at her like a statue. A vehicle came driving into her farm and she recognized it as Harley's. She laid her head against the horse's neck, thinking, trying to sort things out.

As had been the case since meeting Hawkett, confusion ruled her emotions. There was no denying she'd fallen in love with him, and she felt, somewhat apprehensively, that he felt very strongly for her as well. Sometime during their brief time together, she'd began to trust him too, and Jamie knew a person couldn't ask for more than to have a relationship that was based on trust and love. Now, the man she trusted and loved had just finished accusing her of being a murderer. Anger, hurt and guilt were simultaneously playing tug-of-war with her heart.

Was he going to stand there all day, she wondered. She suddenly felt a smidge of hope. She tried to remember what he'd said exactly. He'd said he wanted to help. He'd said he didn't believe it was her. Had he been right? Had his partner been right? Guilt streamed through her soul. She should have told them right away. Told them about the true banker Cordoe, the history about him calling her, again and again, stopping by her house repeatedly, the bastard's unending campaign to get somewhere with her. She shuddered. That disgusting pig.

But she'd finally had enough and the previous Friday evening she'd decided to put an end to it. Doug Cordoe had slowly rolled his Cadillac into her farmyard at suppertime, pulled up to the garden gate and sat there, just sat there, drinking a beer, staring into her house and invading her privacy, like he'd done so many times before. He wouldn't listen to reason. She'd told him politely at first to leave her alone. Then he had forced her to be rude, damned rude. He seemed to love that. It had seemed to turn him on even more. He'd utter some disgusting remark. Oh how she hated that obnoxious bastard!

Enough was enough. Last Friday had been the end. She was unable to endure it anymore. She'd told Andrea to go inside the house and watch television. Then, from the cupboard, she'd extracted Bud's shotgun and loaded it. He'd taught her, years before, how to both load and shoot that gun. She'd left the house without uttering a word. The time for pleading, threatening and insulting was over. He would bother her and Andrea no more. She fired one shot over the top of his car from the front porch before reaching the garden gate. She fired the second shot as he dropped his beer onto his lap and grabbed for the keys. She kept walking toward him, pumping shells and firing the gun over the top of his car. She fired the third shot as he hit the starter. She fired the fourth shot as he shoved the car into reverse, wheels spinning and raced backwards away from her. She fired the fifth shot as the Cadillac roared out of her driveway at a high rate of speed. She pumped the gun again, and aimed directly at the body of the fleeing car. She felt numb, not caring if she hit him as he fled. The gun clicked empty, and she watched his car fly back up the road towards Pigmy.

She was surprised when she saw the Cadillac's brake lights come on as Cordoe approached the bridge and she wondered out loud, "Now what?" The setting sun glared in her eyes. She squinted as she tried to

224

see what had caused him to stall. There was another vehicle parked near Cordoe's. Harley? What was he doing by the bridge?

She was startled when Andrea had tugged her shirt from behind. She had turned, knelt down and hugged the little girl. She'd held her for several seconds, not a word was said. Then, together, they'd walked back to the house. Jamie had returned the gun to its hiding place. They'd had supper and nothing had been said about the incident.

What had happened on the bridge? Had Harley been hanging around on the bridge fishing as he so often did? Well, Harley would have heard the shots anyway. What had transpired on the bridge if they'd had a run in? Could Harley have...? She couldn't bear to consider the possibilities. She could sense something was wrong with Harley, but she thought it simply involved the loss of his other dog. Surely that couldn't have involved the murdered banker in any way. But could it? But what? Had they quarreled? Could Harley have...? No. She couldn't think that, couldn't believe that. What a mess. And it was all Cordoe's fault.

CHAPTER
39

It was well into midmorning. The sun sat majestically high above the southern Iowa farming community. And that's really where one needed to be, high above, to fully comprehend the incredible scene about to unfold on the Chambers' farm below. High above, possibly in a hot air balloon floating slowly above the landscape. Drifting way up there, a person could gaze down and see all the pieces of this story coming to a conclusion.

They would have witnessed the spat between Jamie and Hawkett. They would have seen her racing away on her horse and then, shortly thereafter, Harley driving in. They would see Hawkett walking slowly away from Harley's pickup truck, once again staring up the hillside to where Jamie had reined the horse to a stop. They would see Benjamin's car and hear the tires squeal as it left the county sheriff's office in Pigmy, and headed to the Chambers' farm at a high rate of speed. One might even be able to detect Andrea and her two pets hiding under the rhododendron bush near the garden's edge.

The humidity had given way to a pleasant dry heat. The countryside was responding to the past rainfalls with a beautiful boost of green foliage. The animals grazed contentedly in their pastures. What one couldn't see, couldn't anticipate, was that before the morning was over, three lives would be tragically lost from this usually peaceful little farm.

Hawkett turned once again and observed Harley leaning his chest against the back of his pickup staring into the truck bed. Would he try to run? That would be no problem. Hawkett could just step into the house and call the sheriff. They'd be waiting for him at the edge of Pigmy. Should he question Harley further? That might be a mistake. He needed Benjamin. He needed to start treating this thing in a legal manner. He turned again to look up at the hill where Jamie was lingering. He glanced at his watch wondering how long it would be until Benjamin came back. Too long. He badly needed Jamie to return, so she could witness him getting Harley to confess to the murders. He cupped his hands around his mouth preparing to call out to her, but the yell was interrupted by a sickening sound. A crash of wood against bone as Harley, apparently much stronger than he looked, swung a baseball bat at full thrust, catching Hawkett squarely on the side of his head. Hawkett collapsed to the hard earth like a bird shot out of the sky, so stunned, he couldn't figure out what had happened to him. Blood poured down the side of his face as he tried to regain equilibrium and drag himself to his knees.

The crack of bat to human skull was so loud that Jamie heard it all the way up on the hill. She'd been staring down at the scene and gasped in horror, not believing what she'd just witnessed. With panic in her heart, she gave the saddle girth a yank, leapt onto the horse's back, and dug her heels deep into his sides. Hawkett was on his hands and knees with Harley standing over him, the bat extended above his head, as he prepared to deliver another blow. Jamie, riding hard, knew she couldn't get there in time to stop that killing swing.

From out of the bushes little Andrea sprang like a rabbit, her dog right beside her. It was obvious that she was reacting on instinct alone, as no child would know how to react in such circumstances. With horror she'd witnessed the first hit, Hawkett going down, the blood. With courage possessed by few adults, she hurled her small body head first into Harley's midriff propelling the air from his stomach. Enraged, Harley shrieked a curse and slapped the girl on the side of her head sending her tripping and stumbling over Hawkett. That slap convinced Jack to take action and the border collie drove at Harley's legs, ripping his left calf wide open, teeth buried deep. Harley screamed and swung the bat wildly at the dog, catching Jack squarely in the middle of his back. The dog yelped, mournfully, and crawled away, dragging his back legs on the rocky ground.

Hawkett, still dazed and blinded by his own blood streaming into his eyes, could only comprehend that they were under attack by Harley...Harley and his baseball bat. Unable to rise, Hawkett crawled to the stunned Andrea and tried to cover her, protect her from Harley who was now walking toward them, his glasses knocked off, his pocket pens spilled, his leg bleeding. Harley and his bat.

Benjamin would have gotten there in time. Should have. Less than two minutes had elapsed between him leaving the sheriff's door and the Escort flying down Dead End Road. He grabbed Hawkett's revolver from the car's glove compartment as he drove, thankful it wasn't still locked in the trunk. And he would have gotten there in time had it not been for an innocent act of nature. A rooster pheasant gathering grit for its gizzard along the edge of the road, oblivious to the human tragedy taking place, stood petrified as it watched Benjamin's car bearing down upon it. To fly or to run, that was the question. The rooster decided, too late, to fly. With perfect timing, its takeoff coincided with Benjamin's arrival and at seventy miles an hour, the impact of the bird, shattered the windshield of the Escort. Glass fragments flew into Benjamin's eyes as he hit the brakes, lost control of the car and went flying off the edge of the road, mowing Jamie's mailbox off in the process. Fortunately for Benjamin, the Escort didn't roll, but skidded to a stop just short of a very solid telephone pole as it slid into the ditch. Dazed, he tried to clean the glass from his face.

Jamie, racing her gelding down the hill, her heart pounding, took a shortcut toward the buildings where the tragedy was unfolding. The horse, sensing her tension, ran as hard as he could. A wooden gate lay between her and the farmyard, and she knew, stopping to open it, the seconds lost, could cost her daughter's life. She commanded the horse to charge forward, and Chief obeyed with courage and loyalty. The old horse crashed right through the board gate at full speed, ripping a terrible gash in his neck and left shoulder. Jamie had no weapon, no plan, only instinct. She drove the horse, who was starting to weaken, right at Harley's body.

Chief hit Harley square on, at full speed, then lost his footing, tripped and rolled, throwing Jamie off. She went bouncing across the ground and banged into the side of the barn. Almost instantly she was back on her feet, stumbling, trying to get to her child. Andrea was underneath Hawkett, who had, by then, succumbed to unconsciousness and was nearing shock from his head wound. In addition, he had a broken arm caused, not by the bat, but by Chief's hoof stepping on it. She scrambled to him and he groaned as she rolled him slowly onto his side. Blood everywhere, so much of it. Andrea was covered as well. She glanced quickly back at Harley, flattened by the horse, lying on his side, then back at her daughter. The moaning little girl was conscious. Jamie hugged her and wiped away blood. Realizing that Andrea was not cut, but that the blood had come from Hawkett, she turned to help him. He was unconscious. "My God," she cried, "he's not breathing." She rolled Hawkett onto his back, yelled at Andrea to get some towels and started giving Hawkett mouth to mouth, trying to breathe life back into his body. So scared she could hardly think, her heart still pounding, Jamie forced air into his lungs, counted, then blew again. Lord, it'd seemed so easy in CPR classes. She yelled at him, "Breathe, damn it!"

Suddenly, a shadow loomed over her, the sun's hot glare being broken from her body and she looked up. And there he stood again, wobbling slightly, but baseball bat still in hand, ready to swing. She covered her head and threw her body over Hawkett instinctively. Then came another crash, rather an explosion. Harley dropped to his knees, moaned, and fell dead.

Jamie realized two, no three things, almost instantly. Number one, she'd not felt the blow of Harley's bat. Number two, the loud sound of the explosion had startled Hawkett's seemingly unconscious body. He had shuddered, coughed and was breathing again. The third thing she realized, or rather discovered, was the source of the explosion. A gunshot. She turned and could see Benjamin, bloodied face, leaning across the top of the wrecked Escort, pistol still extended.

Junior, awakened from his nap by the gunshot, sauntered out from underneath the rhododendron bush, stretched and sniffed the air curiously.

229

CHAPTER
40

Benjamin with his blood-stained shirt, loosened tie and bandaged forehead, stood next to the Escort, which was still sitting in the ditch, as he waited for a wrecker to pull it out. He shook his head slowly back and forth still amazed by the events which had unfolded in the normally-peaceful farmyard.

People had come from everywhere. The first county deputy on the scene had reacted with hysterics, screaming over his radio, calling for help. And not surprisingly, thought Benjamin. The place had looked like a battlefield, bodies everywhere, blood everywhere. Pretty quickly the sheriff and two more deputies appeared on the scene. Then came the rescue squad who, after examining Hawkett, radioed for a Life Flight helicopter from Des Moines. Then came neighbors from everywhere, responding as was the tradition in farm country to a neighborhood crisis. And lastly, the local veterinarian arrived.

Attending to Hawkett had been the priority. Harley had already been pronounced dead at the scene. The volunteer emergency medical technicians worked nervously as they tried to stabilize Hawkett. They'd helped Benjamin get the glass fragments out of his eyes and bandaged a cut on his forehead. They'd also bandaged Jamie's cut arm, and Andrea had been examined, but no injuries were found.

Benjamin had watched as the veterinarian told Jamie that the brave old horse, nearly dead from blood loss trauma, had a severely broken leg as well. With tears streaming down her face, she quietly nodded her head in acknowledgement and asked the vet to put Chief out of his misery.

Thelma and Pearl had come directly to the farm from the sheriff's office, and upon hearing Chief's fate, they whisked Andrea to their car, not wanting the child to suffer any more trauma. An emotional conference was held between Jamie and the Oldham sisters. It had involved multiple hugs and many tears. The decision was made to leave Andrea with Thelma and Pearl while Jamie went with Hawkett, who was still unconscious, in the Life Flight helicopter heading for a hospital in Des Moines.

Over near the backyard gate lay Jack. He'd already been put to sleep by the veterinarian. The dog's vertebrae had been crushed during his heroic effort to protect Andrea. The vet said he would never walk again and would always be in pain if he were kept alive, so the decision had been made to end the dog's misery. Benjamin would have to find a shovel. Jamie's only request had been to bury her dog behind the barn somewhere.

The sheriff and his deputies were down the road at the Cordoe place, investigating the scene and retrieving Denny's corpse. It was finished now. This little country caper was finished. Finished except for the paperwork, the damned reports. Finished except for Hawkett. Benjamin looked off into the clouds where the helicopter had disappeared. He said a silent prayer, then went to find a shovel.

Andrea spent the following three days with the Oldham sisters, and judging by the telephone conversations she had daily with Jamie, she was thoroughly enjoying the company, especially Pearl.

Jamie spent the next three days living out of a low rent apartment near the hospital, one of the apartments designated specifically for people with family in the trauma unit. The first night had been the worst. The doctors had wasted no time telling her how serious the brain damage might be, but day by day, Hawkett's condition had improved.

Hawkett still had vision problems in his left eye, but his other motor functions were returning to normal.

Benjamin had been in to visit Thursday, Friday and Saturday night. The investigation in Taylor County had been concluded upon searching Harley's house. Apparently, the old man had been carrying more mental anguish than anyone had initially realized. On his kitchen table lay several pieces of paper on which Harley had tried to compose suicide notes that included his last will and testament. Each attempted letter began, "To Whom It May Concern." His letters graphically depicted the pain he felt from the loss of his other terrier. On tear-stained notebook paper, he'd left the story of his last encounter with the banker, Cordoe. He'd been fishing off the bridge on the dead end road that Friday evening, watching his two rat terriers playfully romp on the creek bank and across the bridge. He'd not heard Cordoe's Cadillac roaring up the road until it was too late. The small dog was already pinned underneath the Cadillac, crying out in pain. It was Cordoe who was first able to reach the injured dog. He got out of his car, knelt and reached under it. Harley had thought he was trying to help, but instead, he'd forcefully drug the whimpering dog out, held it up in the air by its rear leg and heaved it over the edge of the bridge as Harley watched in horror. Harley had tried to save the dog, but it had drowned before he could find it. He'd carried the dog back up to the road, gently laying it in the bed of the pickup. Lying among some of the other tools in the pickup bed was a pitchfork. Cordoe had stood, leaning over the bridge railing and drinking a beer as he watched the rescue attempt. The last line on the letter read, "He took a life; I took his."

By Sunday evening, Hawkett's health had stabilized and he was able to sit up and feed himself.

Jamie had just walked back into his room as he was finishing a bowl of potato soup. She'd been down in the hospital chapel praying for both Harley's soul and Hawkett's health.

She walked over to his side with a look of concern on her face. She reached to the bandage on the side of his forehead. A trickle of blood was inking out. For some reason his cut had been difficult to stitch and was being obstinate about healing. She got a cold washcloth and held it against his forehead.

Hawkett didn't say a word. He was wondering why being

touched by the hospital nurses made him feel uneasy yet, when Jamie laid her hands on him, a peaceful sense of tranquility seemed to fill his very being. He held still, trying to mentally will her to stay near.

"Doctor says you can leave maybe by Monday if I promise to take good care of you. He kept referring to me as Mrs. Hawkett, thinks I'm your wife."

She pulled the washcloth away and inspected the bandage. Apparently satisfied, she took the washcloth into the bathroom, then returned.

Hawkett stared at her and, even with fuzzy vision in his left eye, she still looked beautiful. "Well, I guess it's all over then, huh?"

"What do you mean?" she asked, walking closer to his bed.

"The murder investigation in Taylor County."

"Well, yes...actually no." She sat on the edge of the bed and faced him. "There's more, I should have told you sooner."

She recanted her run in with Cordoe the Friday before he was killed. She left nothing out, the shotgun and her use of it, Cordoe racing away from her farmstead.

Hawkett listened intently, each word of her story filling in missing pieces to the puzzle that had brought him to her farm in the first place. When she finished they sat in silence for a moment, staring into each others eyes.

"Did you see Harley at the bridge when Cordoe took off?"

"No, I saw his brake lights come on and my first thought was he might be coming back. I was thinking my gun was empty and I'd need more shells. About that time Andrea came to me from the house, upset, and I had to deal with her."

"What would you have done if he'd come back?"

"I don't honestly know. I can't think of myself as a killer, but if the situation had come down to the personal safety of Andrea or I, well..." she stopped.

Hawkett nodded, said nothing and waited patiently for her to continue.

"Do you intend to charge me with anything?" Jamie asked, trying to sound brave, but her voice broke slightly nevertheless.

"No, I can't see as anybody would be better off, unless maybe some overpaid lawyers. I think maybe we'd better just keep this deal between you and Banker Cordoe to ourselves."

Relief flooded her senses, and she took his hand in hers as tears welled up in her eyes. "Adam, I'm sorry I didn't tell you about it sooner, but..."

He interrupted her, "You tried, but I didn't really want to know... well..."

Now Jamie interrupted, "Been a really weird relationship, huh?"

"That it has, Jamie, that it has." He sighed, she sighed.

She let go of his hands, stood up, walked slowly over to the window and looked out at a skyline view of Des Moines. "I guess, well, I've been doing a lot of thinking while here at the hospital...thinking three men are dead because of me."

"No, Jamie, three men are dead because of those three men. Each played the leading role in his death. You just got caught up in it. There's no need for you to feel guilty."

She turned and looked at him, as she leaned against the window sill.

"Well it may sound shallow on my part, but I pretty much agree with you. I've already used up a lifetime's worth of guilt over Bud's death. I'm not going to live that way anymore."

He nodded his head silently in agreement.

An uncomfortable silence lingered and the two adults nervously avoided making eye contact. Another crossroad in their relationship was now eminent.

"So, are you going back to the farm? I mean permanently. Are you going to try to keep on with your old way of life?"

"I have to Adam. That farm is as much a part of me as is Andrea. In our crazy, mixed-up lives, everybody has to have something to hold on to. My child and my farm are what I hold on to, will hold on to until I die."

Hawkett nodded his understanding. Being part of her life, being part of her farm, he had, in fact, felt a sense of being in his place, being where he belonged, feeling good about himself. Even at that moment, he would have traded the hospital bed for the solitude of her haymow floor.

"So when are you going back to the farm?"

"As soon as possible, there are animals that have gone unattended for several days. I can only hope that the neighbors have taken care of things. Anyway, now that you seem to be out of danger..." She shrugged her shoulders.

"Yeah, well I guess the doctor told you I could leave the hospital tomorrow if my wife took care of me," he winked as he spoke.

"Well, Adam," now she was smiling, "I'm not your wife, but I wouldn't find it totally unbearable to give you a little assistance in regaining your health. Of course you'd be expected to work off your debt once you got all healed up." She winked at him playfully at that last comment. "Might even give you a real bed in the house if you think you can behave."

Benjamin had checked in repeatedly on his younger partner throughout the week. However, on the day of Hawkett's release, he was nowhere to be found. Hawkett finally called the DCI headquarters and, to his disappointment, was informed Benjamin had left on vacation.

Hawkett asked Jamie to take a cab to his apartment in West Des Moines, where she retrieved a list of items he wanted and returned with his car. From the hospital, they walked hand in hand to the car and drove out of Des Moines and back to her farm in the country.

As they entered Dead End Road once again, Jamie sighed loudly enough that Hawkett heard her and could feel her apprehension, her pain. She was worried about her surviving animals, her farm that had been left unattended for nearly a week. And more importantly, she was worried about how the tragedy had affected her daughter. Would she be emotionally scarred for life?

Hawkett was also thinking of little Andrea and her animals: the brave Paint, guardian Jack and the old bird dog, the lamb, Junior, and the other sheep, the dead coyote, the pigs and her chickens. A lot of lives to tend to. He reached across the seat and tenderly took her hand.

They stopped at the Oldhams' place to retrieve Andrea. A note on the door explained that they were gone but would return by noon, so Jamie climbed behind the wheel once again and continued to her house. She gasped in surprise as she turned the car in the driveway. A banner tacked onto the barn read, "Welcome Home, Jamie." The yard had been mowed leaving no evidence of the tragedy that had unfolded there only days before. Thelma and Pearl were both working in Jamie's garden and another gentleman, who looked familiar for some reason, stood near them, leaning on a hoe handle, smoking a cigar.

Hawkett laughed out loud, when he recognized Benjamin standing there in bib overalls and a denim shirt, with a wide straw hat on his head. Jamie slid out of the car and both the Oldham sisters walked over to her and hugged her, a tearful reunion. Jamie looked inquisitively around the farmstead.

"Where's Andrea? In the house?" she asked.

Benjamin cupped his hands to his mouth and yelled toward the barn, "Andrea, your mom's here!"

And through the barn door came Andrea, running just as Hawkett and Benjamin had seen her the first time they'd entered the farmyard. Right behind her ran her lamb, Junior, and a border collie, but this border collie was smaller, a plump little pup. His short little legs prevented him from keeping up with his new friend. The pup tripped over his own clumsy feet and yelped. Upon hearing this, Andrea turned and gathered the frisky pup into her arms. She ran directly to Jamie and the two hugged, smothering the puppy between them.

"Where did the pup come from Andrea? He's so cute." Jamie ruffled the little pup's ears and he playfully nipped at her.

"I don't know, Mom," responded Andrea. "We just found him in a box in the barn. Somebody mailed his registration papers to us, but we don't know who he's from. I named him Little Jack. Is that okay?"

Jamie didn't reply right away, but nodded her head in approval, tears escaping as she hugged the little girl again.

"And they baled the rest of our hay, Mom. It's already stacked up in the haymow. Somebody fixed the elevator too!"

"What?" A confused Jamie turned around and discovered that indeed, the rest of her hay field had been harvested. "Who?" She turned to Thelma.

"Neighbors," Thelma replied as if it was no big deal and turned her attention to Hawkett. "And how are you feeling, young man? You know you had us all pretty shook up. People been asking about you all week."

"Doin' fine, thank you, Thelma," Hawkett responded as he pulled himself up out of his car and took a deep draw of the fresh country air. It still tasted just as sweet as he remembered, unpolluted by the prior week's deaths.

"Well, come on in the house. Pearl and I made dinner for you. There's tons of food. The neighbors have been bringing things, you know. Pearl even baked you a fresh apple pie this morning, didn't you dear?"

"Damned... uh, yes I did, but it's got two pieces gone already," she turned and stared at Benjamin who issued a "who me?" type of shrug.

"Well come on in. Adam looks like he needs to sit down and..."

"Excuse me," Benjamin interrupted, "Andrea don't you have one more surprise for your mother?" As he spoke he nodded toward the barn.

"Oh der, I almost forgot the big surprise!" Andrea cried out slapping her hand lightly against the side of her head.

"What? Who?" was all Jamie could think to say.

"We don't know who this surprise is from either, Mom. We just found it in the barn this morning." She led her mother to the barn door, then ordered her to close her eyes. Jamie did as ordered and followed the little girl who was pulling on her hand. Jamie heard a soft whinny and opened her eyes. Even in the darkened barn, with her eyes unaccustomed to the darkness, Jamie immediately saw the foal and it was a beauty, a black and white spotted Paint that looked very similar to Chief. Jamie glanced down and noted that it was a filly.

"The note pinned on the barn door says that she is a full sister to Chief, Mom. Isn't that neat? I didn't name her yet though. I thought you could name her. Isn't she cool?"

Jamie patted the filly's head, admiring its features. She felt shocked and overwhelmed by this display of generosity, trying to determine who had been so kind, but she would never know. Turning, she walked toward the smiling Hawkett, and he hugged her with his good arm. Automatically, Andrea stepped up and was joined in the emotional embrace.

Leaning on the barn door, Benjamin smiled broadly, whisked a guilty tear away from his cheek, then turned and walked back toward the garden, the hoe balancing on his shoulder. In his fifty-eight years of existence, he'd never encountered a series of human events as exciting, as generous, as enlightening, as he had witnessed in this quiet little farming community. He chuckled to himself, wondering what tomorrow would bring.